W9-COS-372

PRAISE FOR *THE GHOST PATTERN*

"This story was just THAT GOOD that I kept it in my mind and has made me really think!!!"

"The Ghost Pattern is a great novel well worth the 5-star rating I gave it!"

"The book is well written and the narrative flows smoothly and logically."

"This is one of the best thrillers I have read in a long time."

"Lots of action, battles, tension; kept me riveted"

"This is the best team I have ever read about in books."

PRAISE FOR LESLIE WOLFE

"Leslie Wolfe certainly does her research and can weave a great story around unexpected and almost unbelievable events."

"Another well written, well researched page-turner."

"I don't know what to say other than brilliantly written."

"Another stunning tale of skullduggery and evil from the hugely talented Leslie Wolfe."

THE GHOST
PATTERN

BOOKS BY LESLIE WOLFE

TESS WINNETT SERIES

Dawn Girl
The Watson Girl
Glimpse of Death
Taker of Lives
Not Really Dead
Girl with A Rose
Mile High Death
The Girl They Took

DETECTIVE KAY SHARP SERIES

The Girl From Silent Lake
Beneath Blackwater River
The Angel Creek Girls

BAXTER & HOLT SERIES

Las Vegas Girl
Casino Girl
Las Vegas Crime

STANDALONE TITLES

Stories Untold
Love, Lies and Murder

ALEX HOFFMANN SERIES

Executive
Devil's Move
The Backup Asset
The Ghost Pattern
Operation Sunset

For the complete list of Leslie Wolfe's novels, visit: LeslieWolfe.com/books

THE GHOST PATTERN

LESLIE WOLFE

II **ITALICS**

Copyright © 2016 Leslie Wolfe

All rights reserved.

No part of this book may be reproduced or transmitted in any form or by any means, electronic or mechanical, including photocopying, recording, or by any information storage and retrieval system, without written permission from the author, with the exception of brief quotations used in reviews and articles.

This is entirely a work of fiction. Characters, organizations, agencies, corporations, places, aircraft, and incidents depicted in this book are the product of the author's imagination or are used fictitiously. Any resemblance to actual persons, living or dead, business establishments, or events, is entirely coincidental.

The publisher does not have any control over and does not assume any responsibility for third-party websites or their content.

$\coprod$ ITALICS

Italics Publishing Inc.

Cover and interior design by Sam Roman

Editor: Joni Wilson

ISBN: 978-1-945302-03-9

DEDICATION

For my husband, for being in my life.

He glared at the man standing in front of him and clenched his jaws in an effort to control his anger.

"Speak," he growled.

"*Gospodin* Myatlev," the trembling man articulated in an unsure voice, "I think I found the perfect environment for our next test."

Vitaliy Myatlev let the air out of his lungs slowly. This was not one of his multinational corporations... this was the Russian government. People were slow and stupid sometimes. Most of all, people couldn't just be killed on the spot, especially when they couldn't be replaced that easily. Damn... When the hell did he turn from powerful oligarch into a fucking clerk? A high-ranking one, that's true, but little more than a clerk, serving the almighty Russian president, and running to answer his every call.

The man stood silently, afraid to speak, his back bowing a little more.

Myatlev gestured the man to continue.

"There are 112 men," he said, "all about the same age, height and build, isolated, and vulnerable. It couldn't be better for what we need. They're perfectly contained, and remote. No one will know."

"You're saying this time it will work?"

The man lowered his eyes. "I think so, yes."

"You think...?" Myatlev snapped.

"Umm... sir, with every new pharmaceutical compound there are levels of tolerance, side effects, complications, environmental and metabolic factors to consider. Especially when the drug is aerosolized, the delivery isn't that precise. This hasn't been attempted before," the man added in a timid voice, then wiped his brow with his lab coat sleeve. "We haven't—"

"Save it," Myatlev said. "I've heard it all before, Dr. Bogdanov. Just give me results."

Chief Ramsay paced the room impatiently, muttering curses under his breath and looking out the same window every two seconds, although the view stayed eerily the same. A cold and foggy Aberdeen morning, engulfed in fog so thick it condensed water droplets on everything it touched, including his office window.

He picked up the radio and tried again.

"Nancy Belle, Nancy Belle, this is Shore Base, come in, over?"

He released the radio button, listening intently and hearing nothing. "C'mon, c'mon, where the hell are you?" he whispered impatiently.

His typical mornings were a lot different from that particular one. He'd come in the office a few minutes before 8:00AM, shaking off the humid chills brought by the thick Aberdeen fog, and heading straight for the coffee machine. He'd brew a fresh cup, then enjoy it while making his morning rounds. That was a figure of speech, of course. He rarely left the shore base. Once a rig was in production, barring some unforeseen event, the head of shore base operations had no reason to visit in person. His morning rounds consisted of radio calls with each of the drilling platforms under his purview, making sure everything was running well. He'd check the status of operations for each rig, and receive reports for everything from staff health to outstanding work orders for parts and repairs.

That would have been a routine morning. This time, things were different.

Nancy Belle, or NB64, was one of the three offshore oilrigs he was responsible for, and it was not reading on any comm. The night before NB64 had signed off with a "status normal, nothing to report" code, and now there was nothing, not a single sound coming from the platform on any channel. It was as if the milky fog had swallowed it whole.

A quick rap on the door, and the shift supervisor came in uninvited.

"Boss?" he said, rubbing his forehead hesitantly.

"Yeah, what do you have?"

"Nothing, dead silent on radio, on sat, all of it is dead. I tried a few personal cell phones, none pick up. Even video is down, all of it."

"What?" Ramsay stopped and turned on his heels to face his shift lead.

"Yeah, boss, all video feed is down for 64."

"Damn...bloody hell, what happened to those boys? Have any of the other rigs reported anything?"

"No, nothing," the man replied, shifting his weight from one foot to the other, while the frown on his forehead became more pronounced under the rim of his hard hat. "But they don't have eyes on them either...fog's too thick."

Ramsay went to the window and pressed his binoculars against it, squinting hard against the eyecups, trying to make something out in the milky haze that had swallowed everything like a shroud. His other rigs weren't visible yet either, but NB64 was the farthest one out; it would be a while.

"There's one," he said, pointing in the direction of a familiar shape almost completely hidden in the fog.

"That's 27," the other man confirmed. "If we can see 27, it shouldn't be that long before we put eyes on 64."

"Nancy Belle, Nancy Belle, come in, goddamnit," Ramsay tried again and got no response. "Go try video again, will ya'?"

The man left quietly. He returned within minutes. "Nothing, boss."

Ramsay stuck his face against the cold window and squinted some more.

"There she is," he said, as the fog lifted a little more, enough for him to discern the familiar silhouette of NB64 against the gray mist. "She's still there!"

Ramsay grabbed his binoculars and looked at 64 again. "Yeah, seems to be in one piece, no flames, no smoke."

He made another attempt to raise the rig by radio, then turned to his lead and said, "You know the procedure. We can't wait any longer; it's been almost an hour. We have to assume the worst. Get SAS and emergency response ready, and meet me on the helipad."

Minutes later, the rotor blades of a SA 330E Puma helicopter ripped through the lifting fog as it headed toward the eerily silent NB64.

Vitaliy Myatlev reaped the benefits of being President Abramovich's lifelong friend, and loved it. He took a top floor office in the Russian Ministry of Defense, right next door to Minister Dimitrov, another one of his lifelong friends. Although at the center of a starving, frozen, and desperate Moscow, Myatlev's office was lavishly decorated in Western fashion, with imported furniture and art pieces worthy of the world's finest galleries. He had become accustomed to a certain lifestyle since he had started enjoying tremendous success in business, propelling him on the short list of the world's richest men. He would have settled for nothing less.

This lifestyle contrast was nothing new to the citizens of Moscow, accustomed by now with the gaping chasm between classes. Moscow was the only place in the world where workers dressed in rags crowded on commuter busses that shared the streets with a parade of Lamborghinis and Ferraris. No, nothing new for them.

Since the fall of communism, Russia had quickly replaced one dominant class with another, leading to little quality of life improvement for the average citizen. Of course, it had been the Communist Party's greatest, the KGB's finest who had access to riches, connections, and business knowledge to lay down the foundations of capitalism in Russia. No one else but them, the same ruthless elite had gained access to capitalist power using the same methods as they did back in their communist days. This time they were chasing the mighty dollar, not the political favor of one communist dictator or another.

Myatlev was no exception. He'd come of age in the final days of the old KGB, cutting his teeth in foreign intelligence and gaining invaluable exposure to the West and its ways. He also gained something equally invaluable during those days: the lasting friendship of two young men he met while he was a student at the Dzerzhinsky Higher School of the KGB.

The three of them had a lot in common; they were ruthlessly ambitious; stopped at nothing to achieve their goals; and were bold, unafraid, and brilliant. They all lived to see their dreams become reality, although in different directions.

One, Piotr Abramovich, or Petya for his close friends, had become the president of Russia, and the first to stay in power for more than the typical two mandates after the fall of communism. Abramovich had started his third presidential mandate, and the Kremlin rumor mill suggested he was planning yet another Constitution amendment, to remove any remaining limitations on his path of becoming the first post-glasnost dictator. His ego moved mountains; his bruised ego started wars.

The other one, Mikhail Dimitrov, was Russia's minister of defense, the best and brightest the country had seen in ages. A talented strategist with a cool head on his shoulders and a heartfelt desire to restore Russia's greatness along with Abramovich and Myatlev, Mishka Dimitrov was the voice of temperance keeping impulsive Abramovich from setting the world on fire. He had to walk a fine line to do that, but no one else could do that better than Dimitrov.

Finally, Myatlev, the youngest of the three but not by much, had been born with a natural inclination for big business. Within years after he was set free by the fall of communism, he had amassed billions of dollars and business interests, ranging from banking, imported goods, food, and oil in Russia and the former Soviet republics to investments in technology, natural resources, and real estate everywhere else on the globe. Of course, having his best friends in high positions of power within the Russian government had helped him a little in his business ventures. Myatlev never had to worry about permits, taxes, or even staying on the right side of the law. He had become an all-powerful oligarch, grateful and generous toward anyone who helped him prosper.

Of course, there was a price to pay for all that, like his presence here, in his Ministry of Defense penthouse office. He, out of all people, held a regular day job...the thought of that made him cringe. But no one could say no to Abramovich and live to see the light of tomorrow. Abramovich might have been his friend, but that friendship survived, like with most sociopathic narcissists, just as long as Myatlev did what he was told, and obeyed wholeheartedly. Famous for his unpredictable mood swings, Abramovich could turn on a dime and decide to throw him to the depths of Siberia, or just kill him on the spot. Abramovich was the only man on earth who held the power to destroy Myatlev.

But there was a bright side to his unofficial role in the Russian government. Myatlev enjoyed power more than anything else in the world, even more than he enjoyed money. He also loved his country. He was sincerely committed to serve Russia and help restore its lost greatness.

He was deeply, wholeheartedly grateful to Mother Russia. In service to his country he had gained the skills, knowledge, contacts, and money to get him started on his way to business success; he never forgot that. *Plus*, he thought with a crooked smile, *there are fortunes to be made when rebuilding an empire.*

He and Dimitrov weaved ambitious plans to help restore Russia's long lost greatness and rebuild the decrepit military and technology infrastructure. Dimitrov's military instinct set the vision, the strategy, the ideal. However, Myatlev had an uncanny talent; he manipulated people into doing what he wanted. No matter how complex or diabolical Dimitrov's vision, he found ways to build incredible plans and orchestrate their execution. Most of the times, he was highly successful.

There was mutual benefit from their partnership, and Myatlev made sure the benefit stayed just as mutual as Dimitrov liked. If Russia's defense needed a couple hundred new helicopters, the contract would go to one of Myatlev's companies, and an incentive would find its way into Dimitrov's cash vaults. Then the business genius that was Myatlev would buy a helicopter manufacturer, build the choppers, then sell the plant at the height of its capitalization glory. That was, of course, if no other choppers were needed by the Russian Army.

And that's how the world turns, Myatlev thought, filling a glass with vodka and some ice, slapped carelessly in the cut crystal glass with his chubby fingers.

At 59, Myatlev's physical appearance told the honest truth about the abuse his body had taken throughout the years. He had telling bags under his eyes, and he had lost most of his hair. His skin hung around his jaws as if he were a bulldog, and his eyes were always bloodshot. Vodka was a constant presence in his life, and so were fine cigars and expensive foods. His gastritis was giving him some trouble lately, and the latest sip of vodka immediately bore a hole in his stomach.

"Ivan," he called, summoning his aide and lead bodyguard.

Ivan, a well-built ex-Spetsnaz, walked promptly through the door.

"Boss?"

"Get me something to eat."

Ivan reappeared in the doorframe within seconds, carrying a tray with beluga caviar on ice, surrounded by tiny squares of thin, white toast.

"Thanks," Myatlev said in a rare acknowledgment, chewing with his mouth open. Then he tapped his finger on the empty glass, and Ivan promptly refilled it.

"Dr. Bogdanov is scheduled to arrive in a few minutes," Ivan said. "Do you want me to cancel that?"

"Argh...no, I need to talk to him," he replied, rolling his eyes in exasperation.

Myatlev wiped his mouth with a napkin and lit a cigar. He opened the window and took in the aroma of spring with his cigar smoke. Bogdanov...If this was the best that VECTOR Institute had to offer, Russia was in trouble.

VECTOR, the State Research Center of Virology and Biotechnology, somewhat the Russian equivalent of the US Centers for Disease Control and Prevention or CDC, was home to Russia's most advanced medical research. Some of that research, like in any field for that matter, found its way into military applications, hitting Myatlev's radar.

Myatlev had been laying the ground work for his most recent plan, but his plan required real talent, finesse, genius. He saw none of that in Dr. Bogdanov. Yes, he was a well-educated and highly recommended medical researcher, but he was spineless, a coward trying to read Myatlev's mind and serve him what he wanted to hear, instead of working with him, sharing his vision, and making it happen. But, alas, Bogdanov was the best VECTOR had to offer. *Bozhe moi...*

A tap on the door, and Ivan announced him.

"Dr. Bogdanov to see you, sir."

Myatlev turned toward the door, not leaving his favorite spot by the open window.

Bogdanov stepped through the door, pale, staring at his feet. He held his hands tightly clasped together, probably to keep them from shaking.

"So?" Myatlev asked. "How did it go?"

"The...the results were...umm...less than we expected," Bogdanov started, clearing his throat with difficulty, and swallowing hard.

"What happened?"

"They were...uncontrollable. Once they were exposed to the drug we couldn't stop them, and—"

"So the test was a failure, another one," Myatlev said, slamming his palm against the windowsill. "After all this work, we have nothing, that's what you're saying?"

"Umm...I guess we could say that—"

"Enough with the bullshit," Myatlev cut him off angrily. "Grow some balls and admit you have nothing, or tell me what you have."

"Y–yes, sir, we have nothing. We need to go back to the drawing board."

"Your researchers aren't worth much, are they?" Myatlev asked in a threatening tone. "Why can't you find me better ones? Do I have to solve all your problems for you?"

Silence fell for a second. This time, Myatlev expected an answer.

"No, sir," Bogdanov replied weakly.

"I need to have this done already," Myatlev continued just as angrily as before. "Why is it so hard to get a controlled response in people? The entire goddamned pharmaceutical industry does exactly that, gets controlled responses to chemicals in people. Yet you and your idiots can't. What kind of doctors are you?"

Bogdanov stood quietly, not sure how to respond to that.

"You had the perfect environment for this test. A contained, remote environment with male test subjects of about the same build. That's exactly what you said. Still you screw it up. Why the hell is it so hard? All I am asking of you is to fix me a drug mix with controllable results. Is that clear?"

"Yes, sir."

Myatlev turned his back to Bogdanov, leaving him standing there, not sure what to do, afraid to break the silence and ask. After a while, Bogdanov found the courage to leave Myatlev's office, quietly closing the door behind him.

Myatlev heard the door click shut and whispered to himself, "Impotent idiots...all of them."

Chief Ramsay looked at the men seated next to and across from him. They had the same expression, curiosity mixed with concern, and the determination one sees on a soldier's face before going into battle.

"People, listen up," he said, and everyone turned toward him. "In a minute or two we will be touching down on NB64. The platform has been out of contact and has missed the established communication touch point, which was at 8:00AM today. All video and comm links are down. Our protocol," he said, slowing his rhythm of delivery a little, making sure everyone understood, "our protocol requires us to assume the worst-case scenario, which is a terrorist attack."

Most men knew the protocol well and were not surprised. Two younger men from the emergency response unit lifted their heads slightly.

"An offshore oilrig is strategic infrastructure," he clarified, "hence a prime target for terrorists. It's isolated and immobile, relatively easy to approach despite all security, and therefore vulnerable. Please explain what types of attack we should be mindful of when landing on the rig," he said, inviting one of the veterans to explain it to the team.

"The attack could be chemical, biological, or traditional, with explosives. Do not assume you know what's wrong with the rig's crew or the rig itself until it's actually confirmed, and you hear the clear signal given either by me or by—"

"Chief Ramsay," a young man interrupted in a high-pitched voice, bearing horror written on his face. "Look!"

They looked in the direction of the rig, now in close proximity as the chopper was making its final approach. The deck was stained with blood. Bodies were scattered everywhere. It was the scene of a massacre.

"Masks on," Ramsay ordered. "Keep chatter to a minimum."

They disembarked quietly, then almost all of them stopped in their tracks, taking the details in.

Right next to the helipad, a man lay in a pool of blood with his head split open, the ax still stuck in his skull. A few yards out and to the left, another man had found his demise strangled with a piece of chain. A third man lay on his side, and the unnatural position of his head indicated his neck had been broken violently. Toward the mess hall entrance, a man hung halfway over the guardrail, with a knife stuck deep in his heart. Everywhere they looked, it was the same...countless bodies, all violent deaths, inexplicable. It was as if the entire crew had suddenly turned on one another and fought to their deaths.

Chief Ramsay ordered the teams to split up and go below deck with a few hand gestures. He also gestured the quick unspoken signal for "be careful," a rapid succession of the gestures advising them to listen and watch. Then he led one of the teams below deck, into the mess hall.

The same horrific scene extended below deck. The floor was almost entirely covered in blood, and they had to be careful not to slip and fall. A worker had been killed with a hammer blow to the face, and had fallen on top of one of the mess hall tables, lying there with his eyes still open and mouth gaping in a silent, perpetual scream.

Chief Ramsay advanced cautiously, his weapon drawn, and froze in his tracks seeing a technician alive, eating quietly at one of the tables. The man didn't acknowledge anyone's presence, seeming entirely absorbed in his thoughts. He had some difficulty cutting pieces of a brittle biscuit with his plastic knife, but he continued nevertheless, unperturbed.

Chief Ramsay approached a little more, then asked, "What's your name, son?"

"Jim," the young man answered without looking up from his plate, continuing to chew his food.

"What happened?"

"Something happened...yeah..." Jim replied thoughtfully, as if trying to remember.

"Who did this to you?" Ramsey insisted.

"Everyone...no one..."

Ramsey paused for a second, then changed his approach. The man must have been in shock after all that violence.

"What are you doing, son?"

"Me?"

Ramsey nodded, encouragingly.

"Having lunch with Charlie... He's my best friend. We always grab chow together."

One of the men stepped a little to the side of the table, to see behind a row of pantry cabinets. "Oh, my God..." he exclaimed. He yanked his mask off his face, and pointed at the floor with his other hand. "What the hell happened to these people?"

On the floor, right behind where Jim sat, a young man's body laid still, a bullet hole marking the center of his forehead. His nametag, still intact, read,

"Charlie Hernandez."

Lou Bailey tried his best to make his colleagues comfortable with the exercise he had in mind. He knew them well enough to know they'd be unhappy with the day's agenda. Therefore, he had reserved the entire gun club for the morning, and he even brought everyone's favorite coffee in steaming, tall paper cups.

Alex Hoffmann was the first to arrive, only a few minutes late.

"Hey, Lou," she greeted him and gave him a quick hug.

He made her proud. He was her protégé, although the ex-SEAL had twice her body mass and it was all muscle. She had recruited him from her first client, impressed with his initiative, quick brain, and relentless courage, all great assets for an undercover investigator. Not to mention his amazing hacking skills. Lou could break past any firewall, and crack any encryption.

Steve Mercer was the next one to arrive. Their very own corporate psychologist, the man who helped them think through theories and profile their suspects. The man who brought calm to emotional storms and kept their clients steady and levelheaded during their biggest crises. The man she still loved, but couldn't forgive. She made eye contact with him for a split second, then looked away.

"I thought I had the address wrong, Lou," Steve said instead of a greeting, but accepted the coffee with a wide grin. "What am I doing in a gun club?"

"Wait for it," Lou replied cryptically and winked. Steve smiled and leaned against the wall, sipping on the extra hot mocha latte.

"Good morning," Brian said professionally, entering the clubhouse, confusion written all over his face.

Brian Woods was the business genius of the team, and their very own expert in the gadget technologies they sometimes engaged to help them in their work. His main expertise remained business though, and his classy demeanor made him look every bit the part. On many occasions, he had stayed behind in client organizations, serving as executive officer until leadership replacements were recruited, or until the client finished with the cleanup that many times followed their covert investigations.

That was the team she had joined just a few short years before, as a young executive with a computer science background. Even to this day, she sometimes wondered why they had chosen her; why Tom Isaac, The Agency's owner, had put his faith in her and her abilities. Since then she had accumulated a few decent notches on her belt, a few, yet challenging cases she had worked successfully, causing that self-doubt to start fading away. She finally felt she belonged.

"Is Richard coming?" Alex asked, eager to see the rarely visible financial genius of their crew.

"No, not this time," Lou replied. "He's on the East Coast and couldn't make it."

"If I'd only known," Brian said sarcastically and smiled while accepting his triple espresso from Lou. "Why are we here?"

"Thank you, reluctant colleagues, for being here today," Lou said, earning some chuckles as he spoke. "Per our boss and mentor, Tom, I am now in charge of your fitness, self-defense training, and gun proficiency." The pride in his voice was both amusing and heartwarming.

The two men groaned in protest.

"I work with my brain," Steve said, making a dismissive gesture with his left hand, still holding his latte in his right hand. "I don't need any self-defense...I'm a shrink. I can talk my way out of pretty much anything."

"You're not gonna talk your way out of this one, Steve, that I can promise you," Lou replied.

"I don't need this either, I think I'll head out," Brian said, making a beeline for the exit. "Thanks for the coffee, mate."

"Not so fast," Lou said, cutting across his path. "I was tasked to do a job here, and I will not fail."

Brian stopped and looked him in the eye. Then he relaxed a little. "OK, let's see what you have. Although I have to warn you, I am a total klutz when it comes to guns and fighting. I am a businessman; I fight with numbers."

"What am *I* doing here, Lou?" Tom asked, surprisingly appearing out of nowhere. "I have tasked you to train the team. Why did you call *me*?"

Unperturbed, Lou handed Tom the remaining cup of coffee.

"Well, aren't you a part of the team?"

They all laughed, seeing how shocked Tom looked.

"I'm not...Well...I don't need this, you know. I rarely go undercover any more, I just stay behind—"

"Oh, no, no, no," Brian said, grabbing Tom in a side hug, "what's good for the goose, you know..."

"Yeah, OK," Tom conceded. "Lou, please remind me to train you on how to take direction," he added with humor in his voice.

Tom Isaac was the founder of The Agency, the man who had created their small investigative unit, focused solely on high-profile corporate clients. He was the one who brought them all together—their mentor, and their friend. To Alex, he was more than that; Tom and his wife, Claire, had become Alex's family.

"Ready?" Lou asked, and was immediately rewarded with a variety of grimaces, long sighs, and smirks. He didn't seem to care.

He opened a duffel bag filled with handguns. "Brian, what do you do if you have to fire this weapon?"

"Umm...I examine it and, if available, I read the manual first," Brian replied, and Alex couldn't contain a chuckle. In all fairness, she had been the only one who had discharged a weapon in the past couple of years. However, without Lou's diligent training in Krav Maga and firearms, she would have been toast a few times over.

There was no way of knowing, before taking a client's case, what types of danger they'd be facing. Most of them had worked for The Agency for more than ten years and their lives had never been in any significant danger. Corporate investigations sometimes bordered on boring rather than adventurous, or even dangerous.

Yet Alex had been held at gunpoint on her very first case. Gun proficiency was a good skill to master, even if one's record didn't support that belief. Sometimes, although seemingly benign at first, the cases they worked uncovered significant crimes being committed by people with either too much, or nothing left, to lose. That, in itself, was a recipe for danger. That was the reason why she had accepted to go through the rigorous physical conditioning Lou was imposing on her every week, complete with self-defense, close quarters combat, and timed target practice. Although, in all fairness, she still hated the crap out of that physical conditioning routine.

"OK, that's not going to work," Lou replied, all serious. "You have to be ready at a moment's notice. Today we'll do basic gun safety, gun operations, and you'll all handle these guns until your hand knows what to do before your brain even acknowledges it."

"Lou, please start with these two," Tom said, "I really don't think I need this much of—"

"Nonsense," Lou interrupted, "what would you like to start with? A Sig? Or a Beretta?"

Alex smiled discreetly. Her protégé knew how to hold his ground.

Lila Wallace straightened her flight attendant uniform, getting ready for departure. The same uniform she wore almost every day for work without even noticing suffocated her now. She had tossed and turned for the most part of the night, thinking she'd be stuck on the same flight with Mr. Flying Asshole, the first officer and copilot.

She forced herself to take a deep breath and swallow her tears. Even if he'd been a cheating bastard, fucking anyone in range who registered any life signs, she had to behave at her best, or risk being put on report by the flight's commander, Captain Gene Gibson.

Captain Gibson is a real gentleman, she thought. *Too bad they don't make them like that anymore.* Gibson had tried to warn her, discreetly of course, but she didn't listen. She dismissed the advice for caution expressed by Gibson, who had encouraged her to give the relationship some thought, and she'd fallen hard, head over heels, for the moronic first officer Andrew Klapov. Andy, as she had once loved to call him, had been her very own Prince Charming for about two weeks, which happened to coincide with the exact time it took him to get her in bed.

She thought they had something real, and had never been so happy in her life. That lasted until their next flight together, when she'd assumed she had an open invite for Andy's hotel room, and stumbled onto naked Andy performing cunnilingus on her colleague, Corinne. From between Corinne's legs, Andy had looked her in the eye and smiled, licking his lips and winking at her. Heartbroken and disillusioned, she'd run out of there in tears, without being able to say a single word.

Corinne never learned of Lila's personal tragedy; she'd been carried away on the wings of mindless bliss at that dramatic moment, and hadn't even noticed her coming into the room.

From the scene of that crime, Lila ran all the way to the hotel's business center, where she submitted a request for crew transfer, filled with typos and making little sense. Probably having seen such correspondence before, and understanding implicitly what had caused the request, the airline management had approved it, but it was to go into effect at the first of the following month. One more trip, that's all she had left to endure. One more trip with Mr. Flying Fuck.

On top of it all, their typical route, which was San Fran to London and back, had changed at the last minute, and that last trip had to be to Tokyo and back. Four days instead of three. Great...just great.

She brushed her chestnut hair back and tied it neatly in a ponytail, then applied fresh lipstick and touched up her nose with the powder puff. She gently tapped, without smudging her makeup, the corners of her eyes with a tissue, to absorb the tears that had been welling there. No way was she going to look heartbroken over that prick.

"Fucking bastard..." she muttered. "I *so* deserve better than this."

Then she grabbed her wheelie and walked out of the restroom, watching her reflection in the mirror, noticing in passing how strong, professional, and beautiful she looked. Not bad for a girl from Fayetteville, Arkansas. Not bad at all.

Before stepping onto the jetway, she stopped for a moment to grab the flight's manifest from the gate attendant, and gave it a quick look, hoping for a miracle. Nope, none to be found. Flight XA233, nonstop service from Tokyo to San Francisco, had 423 passengers checked in and ready to board.

Well, it could have been worse, she thought, considering the plane's capacity was 496. But an almost full cabin might be a blessing in disguise, keeping her busy, and making the fourteen hours go by faster.

She trotted with confidence on the jetway, boarded the plane, and tucked her wheelie in the staff closet. She popped her head briefly into the cockpit, greeting Captain Gibson and completely ignoring the dick in the first-officer seat.

Then she signaled the gate crew to start boarding, and took her spot in the first-class cabin, ready to greet the passengers.

They started boarding quickly, first class followed closely by the rest of the passengers, some chatting excitedly about a conference or something like that. The conference travelers were scattered throughout the plane, but they seemed to know one another fairly well.

As soon as a third or so of the passengers had made their way on board, she picked up the microphone and made her announcement.

"Ladies and gentlemen, welcome aboard Universal Air flight XA233, with nonstop service to San Francisco. Today's flight will be almost full, so please be considerate when stowing your carryon luggage. Your smaller bag should fit under the seat in front of you. From the flight deck, Captain Gibson and First Officer Klap welcome you aboard Flight XA233. Thank you for flying Universal Air; we appreciate your business."

She hung up with a wicked smile, happy with the pun she'd made by calling the bastard Klap instead of Klapov, in reference to the sexually transmitted disease. She couldn't resist turning her head to see his reaction.

The bastard didn't seem to care, but Gibson frowned gently in her direction, like a disappointed parent. It made her sad. She pulled shit like that and it felt great for a second, then it ruined her life. Reckless, that's what she was. Reckless in her choice of men, and reckless again in how she dealt with the consequences of her own mistakes.

She stood and filled a few glasses with champagne, the traditional welcome for the first-class passengers.

The woman in 1A had already taken her seat, tucked everything out of sight, and was reading a magazine. She accepted the champagne with a smile and a whispered thank you.

"You're welcome, Ms. Bernard," she replied.

Lila, like all flight attendants who worked the first-class cabin, was required to know the names of their passengers and greet them by name. She only had four on this trip, so it wasn't that hard. This passenger's name seemed strangely familiar, but she couldn't place it. Adeline Bernard...an actress, maybe? She definitely looked like one.

She moved on to 2B, where one Darrell Maldonado was loud on his cell phone. She offered him the champagne and he took it without skipping a beat in his heated phone conversation. She touched his arm gently to get his attention, and said, "You will need to end that call in a minute, sir, and switch your phone to airplane mode."

He dismissed her with a hand gesture, as if she was a bother of sorts, a mosquito buzzing him, or some other form of pest. In his dialogue with the other party on the phone, he inserted casually, "Oh, no, I'm still here, I got time. I just got irritated by something, that's all."

Asshole. Maybe there should be an airline just for them. They already had the right pilots for that.

She heard her colleague announcing roll call and crosscheck, and then she started demonstrating the safety features of the Boeing 747-400. She did one more quick round in the first-class cabin, ensuring 2B was off his phone, then sat on the jump seat and prepared for takeoff.

Vitaliy Myatlev ignored the loud growling in his stomach announcing the buildup of hyperacidity, and washed it down with his third shot of vodka for that morning. After providing a few seconds of deep satisfaction, the alcohol started burning what was left of his stomach lining, causing Myatlev to fidget uncomfortably and cuss under his breath.

"*Tvoyu mat*," he swore in his mother tongue, "this job is going to kill me." He leaned back in his chair, unbuttoning his jacket and putting the palm of his hand on his bloated stomach, in an effort to soothe the pain. Maybe a smoke would help.

He opened a new box of Arturo Fuente Opus X cigars, taking his time removing the clear packaging, and inhaling the scent released by the unsealing of the humidor. Then he chose one cigar, and carefully removed its wrapper, stopping at times to inhale the smell of the exquisite Dominican tobacco. That box of cigars had set him back thirty grand…he wasn't going to let a stupid stomachache stop him from enjoying one.

He clipped the tip with a golden cigar clipper engraved with his initials, a gift from an old business partner. Then he lit the cigar, taking his time, holding the tip above the open flame of his torch lighter, and puffing a few times. Then he let out a long sigh, together with some bluish smoke, but not even that calmed his pain.

He opened the window and let in some fresh air, then took in the cityscape of downtown Moscow, with the massive Kremlin a little to the left, and numerous government buildings crowding the central area of the city.

He used to like this game, but not anymore. For the most part, he still liked playing God, more than anything else, and did so every opportunity he got. But he hated being so close to his friend and unpredictable sociopath, President Abramovich. He hated feeling vulnerable, at Abramovich's whim.

He'd been fearless ever since he'd started amassing wealth at unprecedented rates. He had everything. He had numerous prosperous businesses in various countries, some of which offered no extradition, just in case he'd ever need that some day. Myatlev was one of the richest men in the world, having broken into

Global Fortune 50 a few years back. He had good health, with some minor issues, of course, but still he was doing all right. And he had the same insatiable lust for power and achievement that had propelled him to where he was, and continued to fuel his unrivaled drive.

Only one man could crush all that in seconds, and that man was Abramovich. Myatlev hated how he felt about Abramovich and the power he had over him. He'd heard somewhere that genuine power is held by the person who can destroy what you value the most. How true.

At times, Myatlev had thought of killing Abramovich. It would be so easy. Thirty-five years of friendship didn't mean much to Myatlev, who hated being vulnerable more than anything else in the world. He also knew that, if the right circumstances would align, the same thirty-five years of friendship wouldn't hold Abramovich back from sending Spetsnaz after Myatlev with an order to kill on sight.

Then why not beat Abramovich to it and take him out? Myatlev let out another smoke-engulfed long sigh thinking about it. Yes, it was about money. Lots of it. With a favorable, at least for now, Russian president watching over his interests, and with Dimitrov as defense minister, money kept flowing in from all directions. Tax exemptions, official or unofficial. Countless privileges. Government contracts, military and civilian, they all came his way. In turn, he shared the cash with his two friends, and agreed to help Abramovich and Dimitrov rebuild Russia.

But there was a catch, a wrinkle in this fantastic arrangement. It kept Myatlev awake at night, despite almost being in an alcohol-induced coma every night before his head fell on his pillow.

He'd committed to deliver masterful plans in intelligence and covert operations, to acquire weapons and technologies through a wide net of foreign-based assets, most of which were deployed in America. His unrivaled imagination had delivered strategies that, at a global level, could shift the balance of power in the world in Russia's favor, almost overnight. He had the audacity to deploy foreign intelligence asset arrays in a manner seen only in computerized big data models. He'd crafted unexpectedly innovative solutions to all of Abramovich's frustration with the Americans, and to Dimitrov's military needs.

The problem that was fueling Myatlev's gastritis-soon-to-become-ulcer and his growing fear of Abramovich's retaliation was that his most recent plans had failed to deliver the promised results. No doubt, Abramovich was becoming frustrated with his delivery. No matter how carefully he had planned every single detail, no matter how closely he'd been involved in managing every aspect of the plans—and he hated that—they still failed. It was almost as if he had an unseen enemy out there, one who understood what hid in the deepest corners of his mind and could think ahead of him, taking away the advantage of surprise.

He had thought, at some point, that his identity might have been exposed, that he'd been compromised. No one knew, outside of a very few carefully selected people, that one of the world's richest magnates held a permanent office in the Russian Ministry of Defense. Except that inner circle of trusted friends and appointees, no one knew that he led foreign intelligence, espionage, and military strategy operations instead of focusing on his business empire. No one knew, outside of Dimitrov and, of course, Abramovich, that he was sometimes using his own cash, rerouted carefully though several countries, to fund covert operations on foreign soil. He paid that price to ensure no one associated Russia with terrorism, and, of course, the top two Russian leaders paid him back tenfold in contracts and favors.

But, if his identity had been compromised, why was he still alive? Myatlev wasn't fooling himself; he knew very well that he could become a target the moment the Americans learned who he really was and what he did with his time. Yet the adrenaline rush and the financial windfall were strong motivators for him to continue playing this game.

It felt like a game, and he knew the Americans had no sense of humor; they would have taken him out by now. He actually expected it to happen any day, fueling his adrenaline rush and his growing paranoia. Yet he continued. His ambition couldn't take defeat, then call it quits just because the game had become too dangerous; that was not who he was. Myatlev lived to win, in business or in the service of his country; it didn't matter. Winning was all that mattered. Conscience hadn't bothered him ever in his choice of weaponry or tactics; there was no limit to what his mind could conceive.

In moments like these, when he allowed his mind to wander, he wanted more than anything to find out who was playing games with him. Who was behind the lackluster delivery of new weapons technology through his newly deployed array of agents on American soil? How the hell did the Americans catch his best asset handler so damn fast?

It felt personal; it felt that whenever he had a grandiose plan, his unseen enemy would step in and foil that, but otherwise let him operate. He was sure that the enemy existed; but if he did in fact exist, Myatlev wasn't sure why his enemy hadn't killed him already.

He flicked the cigar butt out the window and turned his attention to the matter at hand. He opened a file folder left on his desk and started reviewing the information it contained.

Doctor fucking lame Bogdanov. *Not such a gift from God after all*, Myatlev thought, referring to the meaning of the man's last name. The file showed the background of a studious young man coming from a solid family with good political connections, who had worked his way though medical school and had graduated top of his class from Lomonosov Moscow State University, then had chosen to become a researcher and had been accepted at the VECTOR Institute immediately. Then he'd proven himself at VECTOR, becoming one of its best researchers.

Myatlev just hated the guy; there was no other word for it. Gutless, spineless little prick, he called him. He could deal with his demeanor better if Bogdanov could bring him some results, but the two months Myatlev had been working with him had been an exercise in frustration.

"Ah...fucking Bogdanov," he said, slamming the file folder on his desk. "Ivan?" he called.

"Yes, boss?" Ivan replied, entering the office promptly and stopping in the doorway.

"Get Bogdanov in."

Ivan stepped aside, making room for cowering Bogdanov to step in.

"Good afternoon, Mr. Myatlev," Dr. Bogdanov said in a hesitant voice.

Myatlev didn't respond. He gave Bogdanov a quick look, then said, "You're going to set up operations near Sakhalin, on the mainland."

"Sir?" Bogdanov said, as his eyebrows shot up in surprise. Sakhalin was an island near the extreme far east of mainland Russia, just a few hundred miles from Japan. It was literally at the other end of the world.

"You're going to pack everything you need to build a full research facility and move it to the new location. Ivan will make sure you get everything you need. You have 48 hours to get ready."

Bogdanov clasped his hands together, rubbing them anxiously. "But, sir, how would—"

"You'll load everything on a military cargo plane. Tell VECTOR to call Minister Dimitrov if there are questions. Take everything you need, you won't find anything there on-site." Myatlev paused for a second, measuring the man from head to toe. "This is your last chance, you hear me?"

"Y–yes, sir, but what's going to...what are we—"

"Bogdanov, it's enough that I have to fix your problems for you. Don't be a bigger idiot than you already are. This is your last chance to get me the results I need. If you fail again, you won't be coming back from there."

Bogdanov turned pale and didn't say another word. Myatlev waved him away, and Ivan took him outside, closing the door quietly behind them.

Good, he thought, *let's hope this time it works. How hard can it be to create a new drug?*

With the Bogdanov issue taken care of, all he needed was lunch, a good, soothing meal that would ease the pain gnawing at his stomach.

Andrew Klapov checked his watch nervously, for the third time within five minutes, then checked the cockpit instrument panel again. Everything was normal on their flight to San Francisco. Altitude, 36,000 feet and holding. Vector 062, as per the flight plan.

Captain Gibson had switched the aircraft to autopilot soon after takeoff, and was flipping through the pages of a magazine, reading quietly. Gibson rarely engaged his copilot in idle conversation. Klapov had always suspected Gibson despised him, particularly because of his numerous flings with flight attendants. But Gibson and his opinions were about to become irrelevant.

Klapov pushed away the coffee cup delivered earlier by Lila, and took a small thermos from his case. Who knows what that bitch might have spiced up that coffee with? He wasn't going to risk it. Some of these broads never understood their role in the grand scheme of things, and had the temporary delusion that they somehow mattered. Strangely enough, Klapov found himself entertained by Lila's bitterness, almost flattered. Ha! If she only knew, she'd probably stop trying to do whatever she was trying to do with her snide remarks and snotty attitude. There was no way in hell he was ever going to care about anything she did or said. In his mind, women were single-use, consumer goods, and he was an insatiable consumer with an eclectic taste. He enjoyed the hunt more than even the sex, and once a woman had fallen prey to his charms, she simply ceased to exist, as he moved on to his next target.

Klapov checked his watch again; two more minutes had passed. It was about time. He checked the horizon line, and this time he saw it. Small, barely visible at first, another jet was approaching.

Then his satellite phone rang, a first ever in all of Klapov's flight hours with Captain Gibson.

"What's that?" Gibson asked, surprised.

"Just my phone," Klapov replied, then picked up the call. "Hello?"

Gibson frowned, and Klapov turned slightly toward him, keeping a close eye on every move the captain made.

"Yes, I can see it, I'm ready to proceed," Klapov said, before ending the call.

"Proceed with what?" Gibson asked, frowning.

"We have traffic," Klapov said, instead of replying to Captain Gibson's question, and pointing toward the approaching Challenger.

Gibson turned to observe the approaching aircraft, and didn't notice Klapov pulling a silenced gun.

"I'll call it in," Gibson said, and reached for his comm.

"No, you won't," Klapov replied, and then pulled the trigger twice, in rapid sequence.

Gibson's head fell on his chest, but he remained strapped in his seat, held back by his harness. Blood started dripping from the two bullet holes in his chest.

Klapov took the Boeing 747-400 off autopilot and, with smooth maneuvers, aligned it with the Challenger, as the other aircraft flew in position right above the Boeing. Klapov changed vector to 070, turning slightly southeast and leaving the assigned flight path. Then he took out a small, encrypted radio.

"Challenger, do you read?"

Static crackled for a second, then a strongly accented voice confirmed.

"Read you clear."

"Maintain course and speed, and wait for my signal to switch transponders," Klapov instructed.

"Copy that."

He put the radio down, and called the flight attendant. Before he could do anything, he had to deal with the passengers.

Lila put in her code and opened the cockpit door, then froze as soon as she saw the blood pooling at Gibson's feet. She gasped.

"You bastard," she said, "what did you do? What did you fucking do?" The pitch of her voice climbed as she spoke.

"Lila baby, you have two options," Klapov said, patting the handle of his gun. "You can go to pilot heaven with dear old Gibson, or you can do your job and keep the passengers safe. What will it be?"

She clenched her jaws and pursed her lips, staring at him with eyes glinting with pure hatred. The bitch's contempt was entertaining.

"What do you want?" she finally asked.

"I want you to tell the passengers we're detouring a little to avoid some turbulence, maximum delay 30 minutes or so. I want them strapped in their seats, quiet, off their fucking sat phones. Flight attendants too. Let's try to avoid more people being shot as part of today's flight plan, all right? Can you do that for me, baby?"

His charm wasn't working on her any more, that was obvious. She would have probably killed him on the spot if she caught a chance. Somehow, despite the job he had to do, the thought of Lila trying to kill him gave him an erection.

He almost smiled.

"Why are you doing this?" Lila asked. "What are you doing?"

"Just taking a little detour, nothing more," he said, grabbing hold of his gun and releasing the safety.

Lila flinched. "All right," she said in a trembling voice, "I will tell them. Then what? You're gonna kill us all? I knew you were a prick, but this?"

"Then you keep the hell quiet and keep everyone calm, seated, buckled, and safe," he said, patronizing her.

Sheesh! Women and their entitled questions, he thought. "Remember, I don't really need you to do this job," he added, liking her reaction to his threat.

She looked past him and noticed the shadow of the Challenger.

"Who are they?"

"Doesn't matter. Go!" Klapov gestured her with his gun to get out of the cockpit.

Moments later, he heard Lila making the turbulence announcement through the PA.

Then he picked up the radio.

"Challenger, do you read?"

"Go ahead," the heavily accented voice replied through static crackles.

"Ready to kill transponder. Fire your transponder up, on my count. Three, two, one, go!"

About two hundred miles away, a Tokyo ATC radar operator saw the beacon code for flight XA233 flicker for a second, then continue on its path across the Pacific. He thought nothing of it.

Myatlev ate seated at his massive desk. He took a couple of spoons of hot chicken soup, dressed with sour cream and feta cheese, and closed his eyes halfway in ecstasy. The soup had filled the room with its unmistakable aroma. Each spoonful took a little bit of his stomach pain away, and he mumbled his appreciation. This cook was good; he'd make sure he never leaves. He took another spoonful, savoring it, and a small bite from a slice of white bread toast with it.

Preceded by a quick tap on the door, Ivan walked in hurriedly.

He watched him walk in and frowned. Ivan needed to brush up on his skills. Myatlev hated to be interrupted from his meals, and his assistant knew better.

"Boss? Major Ignatiev wants to speak with you."

Division Seven Major Ignatiev, one of the rising stars of the new KGB, was leading Myatlev's operations in the Russian Far East.

He wiped his mouth and replied begrudgingly, "Put him through," then picked up the phone as soon as it rang. "*Da.*"

"It's Ignatiev, sir. Just letting you know we're ready to receive them. I have everyone's files, and the Challenger took off an hour ago."

"Good," Myatlev said. "Whatever you need, let me know. And keep that idiot, Bogdanov, in check."

He hung up the phone, and let a cryptic smile flutter on his lips. He loved it when a plan came together, even if this particular one required him to use his own plane, and to push the envelope to unprecedented limits. Hopefully, President Abramovich would never find out.

Lila entered the first-class lavatory and looked at her image in the mirror. Her dilated pupils and frozen lips expressed the terror she felt. What was going on? Where the hell were they going? She swallowed a sob. They'll find out soon enough. *Oh, God...*

She sprinkled a little water on a paper towel and patted her burning forehead with it, then wiped the back of her neck. Klapov was many things, a fuck-fest enthusiast and an incorrigible, selfish bastard, but he was not terrorist material. Or, at least, so she had thought he wasn't. Some judge of character she was...Captain Gibson was dead, at the hands of a terrorist. Her opinion of Klapov, especially her ability to see who the man really was, had miserably failed. Again.

Klapov was a terrorist, by all evidence. And for terrorist attacks in midflight, there were procedures. If only she knew who the air marshal was on this flight. But no, the schmucks had to play it all undercover, refusing to identify themselves to the flight crews.

She needed to think fast and decide the amount of risk she was willing to take. She didn't know where Klapov was taking them, how much flight time they still had left, or what his plan was. This was probably a hijacking, for money or political reasons, like freeing some other terrorist.

Then another thought froze the blood in her veins. There could be other terrorists on the plane, among the passengers, maybe even the flight attendants. No one hijacks a 747 by themselves. It never happens. The anti-hijacking training for civil aviation aircraft crews taught them to assume they don't know who all the players are, and to behave normally. That was going to be hard.

But first, she had to follow procedure and communicate the hijacking to ground control. She opened the hidden panel behind the paper-towel dispenser and retrieved the emergency satellite phone. She dialed and waited, but nothing happened. The phone was dead. Of course...the copilot knew their procedures, and knew where everything was. All in-flight phones were controlled from the cockpit, so there wasn't any point trying any of those.

Maybe she could borrow Darrell Maldonado's sat phone? What if *he* was one of them? She couldn't risk it.

She wiped the back of her head once more, then came out of the lavatory and looked at the passengers. They were starting to fidget. No one was reading or dozing anymore. They were all talking, pointing at the windows, looking at their phones, and trying to connect to the Internet. They were becoming restless, and that was putting their lives in danger.

The man in 9C raised his voice, showing his phone's screen to the surrounding passengers.

"Hey, guys, listen, this plane is heading northwest. See?" He pointed at the compass showing on his phone. "We should be heading east, that's where we're supposed to be going. That's where America is. East."

Lila's stomach churned. *Oh, my God! He needs to shut up*, she thought. There were more than four hundred people on this flight, and panic was the last thing they needed. Whether they knew it or not, they were all going wherever it was that Klapov was taking them. There was nothing they could do about it. Per procedure, she was mandated to preserve the passengers' safety, even if that meant going along with whatever was happening to them.

She approached 9C immediately and placed her hand gently on his arm.

"Sir? Can you please take your seat? We are entering an area of high turbulence and we need you to be seated, with your seatbelt fastened."

He gave her an all-knowing look, then replied caustically, "Yeah, right." But he sat down nevertheless, and fastened his seatbelt begrudgingly.

Lila took the PA microphone in her hand, and took in a deep breath before making her announcement.

"Ladies and gentlemen, we are continuing our small detour to avoid an area of high turbulence and bad weather. Please remain seated with your seatbelts fastened. We have sufficient fuel, the delay will be minimal, and the captain will make every effort to recover any lost time. Please remain in your seats with your seatbelts fastened until the captain has turned off the fasten seatbelt sign."

She moved toward the cabin, and someone grabbed her arm. It was 4B. It was one of her first-class passengers, but his name eluded her.

"Miss? Are we going back to Tokyo?"

"No, we're avoiding a nasty storm, that's all there is."

She heard a familiar chime and turned back to go to the cockpit. The terrorist was calling for her. En route, she locked eyes with Darrell Maldonado, whose eyes fiercely bore into hers in an angry glare. She ignored him and entered the cockpit.

"Ah, you've finally made it," Klapov greeted her with poison in his voice.

"What do you want?"

"Prep them for a rough landing, but don't tell them we're going to land."

"And how exactly would you like me to do that?" Lila blurted.

"Don't know, don't care. Just prove your worth and don't make me do your work for you," he said, touching his gun again as a reminder.

She started to turn, hesitated a little, then asked, "What's going to happen to us once we land?"

"Don't really care, sweetheart. This is where I get my money and my ticket to retirement in a nice, sunny place on a remote beach somewhere."

She knew it was pointless, but the anger rising in her throat suffocated her. "You despicable, rat-ass bastard! You make me sick!"

He smiled crookedly and said casually, as if they were chatting at some party, "Whatever, baby, I really don't give a crap, you know?"

She managed to exit the cockpit and grabbed the PA handset, aware she looked pale. She was struggling to keep her voice from trembling.

"Ladies and gentlemen, the captain has instructed me to prepare you for rough weather."

The passengers reacted to her announcement and their voice levels picked up. Some passengers looked terrified, while others were staring out the windows in disbelief, not understanding how the perfectly blue sky could mean bad weather. A couple of women were sobbing quietly. She raised her voice to cover the commotion.

"Please stow all carryon items you might have taken from the overhead bins. At this time, stow all your personal computers and devices. Remove your glasses and high-heel shoes, and tighten your seatbelts, making sure they are snug around your hips. Please remain calm. This will be over soon, I promise."

Yeah, some promise she was making. Based on what?

"This is total bullshit," she heard Maldonado's irritating voice. "There's no damn storm over the Pacific, I just checked." He was holding up his satellite phone demonstratively.

He was not a terrorist, she dared to assume, thinking a terrorist would not agitate things. That wouldn't make sense. Praying she was right at least about *that* asshole, she took her chances and asked in a whispered voice, "Mr. Maldonado, could I possibly borrow your phone for just one minute? I really need to make a call; it's urgent, and ours is broken."

"Are you fucking kidding me?" Maldonado replied. "You've *got* to be kidding me. Why the hell would I do that? You wanna take my phone away, is that it? Jesus Christ, you people are incredible!"

Lila's head hung, and a rebel tear of frustration formed at the corner of her eye. From the seat in front of Maldonado's, the vaguely familiar Ms. Bernard looked at her encouragingly. In her eyes, Lila saw compassion, courage, and determination at the same time. Adeline Bernard understood what was going on.

Blake lay on his bed, watching her getting ready to join him between the satin sheets. His beautiful wife. His Adeline. She looked beautiful in the warm, dim light coming from their nightstand lamps; she was a vision. Long, sleek brown hair, bright, shimmering eyes, and a secretive smile, reserved only for him.

She came toward him in a flutter of silk and lace, and sat on the bed by his side. She reached out and touched his face, caressing it with frozen fingers. He took her hand to his lips and kissed her fingers gently, tenderly, warming them up.

"I love you, baby," she whispered smiling, then faded away into the darkness that took over the room. He tried to hold on to her hand, but her fingers were slipping from his grasp.

Blake woke up screaming, covered in cold sweat. He jumped out of bed and his eyes fell on the alarm clock display: 5:02AM. He turned on the light and started pacing the room restlessly, trying to shake off the chills sending shivers down his spine and freezing the blood in his veins. The dream had seemed so real…

He threw on a T-shirt and went outside, on the penthouse terrace that overlooked Manhattan from 54 stories up, trying to slow his heart rate. The city looked its normal sleepless self, yet the bad feeling his dream had left wouldn't disappear.

He took a few deep breaths, trying to shake away the memory of the nightmare, then resumed blaming himself. He should have insisted she take the personal jet; that's what it was there for. Even if there was a conflict in their schedules, he should have been the one to fly commercial, not her. Or he should have insisted to charter her a plane. He was the president, CEO, and one of the major stakeholders of America's second largest bank, goddamnit, and he should have done all these things and more.

Well, no point going over those things now…soon she was going to be home. A few more hours, and he'd board his jet to go meet her in San Francisco, and everything would be all right again. And next time, he'd know what to do, and he wouldn't let her talk him out of it.

He took out his cell phone and typed a text message.

"Hey, baby, I know you're in midflight but I miss you. Call me when you get this."

The passengers had remained relatively calm until the Boeing started its descent. That's when they started panicking. They were sobbing, crying, holding one another's hands tightly, asking questions, all in a quagmire of sounds, erratic movements, and emotions out of control. Some were strangely paralyzed, unable to move or make a sound.

Adeline locked eyes with Lila and mouthed to her, "Talk to them."

Lila was already strapped in her jump seat, but she reached out to the PA microphone and managed to articulate an announcement that was supposed to bring a little more calm to the 423 passengers on flight XA233.

"Ladies and gentlemen, to avoid the bad weather the captain has decided to land the aircraft, for your safety. This is a small airport, so please assume brace positions. Please place your feet and knees closely together, with your feet flat on the floor. Bend forward as far as possible, touching the seat in front of you if you can reach it. Keep your hands above your head, one over the other. Bring your elbows close to your body. Remove your high-heel shoes and any eyewear. The runway will be short, and the captain will be braking hard once he touches down. Please remain calm. Universal Air is committed to your safety and to take you to your final destination as soon as possible. Thank you."

Adeline nodded a silent thank you, and Lila smiled weakly for a second. The passengers fell eerily quiet, most likely paralyzed with fear. A woman a few rows back was praying, prayer beads in her hands and eyes tightly shut. Someone's voice was heard coming from the back cabin, "I'm gonna sue you assholes! If I live through this, I'm taking you to the cleaners!"

Adeline gestured Lila to come sit next to her, in the empty first-class seat. Lila hesitated; that wasn't permitted by regulations. Then again, nothing happening on that flight was permitted by regulations, so she unbuckled fast, ran for the seat next to Adeline, and buckled up just when the jet started its final descent.

The aircraft dropped altitude abruptly, then finally touched down on a bumpy, decrepit concrete runway, almost too narrow for its wheels to fit. The Boeing's brakes hit so hard they made a screaming noise, exacerbated by passengers screaming and wailing, covered by the roar of all four engines in full reverse thrust. The huge jet shook hard as it rode over the potholes and cracks in the concrete surface, making the passengers bounce around in their seats as if they were broken puppets.

The jet finally came to a screeching stop, through some miracle remaining intact after the rough landing. The passengers lifted their heads slowly, as if finding it hard to believe they survived, and started looking out the windows.

The plane started a very slow taxi on a narrow extension of the runway, its massive wing wheels rolling on the grassy grounds on the sides of the strip. After what seemed to take forever, the jet entered a decrepit hangar buried in the side of a hill. It was dark, poorly lit by some improvised projectors and whatever light made it through the doors. It was lined with rusted metallic panes that had originally been painted army green, now stained and falling apart.

Then someone's yell froze the passengers' blood in their veins. "Oh, my God, they've got guns!"

Lila grabbed Adeline's hand and both of them looked out the window.

"Oh, God..." Adeline whispered, "where are we? Do you know?"

"We must be in Russia somewhere. There's nothing else here other than Russia and Japan, and this doesn't look anything like Japan," Lila answered, shuddering.

First Officer Klapov exited the cockpit and unlocked the cabin door. Through the open door and through the starboard windows, the passengers watched in terror how armed men pushed mobile stairs toward the jet's door.

A woman shrieked and said, pointing at Captain Gibson's body, now visible through the open cockpit door, "Look, he's dead!"

Then all hell broke loose.

Armed men climbed onboard the aircraft and took positions inside the cabins. Two remained by the cockpit, two more made their way toward the back of the plane, shoving hard anyone who stood in their path.

They looked military, but their uniforms were in bad shape and mismatched, as if they had put on whatever pieces of leftover uniforms they could find. Most of them were heavily tattooed and looked like ex-cons, escaped after many years of doing hard time. They were dirty, most of them unshaved, and, on whatever parts of their bodies were showing, covered in scars. They looked more like a hard-core paramilitary gang than a military unit.

Within seconds, the entire cabin commotion fell to a deafening silence, sprinkled here and there with muffled whimpers and quiet sobs.

One of the armed men picked up the PA microphone and spoke in heavily accented, rough English.

"Welcome to Russia," he said, smiling wickedly and exposing two rows of dirty, decaying teeth. "This is how it will work. I say, you do. If you do what I say, you live. If not," he added, shrugging his shoulders with indifference, "you die."

Passengers and flight attendants watched what was happening with eyes wide open in terror, speechless.

"Now we get off the plane," the man continued. "Move!"

The two men in the back of the cabin started pushing the reluctant passengers out of their seats. A man tried to grab his briefcase and was punched hard. The blow brought him to his knees in the aisle between the seats.

"No time for bag, leave it!" the man with the gun ordered. Then he prodded the kneeled passenger with the barrel of his gun, forcing him to get up and walk toward the exit.

One of the armed men at the front of the jet started his way toward the back, but stopped halfway, and started pushing and shoving passengers, forcing them to disembark. Scared and helpless, passengers clung to their seats, afraid to leave the relative safety of the aircraft and brace the terrifying unknown that awaited them at the aircraft door.

Lila and Adeline still held hands tightly, holding on to each other. Still holding hands, they were pushed out of the plane, and down the stairs, where more men with guns barked orders and pushed everyone toward the hangar door. Outside the hangar, several Army trucks stood by.

One of the Russians held a clipboard in his hand, and directed disembarking passengers toward the trucks.

Lila and Adeline waited in line behind passengers who had disembarked before them. The man with the clipboard asked everyone their name, then flipped though the papers attached to his clipboard, then pointed at one truck or another. He was sorting them, executing some form of triage. They had the flight manifest.

"Theo Adenauer," the next passenger in line identified himself in a discernible German accent.

"Dr. Adenauer, yes?" the Russian asked.

"Yes," the German confirmed, slightly surprised.

The Russian pointed him to the nearest truck, parked right next to the hangar door. The German complied.

The next few passengers were pointed toward other trucks, which were filling fast. Used to counting passengers, Lila fell into her work habit and determined that a truck could take roughly fifty passengers. They were the types of trucks most commonly seen in World War II for supply transport, a cargo hold was covered with a soft top made of military drab fabric on a wire frame. Fifty people would fit in there, standing room only, packed closely together like sardines. Even so, the Russians needed nine or ten trucks to haul all of them out of there.

"Alastair Faulkner," said a proud man with a British accent.

"Dr. Faulkner?" the Russian confirmed.

"Yes," the man replied, raising his eyebrows.

The Russian showed him the truck parked closest to the hangar door.

"Did you notice that?" Lila whispered, wondering what the hell that was all about.

"Uh-huh," Adeline whispered back, "they're sorting passengers; they're putting all the doctors in that one truck." She squeezed Lila's hand.

An Asian family was next in line, a man carrying his toddler and holding on to the hand of his wife.

"Wu Shen Teng, Lin Teng, and Yun Tsai Teng," the man said quietly, not daring to look the Russian in the eye.

"Dr. Teng from Taiwan?" the Russian asked, after flipping through his papers.

"Y–yes," the man replied.

"You, go there," the Russian said, pointing at the nearest truck. "The woman and child will go there," he added, pointing at one of the other trucks.

"No," Dr. Teng said, "I'm going with them, they are my family."

The Russian remained quiet as he handed his clipboard to another man, then took his Kalashnikov off his shoulder. Lightning fast, he hit the Taiwanese man in the groin with the weapon's butt stock. Dr. Teng, still holding his daughter, shrieked and fell to the ground, managing to turn and land on his side, his daughter on top of him, unharmed. His wife cried and grabbed the baby, then kneeled next to her husband, saying something fast in Chinese in a pleading tone of voice.

"You, go to that truck, they go in the other one," the Russian repeated. "OK?"

Another Russian grabbed Mrs. Teng and her baby and pushed them toward a truck, while Dr. Teng managed to stand up and walk on his own, bent forward, crouched in pain.

The next few passengers boarded their trucks in silence, and none of them was selected for the closest truck.

Lila and Adeline were next.

"Lila Wallace," she said, anticipating she'd be sent to the trucks to their right.

"You go there," the Russian said after checking his papers, pointing at the doctors' truck. "Someone needs to feed them and wipe their asses, and it will not be me."

Adeline was sent to the other trucks, with the rest of the passengers. They parted ways reluctantly, with a final hand squeeze and quiet, whispered words of encouragement.

Then an American accent was heard, coming from a middle-aged woman who held her head up high. "Jane Crawford."

Same routine...the Russian checked his papers and confirmed. "Dr. Crawford?"

"Yes," she answered. "Yes, I know, that truck," she said. "But tell me, please, what's the deal with the separate trucks? Where are you taking us?"

"To the lab, where you have work to do," the Russian replied.

"And them?" Dr. Crawford asked, pointing at the rest of the trucks.

"Them? They are your lab rats. We will cage and feed them until you are ready to run your tests."

Alex took her seat on the restaurant's patio, enjoying the warm April sun, the happy chirping of the birds, and the fresh green of the palm trees. Although almost irrelevant to talk about spring in southern California, Alex still enjoyed the tiny differences between seasons, bringing new flavors and new sounds to the landscape with each season.

She'd arrived a little early for her lunch with Claire Isaac, Tom's wife and her best friend. She and Claire had become close after Alex had joined The Agency. She found in Tom and his wife a new family, support, encouragement, and warm friendship.

There she was, walking with a spring and looking happy and full of life. Alex admired Claire's looks, from her fit body, to her hairstyle, her choice of elegant yet casual clothing, and her overall demeanor. She hoped she'd look that good at Claire's age.

"Hello, darling," Claire greeted her, and then gave her a warm hug and a kiss on her cheek.

"Good to see you," Alex replied cheerfully. "I've got some stories to tell."

They both chuckled as they took their seats at the table. A waiter appeared and took their drink orders.

"So, how did it go?" Claire asked. "Your team self-defense training."

"It was hilarious. You should have seen them all protesting. It was fun to watch. Steve and Brian said they never get in fights, which, for the most part, is actually true. But Tom was the best. He didn't want to be there at all, but he had no way out. Lou wouldn't let him off the hook!"

They both laughed, then Claire said, "It was about time you all did this, you know. As Tom's wife and den mother for this crew, I have spent many hours worrying for your safety. Things could go wrong in so many ways, I can't even—"

"Excuse me just a second, Claire, look!" Alex pointed in the direction of the restaurant's TV, displaying Stephanie Wainwright's familiar face under the headline, "Disappeared over the Pacific," while the "Breaking News Alert" sign was rolling at the bottom of the screen. "Let me see what that's about."

She waved at a waiter and asked him to turn up the volume on the TV.

Stephanie's voice came to life. "Disappeared while in flight above the Pacific. The aircraft, a Boeing 747-400 operated by Universal Air, presumably crashed into the ocean with 423 passengers and 18 crew onboard. Search teams have been dispatched from Tokyo and Sapporo, Japan, to search for the missing aircraft. The flight's transponder was last recorded at these coordinates, putting XA233 at least four hundred miles out to sea."

Alex turned her attention back to Claire.

"I'm sorry, Claire, I interrupted you," she said, a little absentminded, a deep frown lingering on her forehead.

"It's all right, my dear," Claire replied. "Such a tragedy...Did you know anyone aboard that flight?"

"No, I didn't. I don't think so."

"Then what's on your mind?" Claire probed.

Alex frowned and fidgeted a little before answering.

"Umm...I was just thinking. How is it possible that these aircraft don't even have the GPS and remote-tracking system that an OnStar has, for example? If we can have it in our cars, how come we don't have it on our planes? They should be able to know precisely where it crashed, and what went wrong." She stopped talking for a few seconds, deep in thought, then added quietly, "Probably no one will find that wreckage for years to come, no matter how hard they'll look. What a waste, in the age of technology."

Alex loaded her Walther PPK and put her earmuffs on. Then she took a big gulp of coffee and rubbed her eyes. Shooting exercise at night...only Lou could come up with shit like that. Yeah, yeah, she understood that bad guys don't make appointments during business hours, but this was hard. Her eyes were screaming to stay shut, and the targets danced in front of her. She was doing little else than wasting bullets and making noise.

"Yo, Alex, wake up," Lou said, snapping her out of her reverie. "I've started the clock already!"

In a mock-up of a house, built on one of the club's ranges, targets on springs were popping left and right from behind doors or corners, and, if they would have had real weapons, she'd been dead and buried by now. She touched the red button that stopped the simulation and took her earmuffs off.

"Lou..."

"What, if anything, could get you to focus tonight?" Lou asked, ignoring her plea.

"Never mind that," she deflected masterfully, "tell me where the others are, and why I am the only one taking this abuse from you right now."

"You were the most advanced in your training. They have a lot more to endure before they can even attempt to pass this certification."

"Free translation of what you just said is that I'm the only one who got suckered into being here tonight, right?"

"No, I meant it when I said—"

"Lou? Don't lie to me," she said, waving her index finger at him and noticing he couldn't control a chuckle. Busted!

"OK, now that we know where we stand," Alex continued, "let's just go home and sleep. Morning is when sleep is the sweetest, and we're wasting that, and lots of ammo."

"Nope, we're staying and finishing this," Lou replied, turned all serious.

"Really?" Alex protested in a childish voice. "I mean, really?"

"Yeah, really, 'cause otherwise you'll have to start this all over again some other night, and it will be just as painful. Finish this exercise and I'll stay off your back for a year!" Lou said, offering her a bone. "Well," he immediately corrected himself, "except for the monthly gun proficiency, and the weekly self-defense training exercises that are mandatory."

"Argh..." Alex replied, her face taking an exaggerated expression of frustration. She reloaded her weapon with a new clip.

"How can I get you to focus?" Lou asked again.

She thought for a little while, then turned to the range master who waited patiently behind the yellow line, and asked, "Do you have a red marker?"

"Yeah, sure, here you go."

She took the marker and went inside the range, where she drew the letter V on all the targets.

Then she came back and grabbed her gun, assuming position at the start of the simulation. "There! That will get me focused."

"Your mystery Russian?" Lou asked. "You really think he's still out there?"

"I'd bet my life on it," she said, frowning.

Her mystery Russian had been on her mind for more than a year, yet she'd made no real progress in finding out who he was. He was the one she couldn't catch, not yet, anyway. He was a genius mastermind of terrorist plots, creating strategies that sent everyone else hunting shadows and looking in all the wrong places. He was bold, he was majestic, he was grandiose. His plans were spectacular in size and scope.

She'd come close one time; so close that she almost found out who he was. But no, he was gone again, disappeared, and even Mossad had failed to find out more about him. All it knew was that he was Russian, despite his association with Islamic terrorist factions, that his name started with the letter V, and that he was brilliant.

He never used his credit cards for anything; he rotated through his staff, team, or people to pay for things, or however else he could manage to exist in places without leaving a shred of financial evidence. She had tried to identify him like she'd caught others, by running financial tracking software against known locations of terrorist activities, and seeing which names showed at more than just a few. But no, he was too smart for that. All she could find was that at every location of such an attack or conspiracy, there was always one or more Russians traveling, but never the same ones. She tried to find out what, if anything, all these Russians had in common, and came up empty. Nothing. Coincidence? No. The bastard was *that* good.

And he was *that* dangerous...In one case, she had definite proof of V's anti-American interests. That's the closest she'd ever come to catching him. Then, in her latest case, she couldn't prove anything, but it felt like him. The terrorists she did catch wouldn't talk, but their plans had that greatness. Their strategies had that exceptional quality, an uncanny brilliance she'd since learned to associate with him, with the mystery Russian whose name started with the letter V.

She wanted nothing more than to catch him, and her mind could barely focus on anything else. At her house, she had a timeline wall with notes, dates, and entries of all related incidents and bits of information she could gather. She spent countless hours staring at the crazy wall covered in pictures, paper clippings, and sticky notes, all tied up with colorful yarn showing the correlations among them. She stared at that wall for hours, making zero progress. In the meantime, she felt she somehow managed to disappoint everyone, let everyone down. Her team, her Agency family, they all thought she was becoming obsessed with him, with her Russian ghost, and they were losing confidence in her. Because of her obsession with V, she'd broken up with Steve, and her heart still ached. V was ruining her life. He was real, dangerous, and, for sure, keeping busy. And she couldn't goddamn catch him.

She felt a wave of anger rushing adrenaline through her veins, switching her brain into high gear, rendering her wide-awake. She checked her clip with a couple of quick moves and said, "Ready." Lou started the simulation, and she went in, taking down target after target. She moved fast, left no survivors, and wasted no ammo.

"Cease fire, cease fire," she heard the range master's voice, followed by the familiar alert horn.

"Oh, God...what now?" She just wanted the exercise to be over with. Two more minutes and she would have been done.

She approached the range master. "What's up?"

"It's your phone, miss. It's been ringing nonstop. I thought it would go to voicemail, but it keeps on ringing. Must be an emergency, at this time of night."

She unzipped her duffel bag and took out her phone. Seventeen missed calls! Before getting to see whom they were from, the phone rang again, and Blake Bernard's name and picture displayed on the screen. She picked up.

"Blake!"

"Alex, thank God!"

"What happened? What's up?"

"No time now," he said, his voice sounding desperate. "I need you badly. I'm flying in; I should be landing in 45 minutes or so at San Diego International. Come meet me, please."

"Sure thing, on my way." She hung up and stared at the phone's screen, concerned.

"Who was that?" Lou asked.

"Blake Bernard, our former client, the financier. I'm sure you remember him. He's in some kind of trouble. We're leaving now."

Dr. Gary Davis shifted his weight from one foot to the other, tensing his muscles to restore blood flow. He trotted gently in place, then stretched on his toes and extended his arms above his head, as if reaching for something hanging high from the ceiling. Then he relaxed his arms and shook them gently, welcoming the refreshed blood flow in his veins.

He didn't dare to move; he couldn't see anything in the pitch-black darkness of the hole they'd been thrown into. He didn't want to step on any of his cellmates. The other two were lying somewhere on the cold, concrete floor. In the time that had passed since they left the aircraft, they had learned to sense each other's presence in the nightly blackness of their confinement.

During the daytime, faint slivers of light made their way through two tiny vents at the joint of the back wall with the stained ceiling, making their lives a little more endurable. Those vents were the only source of fresh air and light they had. At nighttime though, no shred of light made it in.

Their cell was about ten by ten feet, and the ceiling was quite high; he could sense an echo when they spoke. The two vents cut in the concrete wall were the only openings; there were no windows, and the massive, green, bolted metal door was always closed. It had stayed closed since they were brought there, despite sustained, repeated banging and yelling, in their attempts to get someone's attention. Anyone.

Daylight, fading into darkness, and back into light again had helped them keep track of the days going by. Growling, aching stomachs and parchment-dry throats kept track of time with equal accuracy. They'd been in that hellhole for three days, living off moldy, musty bread and stale water from a rusty pot, now empty.

"You know what I appreciate about this place?" A woman's voice, with a strong French accent, and a husky, guttural pitch asked, resonating strangely in the thick darkness.

That was Marie-Elise Chevalier, Dr. Chevalier to be precise, professor, researcher, and thought leader in the field of molecular neuroscience and neuroanatomy. Since they'd been sharing a cell, they all had time to become properly acquainted. Although in the past their paths had crossed, at medical conferences and scientific events, they had never spoken to one another before their detention.

"You actually *like* something about this place?" The British accent of Dr. Declan Mallory spiced up the dialogue. "I know a good therapist, he might be able to help you," he added, a trace of cynical humor in his voice.

Dr. Mallory specialized in ADHD and neurodevelopmental disorders. A great guy: calm, focused, supportive, yet sometimes moody. *Great scientist and partner to be abducted and incarcerated with*, Gary Davis couldn't help thinking, a grim sense of amusement tinting his otherwise clinically dry judgment.

"*Oui, absolument*," Dr. Chevalier replied. "But can you guess what?"

Gary chuckled quietly. This exercise of theirs had kept them sane for a while, and it was probably bound to continue to keep them sane for a little while longer, but not more. They had played word games, engaged whatever remnant of their sense of humor they could muster, and counseled one another. Cried on other's shoulders, and told stories of their families. Shared hope and hopelessness, both equally volatile in the hell they'd been confined to.

"I give up," an almost morose Dr. Mallory said. "I cannot fathom what you could possibly like about this place. You win."

"Bugs," an almost cheerful Dr. Chevalier said. "There are no bugs here. *Oui?*"

"Right," Gary agreed. "Roaches could have made this *sejour* much worse."

"Or rats," Dr. Mallory added.

A moment of silence followed, interrupted immediately by Chevalier.

"*Oh-la-la*...rats are worse," she said, thoughtfully. Then she changed her mind. "*Mais non,* bugs are worse!"

"Let's put this to a vote," Mallory quipped.

"Shh..." Gary whispered, "I hear something. Footsteps."

They all fell silent, holding their breaths. They could hear footsteps approaching; two, maybe three men, closer, louder.

The sound of the door latch being pulled startled them, and the light that burst inside blinded them, making them squint as their eyes tried to adjust to the brutal invasion of powerful fluorescent light.

"*Yebat,* move it!" One of the men, a six-foot tall, heavily tattooed goon, dressed in mismatching uniform parts, stepped inside their cell and prodded him with the barrel of an AK47. The sleeves of his uniform were rolled up, showing muscle fibers knotted under his grimy skin, and making the inked king cobra curled on his right forearm seem alive.

"All right, all right," Gary replied, holding up his arms in a pacifying gesture, and stepping out of the cell. Drs. Chevalier and Mallory followed closely, still squinting badly from the intense light.

They walked behind King Cobra on an endless, slightly curved corridor, while the two other armed men ended their procession. After a few hundred feet, they came to a stop in front of another green, massive metallic door. King Cobra unlatched that one, and immediately prodded the occupants to step outside.

Four more squinting, wobbly prisoners stepped out of that cell. Dr. Gary Davis recognized two of the speakers from the conference they had all attended what seemed like years ago. Dr. Theodore Adenauer, a top-notch researcher from Germany, had presented his thesis on molecular psychopharmacology in his typical arrogant manner. Yet not even his irritating arrogance was able to diminish the value of the work presented. Arrogant or not, the man was scintillating, and his work had been recognized as foundational research for recent advances in drug research, leading to significant progress in antidepressants, SSRIs, and the overall understanding of synapse chemistry.

Dr. Howard Bukowsky, a kind and easy-going Canadian, had shown no trace of arrogance when he'd spoken to a jaw-dropped audience about the results of a newly introduced therapy regimen, a combination of sensory-motor therapy and minimal drug support, engaged together in the treatment of PTSD. Dr. Bukowsky was the only clinician on the speakers' list, and the only practitioner Gary would have chosen as his personal therapist.

Right behind Howard Bukowsky followed a young woman, her face stained and smudged from tears and makeup. She blinked repeatedly, trying to adjust to the blinding light, while straightening her clothing. She'd obviously been sleeping on the concrete floor, like the rest of them, curled up in the dirty blankets their captors had thrown in their cells before slamming the doors shut. She seemed familiar, although she was too young to have been in medical research. Then she put on her jacket, bearing the Universal Air logo, the "X" with a curvy, extended left arm, and Gary immediately remembered her. She was one of the flight attendants, most likely the one servicing first class, if he remembered correctly.

The fourth to come out of the cell was a woman in her mid-fifties, needing some assistance to walk, which Dr. Bukowsky immediately offered, calling her "Dr. Crawford." She looked pale and sick, too weak to walk.

One of the goons prodded her to move faster, and she groaned in pain.

"Hey," Dr. Bukowsky said, holding her and helping her walk. "Take it easy, will ya'? She can't move any faster, can't you see?"

King Cobra resumed walking farther on the endless corridor, while the two Russians at the end of their procession talked angrily among themselves, gesturing toward the prisoners. Gary Davis didn't understand a word they were saying. For the first time in his life, he regretted not studying Russian as an elective in school. He'd chosen French; not very useful under the circumstances.

"Where are you taking us?" Dr. Adenauer's strong German accent echoed in the hallway. "I demand to know."

The two Russians looked at each other and burst into laughter.

"*Vy yebat!* You demand to know? This is all you need to know," the Russian continued, slamming the stock of his weapon in Adenauer's back, making him keel over with a loud groan. Mallory picked him up quickly, in the roars of laughter sprinkled with expletives coming from the two Russians.

A few more yards, and another green massive door unlatched, its four detainees pushed outside in the blinding light.

Dr. Teng, from Taiwan, emerged with tears that streaked his face, and with hollow, expressionless eyes. His achievements in psychosomatic medicine and his latest research in brain imaging had made the thin, fragile man well-known in their circles. He was barely recognizable now.

Dr. Alastair Faulkner, a British national and the world's foremost authority in regional and seasonal affective disorders, was grayish pale and a little unstable on his feet. He touched the walls a number of times to gain stability. Definitely not a good sign, and, by the sad, accepting look in his eyes, he was well aware of it.

Dr. Fortuin, Klaas Fortuin, if Gary remembered correctly the Dutch man's first name, professor of biochemistry and neuropharmacology, held his spine upright, in typical Dutch manner. Gary remembered he'd read somewhere that the Dutch are tough, almost harsh in their parenting, being focused on building character and resilience in their offspring. Dr. Fortuin definitely displayed character and resilience in the face of adversity, walking tall and almost proud, calm, unfazed, as if not noticing he walked between two loaded machine guns, not reacting to the barrel of the AK47 bruising his left ribs.

The last to vacate the cell was their pilot. His uniform was wrinkled and stained; most likely, he'd slept in it despite how warm it was. As usual, Gary noticed the most unusual details for the respective moment, and that time he noticed the wear and tear on the man's uniform. The sleeves shined at the elbows, and the cuffs were almost fringed with wear. That level of wear couldn't have been from just three days of incarceration; that was months' worth of daily use. There used to be glamour about a pilot's job; apparently, not anymore.

Gary found himself counting the members of their group, as King Cobra had resumed his walk down the endless corridor. They were nine scientists and two flight crew. So far.

King Cobra opened a massive door, but this time gestured his followers to walk in. Gary entered a large room, organized as a makeshift lab. As soon as he stepped through the door, he found himself at the top of a five-step flight of descending stairs, leading to the main floor.

He hesitated a second, taking in everything in the huge lab. More than two hundred feet wide by maybe one hundred and fifty feet deep, the space had tall, dark gray, concrete walls, one of them curved, matching the curvature of the hallway they'd just walked through. The opposite wall had windows, placed at least ten feet high above the ground, with rusty frames holding dirty, almost completely opaque glass. The room seemed to be a part of a larger, round structure.

Rows of tile-covered tables lined up almost wall-to-wall, covered with equipment and chemicals. Autoclaves, incubators, Bunsen burners, and refrigerators took the first row of lab tables. Microscopes, scanners, centrifuges, a liquid chromatograph and a mass spectrograph lined another row of tables. Against the wall, there was a surprising collection of modern lab equipment: a Hitachi 917 automatic analyzer, a microscale, a recent model Belson biochemistry machine, Chinese but decent, state-of-the-art pharmacology analysis equipment, and a digital amalgamator. Some of the equipment was antiquated, but most of it was modern, the latest the industry had to offer.

Supplies were neatly organized and stored against the right wall, labeled in English. Almost forty feet of refrigerators filled with drugs, chemicals, reactives, and serums covered the wall. Past the refrigeration area, several tens of feet more continued with room-temperature shelving, holding thousands of drug formulations and chemical compounds. It was, by all appearances, a well-equipped lab. Where the hell were they? What was this place?

Some sleeping cots stood against the back wall, leading Gary to assume they wouldn't be leaving the lab anytime soon. Simple, folding military cots, with dirty blankets on each one. In the far corner, an improvised separation for personal use, probably the Russian version of a port-a-potty. And everywhere, the same insufferable, inescapable, musty smell of moldy concrete.

"What is this place?" Dr. Chevalier whispered, her French accent stronger than usual.

"It's a nuclear missile silo by the looks of it," the pilot replied. "This facility is half-buried underground."

"Nuclear?" Dr. Adenauer jumped in the conversation. "Does that mean there's radiation here?"

"Oh, my God..." the flight attendant whispered, tears running freely from her red eyes.

"Quiet," King Cobra shouted, punctuating his words by pounding his weapon into the ground. "No talking."

A middle-aged man wearing a lab coat walked through the door and closed it. The noise of the massive door latching got everyone's attention. They turned toward him.

"I am Dr. Bogdanov," he said in harsh, heavily accented English. "This is your lab. You all work for me now."

They shifted their weight nervously, some gasping, others wringing their hands.

Forced labor, Gary Davis found himself thinking, *doing who knows what for the Russians. We are so screwed.*

"Make no mistake," Bogdanov continued. "If you are not worth keeping in the lab, we will use you as lab rats for the test batches. One way or the other, you *will* work for us."

A deathly silence engulfed the small group. Bogdanov smiled, satisfied.

"Now get to work. Organize everything, make a list of what you're missing, make sure you're ready to produce the chemicals we need. Is that clear?"

No one replied. He waited a few seconds, then turned to leave.

"Dr. Bogdanov, if I may," Dr. Bukowsky spoke, his Canadian politeness intact despite the circumstances. "We need insulin. Dr. Crawford is diabetic, and she ran out of supplies yesterday."

Dr. Crawford grabbed Bukowsky's sleeve, as if asking him to stay quiet.

"We will see about that," Bogdanov replied. "How useful is she? What does she do?"

Someone gasped behind Gary. As if hypnotized, he heard himself speak.

"She is quintessential to any neurochemistry research," Gary spoke clearly, calmly, and sounding sure of himself. Although he was making it up on the fly, he hoped he was right about the Russian's intentions. "Her dissertations on the clinical aspects of applied psychopharmacology, and her fellowship experience with the University of Virginia make her irreplaceable to any drug study."

Dr. Crawford looked at him with amazement, a hint of a smile fluttering on her lips as she mouthed, "Thank you."

"I will bring insulin," Bogdanov said. "Now, get to work."

Dr. Faulkner, still weak on his legs, stumbled forward and said, "You can't do this! You can't force us to work for you! What kind of doctor are you?"

Bogdanov turned and stared at Dr. Faulkner in disbelief, then gestured at King Cobra with a swift head movement.

Cobra took three large steps and, as he reached Faulkner, struck him in the stomach with his knotted fist. Dr. Faulkner gasped, then keeled over, curled up on his side. He moved his legs spasmodically, and, as Gary and a couple of others rushed to assist him, he drew his last breath with a terrifying groan.

Gary put his fingers on Faulkner's neck, searching for a pulse.

"He's gone; probably a massive coronary," he said bitterly. "Great job," he turned and said to Cobra. "At this rate, you'll kill us all before we do whatever the hell you got us here to do, you stupid moron!"

Cobra took a step toward him, cussing in Russian, his face congested and scrunched in anger, wielding his fist in a threatening motion. Gary stood there, not even flinching. *Que sera, sera*, he thought, bracing himself for the beating that was to come.

Cobra's fist never came down on him.

"Enough," Bogdanov said, then left the lab, followed closely by his men.

Alex waited on the tarmac, oblivious to the early dawn coloring the sky with a reddish palette of hues, and to the fresh morning breeze. Her eyes scouted the runway, waiting for the plane to appear, worried about her friend, Blake Bernard. The calm and composed Blake, who held his own impeccably while transacting billions of dollars without breaking a sweat, would never give anyone seventeen missed calls. Yet he'd done just that.

The familiar silhouette of his Phenom 300 taxied quickly and came to a stop right in front of the VIP terminal, where she waited. The door opened immediately, and Blake stepped down, rushing toward her. She met him halfway, registering briefly how disheveled he looked. Dark circles under his eyes, clothing and hair in disarray. His signature elegance was completely gone, replaced by the aspect of deep distress.

"Alex," he said in a broken voice, and hugged her tightly.

"Blake, my goodness, what happened?"

"Adeline, my wife, she was on flight XA233," he said, his bleak, dejected face still buried in her shoulder.

Her eyes welled up instantly. *Adeline...oh, no!*

"Oh, my God, Blake, I am so sorry! Please accept my deepest—"

"No!" Blake snapped angrily, pulling away from her. "No condolences, that's not why I'm here."

"Then what can I do?"

"I want you to find her," he said, looking her straight in the eye. "You're the only one who can."

He couldn't be serious. The entire world was looking for that plane; what could *she* do?

"Blake, I–I can't, there are—"

"No!" Blake almost yelled. "You don't understand. She isn't dead. She can't be! I'd feel it in here!" He pounded his chest above his heart with his closed, white-knuckled fist. "I'd know it!"

She took a step forward as to attempt to console him. He was crazy with pain over the loss of his wife, and he wasn't thinking straight. She wished Steve were here; he'd know what to say and do to help Blake. She was going to have to do her best, and hope her best was good enough.

"Blake," she spoke softly, "such a loss can be devastating, I understand. And I am here for you. Why don't we go to Tom's, get you a hot cup of soup, and help you get some rest?"

His eyes shot her a glare filled with disappointment.

"Not you too! Not after everything we've been through together, Alex! Do you think I lost my mind? Is that it?"

She shrugged a little, involuntarily, and felt her cheeks catch fire. "Blake, I—"

"No, I'm still sane, Alex, and I am appealing to that fantastic brain of yours! You who found a ten-billion dollar, money-laundering scheme hidden so deep inside my bank's business systems that no one else had managed to find it before. I am pleading with my friend, Alex Hoffmann, the best investigator I have ever met, to just hear my case for a minute. Can you do that for me? Give me one minute of unbiased attention?" Blake's pleading voice reached a higher pitch, while he still struggled to stifle heavy sobs. "Do you still trust me that much?"

She considered his words, embarrassed she'd jumped to conclusions and dismissed Blake so quickly. She shouldn't have made that error in judgment; she knew better.

She managed to look at Blake, unable to hide her embarrassment. "I am so sorry, Blake, please forgive me. Can we please start over?"

He let out a pained, long sigh. "Don't apologize. I sometimes think I'm crazy, too. But believe me, she isn't dead. She can't be. Oh, God…"

"OK, let's talk. I am all ears. Why do you think she's not dead? The authorities confirmed the plane went down over the Pacific."

"I'd feel it…I *know* I would," Blake said quietly, looking Alex in the eye with an unspoken plea to believe him, to trust his call. "And…and I had a dream right about the time her plane went missing."

"A dream?" Alex couldn't hide the doubt in her voice.

"Yes, a dream, and I know just how this sounds. But Adeline and I are very close; we're what people refer to as soul mates. We've always had our ways to feel each other's pain, stress, or fear."

She didn't dismiss the thought so easily the second time. Although the science behind it was blurry to say the least, there were numerous documented cases of such mental connections existing between closely connected human beings, able to transcend thousands of miles.

She decided to believe that was a possibility in Blake and Adeline's case. Steve would have been a great asset to her right now…damn it! And Blake wouldn't move from the damn tarmac. No way could she get him to Steve. She refocused her attention.

"What was the dream about? Was she saying anything to you?"

"She said she loved me, and then…" Blake almost choked, "well, I don't know how to describe it, but the message was that I shouldn't let her go. I shouldn't give up."

"OK, good enough for me," Alex replied, her usual analytical self taking over. "What do you think *I* could do, that the authorities aren't doing already?"

"Believe," Blake replied. "Believe that it's possible that plane didn't crash into the Pacific. During the past 48 hours, I've been traveling like crazy, speaking with everyone. Airlines, the FAA, no one would even listen to me. It doesn't matter who I am, or how much money I'm willing to spend. No one even wants to hear me out; they all dismiss me and recommend some shrink or another, after expressing countless regrets."

She blushed again and looked at the tarmac for a minute, trying to hide it, disappointed with herself at how narrow-minded she'd been about the whole thing. She'd done the exact same thing the airlines had done. She, too, had wished she had a shrink present to help Blake. Must be the early hour to blame for her atypical shortsighted logic. Forget Steve. Blake was there to see her.

"OK, let's talk scenarios," she managed to articulate.

"Yes! Thank you!" Blake said, hugging her tightly. "I knew you would hear me out. What do you want to know?"

Where the hell do I even start, Alex asked herself bitterly.

"Umm…" she said, "what do you think could have happened to that plane?"

"I don't know," Blake answered with sadness, "but I just need you to consider the possibility that it hasn't crashed in the Pacific, and start looking for it."

"That I can do," Alex replied, "but why do you think that's even possible? You think the entire world that's looking for it is just plain wrong? Everyone's looking for it in the middle of the Pacific."

"Where they fail, you can succeed. It's happened before. I have that much confidence in you, Alex."

Oh…OK, no pressure, she thought, a little flattered, yet feeling overwhelmed.

"Blake, I don't even know where to start," she admitted.

"Maybe…but you'll think of something. I'm willing to bet a ton of money that by the end of today you'll have a few ideas. Only you can find her."

She smiled. "Thank you for your vote of confidence, Blake. I hope I'll earn it."

"You will, and I will help you. Any resource you need, you got it. All my money, all my influence, you can use at will, no questions asked. I will sign blank checks, I'll do anything."

"Anything?"

"Just name it," he confirmed.

"Park your plane somewhere and let's go to Tom's. I need breakfast, and I need to think. You need to come with me," she added, feeling uneasy for manipulating him like that. "Just in case I have questions or I need resources, or something."

"Done," he replied, then turned toward the plane and signaled his pilot.

Minutes later, he was fast asleep in Alex's car, as she drove on the Pacific Highway, heading north in the dawn's brisk light.

The massive door unlatched noisily, startling them.

One of the armed men walked in, his weapon hanging loosely, strapped on his shoulder. It was the one they called One-Eye. He still had both his eyes, but a long, purplish scar extended from his left ear to under his left eye, putting a deep ridge into his cheek, making them wonder how his eye survived that terrible knife wound.

One-Eye extended his hand, holding a small packet with insulin vials.

"Insulin," he spoke harshly.

Dr. Gary Davis stepped forward, grabbing the box.

"Thank you," Gary said, then opened the box. "Hey, this is just two days' worth," he said, showing the man the four vials.

One-Eye shrugged and replied dryly. "If you all behave, she'll get more." Then he turned and left, latching the door behind him.

He rushed to Dr. Crawford's cot, while Dr. Adenauer brought a hypodermic and some alcohol on a piece of gauze. Dr. Crawford sat with difficulty on the side of her cot, preparing her insulin shot.

"Thank you," she said, speaking weakly. "This will help."

She shot the insulin into her thigh, then massaged the spot gently, while everyone kept their backs turned to give her some privacy.

"Thank you," she repeated, "I'm done."

They all huddled around her cot except the pilot, who remained crouched on the floor, not moving much or saying anything since they'd entered the makeshift lab. Lila, the flight attendant, kept as great a distance from the pilot as physically possible, quiet and grim, crying at times.

"Do you understand what they want us to do?" Dr. Crawford asked. "I was a little out of it and I couldn't focus," she explained apologetically.

They stood silent for a few seconds, looking at one another, various degrees of concern marring their expressions. It was as if the nightmare would become more real if one of them would put it into words.

"They want us to build a drug formulation," Gary spoke, "a drug that will increase the violence drive in subjects in a controlled manner. Not too violent; just enough to cause damage, and controllable with an antidote. They also want the drug to be aerosolized, yet have precise, controllable response in subjects."

"This is insane," Dr. Mallory spoke. "I don't even think that can be done. Not here, not like this. What they're asking for requires years of work."

"Don't say that, please," Dr. Teng spoke, his voice strangled by tears. "I–I have my family with me. My wife and my little girl…they have them. We can't say no."

"Indeed," Dr. Adenauer spoke, arrogance seeping in his voice. "We all know we cannot say no to the malignant, sociopathic narcissist without taking considerable risk. We have to be judicious about our approach to this research."

"Approach to research?" Gary snapped. "Are you seriously considering doing this? It's against everything we have sworn to do as doctors."

"What choice do we have?" Adenauer replied. "Compliance, in this case, is the logical, self-preserving thing to do."

"But consider the consequences, for chrissake," Gary insisted.

He felt Dr. Teng's hand grabbing his sleeve. "Please," the tiny man whispered, tears welling in his eyes.

"Ah, you are forgetting," Dr. Adenauer replied, pedantic as if he were lecturing in front of young students, "I said research…I never said delivery of a drug formulation."

"What do you mean?" Dr. Mallory asked.

Gary was starting to see Adenauer's point. He was, indeed, brilliant, and, he had to admit, he stayed cool and rational better than most. Better than himself even.

"I mean we comply, we do the research," Adenauer clarified with a parental tone, "but we will not be able to deliver results very soon," he ended his phrase in a whisper. "We…stall. Isn't that the right word in English?"

"It shouldn't be too hard, considering how insanely absurd and complex this task will be," Mallory added.

They nodded in agreement, and remained silent for a while.

"What are we hoping for, though?" Dr. Klaas Fortuin asked. "They'll never let us go. If we are worthless to them, they will kill us all. There is no doubt about that."

The harsh reality expressed so simplistically by the direct, almost blunt Dr. Fortuin hit hard. They bowed their heads and hunched their shoulders, desperation taking over.

"We don't know that. We don't know anything," Gary said. "For now, let's focus on immediate survival, right? Dr. Bukowsky, what would you say to a patient in this situation?"

"Exactly true, let's focus on survival," Howard Bukowsky confirmed. "Our situation has definitely improved," he continued, trying to focus everyone on the very few positive aspects of their confinement. "We slept on cots last night, not on the floor, we have water, and we had warm food last night. Dr. Crawford has insulin for a while, and that demonstrates a very important point."

"What?" Dr. Crawford asked.

"That we were able to negotiate with them. We asked for something and we got it. It's important we keep that in mind," Bukowsky concluded.

"Ah..." Gary said. "You're right. Then let's ask them to keep our lab rats healthy and well-fed, to ensure the tests will be relevant and successful."

"You're not saying...you're not seriously considering testing on human subjects, are you?" Dr. Fortuin asked, barely containing his apprehension at the thought.

"No, of course not," Gary replied. "But they expect us to use them as test subjects. If we ask for it that way, we can hope to negotiate better conditions for the rest of the passengers."

"We might not have a choice, you know," Dr. Adenauer said. "We might be forced to test on them. Who knows what they'll do if we resist?"

"Then how do we prevent harm from coming their way?" Dr. Mallory asked. "We formulate weak batches?"

"Uh–huh," Gary said, pensively, shoving his hands in his pockets. "That would work. Weak batches, using low-toxicity components with small halftimes."

Dr. Crawford stretched her legs, as if to see if she was able to stand on her own. Then she spoke in a quiet voice, just above a whisper. "Let me ask you all something that might seem unusual. Are any of you good with hypnosis? I mean, really good, as in hypnotizing someone against their will?"

"Hmm..." Gary said, "interesting thought."

"I've had some results," Dr. Mallory replied, "but, of course, I've never tried it against a patient's will. It's unethical, illegal even."

"Here, it doesn't matter," Dr. Crawford said. "Try, try it whenever you have a chance, let's see what happens. Maybe some are more susceptible than others. It could be a way. But be careful," she added. "They can't suspect a thing."

She stood and stretched her back a little. "In the meantime," she added, "I will ask for any documentation they might have on previous research. Something tells me this isn't the first time they've tried to formulate this drug."

She stood in front of the whiteboard again, staring at the only thing written on it. XA233 and a question mark, that was all, scribbled at the center top of the board.

Alex paced Tom's den nervously, sipping her fifth French Vanilla brew of the day and occasionally glaring at the almost completely whiteboard on the wall. Tom sat quietly, slouched in his chair, appearing entirely absorbed in his reading of the latest edition of *TIME* magazine. He hadn't spoken a word in almost an hour, nor had he looked at her.

She'd heard about authors having writer's block in front of a brand new, white, untouched manuscript page, but never in front of a whiteboard. Although the psychology could very well be quite similar.

Argh...damn this fucked-up shit to hell and back! Alex thought. *I'm babbling here, wasting time. I need to think. I need to come up with something.*

"Tom?" she called. "Can I interrupt your reading for a minute?"

He smiled and put his magazine down. "Absolutely, my dear. What can I do for you?"

"Let's bounce some ideas around, what do you say?"

"I thought you'd never ask," he said with a smile. "I was running out of good stuff to read, you know."

She chuckled.

"I—I just need to let some steam out, for now. Just for a few seconds."

"OK, let's hear it," Tom replied all serious, but with a parental smile in his eyes.

She paced the room a little more before speaking, then spoke in a high-pitched, machine-gun rhythm, showing how frustrated she was.

"How in the red fucking hell am I gonna find the goddamn plane that no one else can find? This is not a case, or a challenge; this is insane! I can't be expected to—to deliver on this!" She stood right in front of Tom, with her hands firmly stuck in her jeans pockets.

"Seems to me you're afraid of failure, and you're presenting me with a disclaimer, a waiver of liability or something," Tom replied quietly.

"No...What I meant was...Well, yes, I guess I am. And? What if I am? You find that absurd?" She sounded argumentative, ready to fight, her frustration taking over.

"I never said that, now did I?" Tom said, his voice taking that kind, fatherly tone that always helped her get grounded and be prepared for anything.

"No, you didn't," she admitted, aware she was blushing and hating it. Lately, her brain had misfired a lot.

"OK, so consider it signed," Tom said and winked.

"Consider what signed?"

"The waiver of liability. You are off the hook if you fail. Isn't that what you wanted to hear?"

Now she was blushing big time, her face burning red and seeding tears of embarrassment at the corners of her eyes. *Damn!*

"You really see right through me, huh?" she found the courage to ask.

"Like reading an open magazine," he acknowledged, rapping his fingers humorously on the cover of *TIME.*

"OK, so I need some improvement in that area," she admitted and smiled widely.

Tom nodded his approval, then frowned a little and asked, "Why did you take the case, Alex?"

"Huh?"

"Why didn't you express your regrets to Blake, and send him on his way?"

She bit her lower lip, thinking hard. Great question. Tom was making an interesting point.

"I guess I thought I could help. I thought I should at least try," she said in a weak, unsure voice. "I thought I had some ideas, but..."

"Then what changed?"

"Nothing, really. I just...well, I'm just having a moment of self-doubt, I guess," she conceded with a tentative smile, feeling her mind become clear again.

"Is it over, then? Your moment of self-doubt?"

"Yes, thank you," she said, shifting her weight from one foot to the other, sipping more coffee.

"OK, then, let's find us that goddamn plane, as you like to call it." He threw her a blue dry-erase marker.

She caught it and turned toward the whiteboard.

"This is what we know," she said, and drew a vertical line on the board to create a column, then labeled it "Known." She added the information in the form of a bulleted list.

- 423 passengers

- 18 crew
- Tokyo to San Fran
- Took off on time
- All communication normal before it disappeared

"These are the coordinates where they think it crashed," she added, transcribing those from a handwritten note she had in her pocket. Then she added the word *manifest* in the "Known" column.

"We have the manifest?"

"Yeah. Lou grabbed that yesterday from the airline's system. He was able to break through their security in less than ten minutes; I was impressed."

"So, what do you want to do next?"

"Start from the manifest," she said, her voice firming as she regained her self-confidence. "We looked at it yesterday and this morning, but we need more than human eyes and brains to draw any conclusions."

"What do you mean?"

"We were able to figure out the passengers' nationalities and final destinations, their dates of birth and genders, but that's about it. We need more. Lou is modifying a piece of software he wrote to extract background information on all passengers and crew, and then we can look for commonalities, for anything we can find. It's pattern recognition software he's adapted for any type of data," she added, seeing how confused Tom looked. "It will extract deep background on all passengers, then compare the data and look for things they have in common."

She paused for a few seconds, seeing how Tom looked at her pensively, creases forming on his forehead, right above his bushy salt-and-pepper eyebrows.

"I am grasping at straws, I know," she added.

"No, you're not. This is the best way to start. Who else is helping you?"

"Steve is helping Blake deal with everything."

"Good. What do you expect to derive from the manifest analysis?"

"If anything other than a crash has happened to XA233, then it must have been intentional. Even if the plane made an emergency landing due to some failure, someone would have found it by now. We would know. I'm hoping that the manifest will give us a hint as to what, or who, had XA233 in their crosshairs, and why."

Tom leaned forward, his interest piqued.

"When do you expect that to be completed?"

"The manifest analysis should be done by the end of today. Then we'll look at commonalities and formulate scenarios. At that point, Lou will run his adapted pattern recognition software and get deeper data, but that might take some time."

She took the marker and wrote a new column heading, "Scenarios."

Dr. Theo Adenauer pushed his food around with his spoon, too deep in thought to be aware of how hungry he was, or to register the annoying sounds made by the aluminum spoon scraping against the aluminum plate.

For the third time in as many days, they've been served cabbage. Chopped, boiled, and tasteless, with about zero nutritional value. He had to admit that today's serving tasted better due to the clever Dr. Fortuin, who played in the lab a little and came out with salt, chunks of salty deposits on the bottom of a Petri dish, but edible salt nevertheless.

Fortuin had joked while handing them the salt, saying that he'd graduated from biochemistry and pharmacology to molecular gastronomy, and was committed to get them some oil and some protein next.

Theo looked at his prison mates, scrutinizing them one by one. How different people were! Some took their abduction really badly, cried a lot, or let themselves spiral into worry and depression. Lila Wallace, their flight attendant, was one of those. Dr. Teng, for understandable reasons, considering his family was in the test subject population, was another. Dr. Chevalier, who had held on bravely for a couple of days, was coming apart, thinking of her husband with advanced coronary artery disease.

Others were calm, probably keeping their feelings bottled inside, or engaging the use of reason and logic to fight the feelings of terror and absolute powerlessness brought by what was happening to them. Drs. Mallory and Davis were like that. Calm, composed, holding it together, at least on the surface.

Finally, Drs. Fortuin, Bukowsky, and Crawford were irritatingly accepting of the entire situation, applying the precepts of positive thinking to the point where he wanted them slapped back into reality. Yes, people, even if you're still alive now, that doesn't mean you couldn't be dead the next minute!

And then there was him, struggling with the huge burden of guilt he felt, so overwhelming he couldn't even breathe sometimes. To be responsible for the abduction of hundreds of people, for the death of Dr. Faulkner and who knows how many more to come...He didn't know how he could live with that burden, even if they somehow made it out of there alive.

Because it was him, Dr. Theo Adenauer, who the Russians had hijacked the plane for; he knew that for sure. After all, he was the world's highest regarded expert in molecular psychopharmacology and transitional addiction. Whom better would they choose if they wanted a psychotropic drug formulated? It was him they put in charge of the research team. That Russian doctor, Bogdanov, knew exactly who he was and what his lifelong work was about.

The latest antidepressant that had hit the market, the first one in history to reduce suicide risk in patients by more than 90 percent, was his formulation, the result of five years of research. The pharmaceutical company had valued it at more than four billion dollars within a week of the drug obtaining FDA approval for release in the United States. Yes, whom else would they have hijacked the plane for?

His head hung low and deep ridges formed around his mouth, underlining the tension in his lips. He was no longer proud of his professional achievements. It was the first time in his life he'd felt such overwhelming guilt. Shame. Despair.

"Do you think they're looking for us?" Dr. Bukowsky said, chewing vigorously his half-cooked cabbage with added salt.

"Who?" Gary Davis asked.

"You know, the people who normally search for missing planes," Bukowsky replied. "Don't they have crews, teams who search for planes? There's always someone…A plane doesn't just disappear, and no one's looking, right?"

Theo Adenauer put his plate down noisily. He hadn't even eaten half his food.

"No one will come rescue us, because no one is looking," he said.

"What do you mean?" Gary Davis asked, blood visibly draining from his face. The American was so impressionable.

"If the plane appears to have crashed in the Pacific, that's where they'll be looking," Theo replied, "for bodies and debris, not for people to rescue. Not for us."

"So…you're saying there's no hope?" Dr. Chevalier's voice reached a high pitch, conveying her desperation and anguish in just a few words.

Dr. Bukowsky reached out and grabbed her hand, trying to comfort her. Tears started running on her face, and her hands started shaking uncontrollably, as she muttered, "It can't be…It can't be…"

*Mein Gott…*Theo thought. He should have known better than to eliminate all the hope these people had, even if it was built on a false, delusional foundation. Some bedside manner he had.

"There's always hope, Marie-Elise, you know that. Life is a mystery, *ja*? You don't know what's going to happen next. Correct?"

"I definitely didn't know what was gonna happen when I boarded the damn flight," Dr. Crawford said bitterly. "But I, for one, ain't giving up hope, no matter what *he* says," she added, pointing at Adenauer. "They'll come looking, don't worry. You'll see."

They chewed silently for a little while, as he studied them some more. His victims, all of them, suffering through hell.

His fault.

Tom's den looked more and more like a war room, and the air was getting stuffy, hard to breathe. The walls, long since stripped of their artwork, were covered with sticky notes, a six-foot wide wallboard, and flipchart paper. Two laptops took the small table. Alex and Lou kept their heads close together, looking keenly at the screen of one of the laptops.

"See?" Lou said. "This is how it appears. It gives categories of commonalities with other passengers or crew. Crew names are in blue, the rest are in black. And whatever pattern the software sees, it will add as parameters after the name, with numbers indicating occurrences."

"Got it," Alex replied.

"Not me," Steve said. "Let's walk through an example."

"Sure," Lou replied. "See this guy? Mark Atchkins? After his name, you have San Francisco (47), engineer (5), married (219), two children (98), 47 years old (19). That means he's from San Francisco, like 47 other passengers, he's an engineer, just like five other individuals, and so on. Got it?"

"Yes, got it, thanks," Steve replied. "Do we think age, number of kids, marital status are relevant?"

"No, I don't think so," Alex said. "Good thought, Steve. It clutters the results. Even location, I don't think it's that relevant. But I'd love to see income bracket."

"All right," Lou replied. "Give me a few minutes to reconfigure."

"Can you summarize the data somehow? Scrolling through 441 names like this would take forever."

"On it, boss," he replied with a wide smile, and started to type.

Alex sprung off her chair and took a rolled-up sheet of paper from the corner of the room.

"Steve, will you please help me hang this?"

"Sure, what is it?"

"The biggest map they could print at the local print shop," she replied, handing him a couple of pushpins and unrolling the four-foot wide print. They grabbed the corners of the printout and stretched on their toes to pin it as high up on the wall as possible.

"There, excellent," she said, then grabbed a bunch of blue pushpins. "Let's map XA233's flight plan."

She browsed the Internet a little until she found a site that showed all the main flight routes. She started pushing pins into the map to match the flight route shown on the Internet, all the way to its destination, San Francisco. It wasn't a straight line. The flight routes were smooth curves, arcs, optimized distance against the Earth's curvature. When it came to flight routes, the shortest distance between two points was not a straight line.

From Tokyo all the way to its destination, XA233 was supposed to be above water. No land anywhere in its flight path; just a massive expanse of blue water. The closest XA233 was supposed to come to land was within 100 miles or so of the Aleutian Islands, but the plane had never made it that far. *Damn...*

She scribbled on a sticky note, "Verify flight path," and then stuck it on the whiteboard. Then she took a handful of red pins, put one in Tokyo, a second pin where the plane was last seen on Tokyo ATC radar, and another one at the coordinates where the plane had presumably crashed. The last red dot was a little south of the designated flight route, causing her to frown.

"Lou? How sure can we be of these flight routes, or even the crash coordinates?"

"Huh? Not 100 percent, that's for sure. Let me poke around a little in Universal Air's servers, see what I can find."

"I want to understand how they came up with those coordinates for the crash. They didn't find any wreckage there, right? So...what are we missing? Is it a projected point based on the last confirmed set of coordinates?" She clenched her fists and stuck them firmly on her hips, and ground her teeth, letting out a groan of frustration. Then she started pacing the little room, absently avoiding table corners and chairs. "Shit...there's so much we don't know about these planes. We have more questions than answers."

The door opened and Tom walked in, carrying a tray with coffee and cookies, followed by Blake.

"I come bearing treats and bringing friends," Tom started to say, then abruptly changed his tone and subject. "How can you guys breathe in here? Steve, crack open that window, will you? Whew!"

Alex turned and gave Blake a scrutinizing look. He looked a little better, some of the despair in his eyes having been replaced with a shred of hope. He wore one of Tom's checked shirts, a complete departure from his typical dress style.

"Blake, are you sure you want to be here for this? It could get difficult for you to hear." Alex asked, a little worried.

"Yes, Alex, please. Don't shut me out. I'd go crazy."

"OK, that's understandable," she replied, then turned her back to all of them and started analyzing the map.

How is a plane's position tracked from ground control? *Lamely*, she thought, remembering her conversation with Claire about the need for planes to have GPS tracking and a sensor array at least at the level of those installed in common vehicles. *Lamely or not, but how?*

She turned toward the team, and saw them all seated at the table, with their eyes on her, all except Lou, who typed quickly and quietly on his laptop's keyboard.

She took a sip of steaming coffee, a Turkish recipe Claire liked to make, brewed over an open flame. It was murky and strong, and made to wake up the dead, as she liked to say.

"All right, let's treat this as if it were a murder case—or a kidnapping, not sure yet," she added quickly with a faint apologetic smile. "We'll do full victim backgrounds," she said, then cringed when she saw Blake's reaction to her choice of words. She corrected herself, "We'll do full passenger and crew backgrounds, and establish commonalities."

She took another gulp of coffee, already feeling the effects of Claire's special brew on her brainpower.

"Let's talk scenarios," she said, grabbing the blue dry-erase marker and focusing on the respective column on the whiteboard. "The scenario in which the plane actually crashed in the Pacific doesn't interest us, so I will write it down here, then cross it out, so we can stop thinking about it." She stroked through the word "crash" with a thick blue line. "If XA233 really crashed, there's nothing we can do. So we'll simply ignore that scenario. Any objections?"

No one said anything. Lou lifted his gaze briefly from his computer screen to signal his quiet approval, while Blake mouthed a silent thank you.

"Then what else do we have?" Alex continued. "If a commercial jet doesn't make it to the final destination, doesn't emergency land, and doesn't crash or explode in mid-flight, there's only one scenario left." She wrote a word in all caps on the whiteboard. "HIJACK."

The room fell completely silent, as if everyone there held their breaths. Lou had stopped typing, and everyone watched her intently.

"Two hijack scenarios I can think of right now," she added, as she wrote, "for money, and for political reasons."

"To your point, Alex, could this plane have made an emergency landing somewhere, due to some technical issue?" Steve asked.

Blake shook his head in a silent no.

"Highly unlikely," Alex replied. "It's been five days; the crew would have made contact by now. And someone would have communicated the emergency to ground control before landing, wherever that ground would have been."

"But there's been no ransom call, right? Do we know for sure?" Steve pressed on. "Officials aren't exactly open about these things, you know."

"None that we know about," Alex replied. "And Lou's been looking."

"I've been checking the airlines, and talked to some friends in the FBI. There's nothing that we know of, not a whisper of anything."

"But there could be some hostage negotiation going on that we don't know about."

"If it's about money, wouldn't Blake know by now?" Tom asked. "Adeline would have been a prime target in that case, right? I'm sorry, Blake, I didn't mean—"

"It's OK, Tom, don't apologize," Blake cut him off. "You're right. And they would have called me, I guess."

"Then it's political?" Steve asked. "If it's political, what would they be looking for?"

"We can't even formulate that until we know who they are," Alex said, as she wrote UNSUB on the board, using the abbreviation for *unknown subjects* common for many law enforcement agencies. "Depending on who the UNSUB are, they could ask for the release of incarcerated terrorists, or the withdrawal of American troops from who knows where. They could be looking for military or diplomatic action against their enemy, and so on. It could be anything. In that case, the officials would keep this matter highly confidential. After all, America doesn't negotiate with terrorists, remember? The public would be frantic at the thought of sacrificing 441 people to maintain such a statement."

"Yeah, we'd have no way of knowing," Tom said. "What do you want to do next?"

"I'm going to ignore what I don't know, like what they're looking to gain from the hijacking, and focus on finding them." She wrote on the whiteboard. "No matter who the UNSUB are, this is a crime, and crimes follow the rule of *means-motive-opportunity*. We know nothing about motive, so we'll ignore that for now. Let's focus on means, the opportunity—how they grabbed it—and then we'll figure out on why XA233 was the UNSUB's best opportunity. Why XA233 and not any other plane? What made it special?"

She paced what little room she had in front of the whiteboard, then added, "I'll need an aviation consultant of sorts, to teach me how someone would be able to hijack a Boeing 747-400 and leave no trace. I want to start focusing on the means, while Lou is deep-diving into everyone's background to understand the opportunity."

"Consider it done," Tom replied. "I'll find someone ASAP."

"Thanks," she said, then she turned toward the map, looking at it intently. She was too close, and the map print was huge, taking almost the entire wall. She took a few steps back, not taking her eyes off the map, and suddenly, her blood froze. "Oh, my God…" she whispered.

"What?" Blake asked, and everyone else locked their eyes onto her.

"What do you see here?" Alex asked, pointing a laser dot onto the main piece of land visible on the map, west and northwest of the flight path.

No one replied. She took the laser pointer and underlined the letters S, I, and A, printed in large, bold font on the section of the Asian continent that had been caught in the printed map section. "Russia! This is Russia, people, right here! Just a couple of hundred miles from this plane's flight path! In 747 flight time, that's nothing!"

They all stared at her quietly. No one followed her chain of thought yet.

"I'm adding a third scenario, guys, I have to," she said, then went to the whiteboard, and wrote the letter V under the two other scenarios.

"Alex," Tom said, "are you sure? I know you're—"

"Obsessed?" Alex fired right back. "Is this the word you're looking for, Tom?"

"N–no, I wanted to say, umm…motivated," Tom replied hesitantly.

"What am I missing?" Blake asked.

"V is a Russian terrorist, the leader of the network you helped me track down. But him? We never caught him." Alex said, turning her attention to Blake. "He's a brilliant mastermind, and his plans are not the ordinary terrorist agenda; they are majestic somehow. It's as if the entire world is that bastard's playground. I've been trying to nail him for a long time, but I don't even know his name, just his initial, V."

"Alex, we talked about this," Steve intervened. "You can't make all your cases about V. You will screw up. It clouds your judgment."

"But what if it's a viable scenario?" Blake pushed back. "I, for one, trust her judgment, clouded or not. That's why I'm here."

"Blake, you don't understand," Steve continued. "She's completely—"

"Obsessed," Alex cut him off, laughing bitterly. "OK, yes, maybe I am. I don't think any of us are safe until that son of a bitch is dead and buried, maybe not even then. But I also know I can't ignore a plausible scenario, no matter how much I would just *love* for Tom and Steve to not think me obsessed."

Silence fell heavy among them. Steve broke it first, saying in an apologizing tone, "Yeah, I guess you're right."

She turned to Tom and said, "Tom, I need Sam to join us."

"Boss?" Lou said, lifting his eyes from the computer screen for the first time in minutes. "Look!" He turned his screen toward her and highlighted a name with his mouse.

"Oh, crap," she reacted. "Here's the opportunity. One of the XA233 pilots has dual citizenship. He was born in Russia."

They had set up a room just for Myatlev and Dimitrov. The two massage beds were placed closely together and covered with sparkling white sheets. As such, the two men could have quiet, exclusive conversations during their massage sessions, in the complete privacy of their dedicated spa room.

Two bodyguards secured the door on the outside, and Ivan and two more men were on the inside. Those guarding it on the inside had gotten a better deal, being able to let their eyes wander on the naked bodies of the two young masseuses. It was quite the view, especially if they managed to keep their eyes off the nakedness of the two chubby, hairy, older men lying on their beds.

That's the way Myatlev liked his full-body massages: delivered in privacy, by completely naked young women, not a day older than eighteen, with their pussies completely waxed. He didn't touch them; well, not that often, anyway. And not when he had guests, like today. He just took in the sensation and the view, reflected by wall-sized mirrors in the warm, relaxing light of the spa.

"This goddamned music makes me want to take a piss," Dimitrov said grumpily.

Myatlev gestured to the bodyguards, running the edge of his palm against his throat. Ivan obliged immediately, and the tropical forest sounds that had played in the background left the room in complete silence.

"Better?" Myatlev asked.

"Yeah…it's heaven, my friend. And this *devushka* is giving me a hard-on, and she only just worked on my neck so far," Dimitrov laughed.

"Speaking of hard-ons, I just heard a joke from one of my men," Myatlev said. "It goes like this: Can you fuck at a distance?"

"Huh?" Dimitrov turned his head toward Myatlev, intrigued.

"Yes, if your cock is at least five inches longer than the distance," Myatlev said, and they both burst into laughter.

"Five inches is all you need, huh?" Dimitrov quipped.

"These days?"

Both men started laughing hard. Myatlev signaled Ivan, who brought them shot glasses with chilled vodka.

"*Ura!*" the two men cheered as they clinked their glasses together, still lying on their bellies, just extending their arms toward each other enough to make their glasses come together.

"OK, here's one," Dimitrov said, after gulping down his vodka. "There was a destroyer sailing in the Barents Sea, north of the polar circle, and the XO got sick and died. The captain said he was only going to promote someone in his place if they were a real man, proving they could get an erection in the Arctic cold."

"Brr…" Myatlev laughed.

"All candidates were there, on deck, with their pants down in the icy blizzard, masturbating furiously, hoping to get a boner stiff enough to please the captain and get the XO's job. Nothing…they tried, and they tried, and nothing, one by one they gave up and went back below deck, defeated and impotent. Just when the captain was about to give up, a lowly sailor steps forward and asks if the job was still open for the man with the strongest erection onboard. The captain says, 'Yes, it is.' Then the sailor drops his pants and there it was, a strong, erect organ, standing proud, oblivious to the ice storm. The captain gives him the XO stripes and congratulates him, then asks, 'Son, how did you manage to get that erection in such cold weather?' The sailor replies, 'Easy, sir, that's the way it froze back in Murmansk!'"

They roared with laughter, then gulped down some more chilled vodka. Their masseuses moved to their lumbar section, working thoroughly on their contracted muscles.

"Vitya," Dimitrov asked in a serious tone of voice, "are you going to tell me what you're doing with all that lab equipment you took from VECTOR?"

Myatlev repressed a frown and turned slightly to his left, to see the expressions on Dimitrov's face as he was sharing his plan.

"I've built a lab, a research facility buried deep in the far eastern territories. I'm building a new weapon."

"Are we finally going to war? What are you building?" Dimitrov asked, his interest piqued.

"Not in the traditional way, but, yes, we are going to war. Just imagine one day, all the police force in one city becoming a little more aggressive, enough to beat and kill people in the streets and wreak havoc, enough to become a menace."

Dimitrov frowned.

"What are you trying to do, Vitya?"

"Keep our enemy busy from within. I want to ignite deep dissent in the ranks of the American people. It will be as if a cancer they can't control is attacking them from within. They can't control the attack, but we can. I want them killing one another in the streets. I have the best researchers in the world working on this."

"*Bozhe moi!*" Dimitrov replied. "Oh, my God! Another one of your genius ideas…Abramovich might like it. Does he know?"

Myatlev cleared his throat before replying.

"No, not yet. His mind is set on a traditional war. He wants us to drop a few nukes, attack frontally. But I think this is better, more prudent. Radiation is tricky once it's released into the atmosphere. It can go anywhere; it could come all the way here. I don't want my dick to fall off."

They were silent for a while, both frowning, deep in thought.

"How the hell did you pull this off?" Dimitrov finally asked.

"Trust me," Myatlev replied, "you might not want to know."

Dr. Gary Davis sat in front of the idle mass spec, watching his colleagues engaged in a bitter debate. The weather had gotten hot, and the air in the lab was stuffy and hard to breathe. They were all sweating, and, in the absence of daily showers, that heat was becoming increasingly difficult to endure, making everyone irritable.

To make things worse, the Russians had put Adenauer, Dr. Arrogance himself, in charge of the team, and, for some reason, everyone obeyed that decision. Of course, one of the reasons they obeyed was that Adenauer instantly started behaving as project lead, taking his responsibilities seriously. Yet something was eating at Adenauer. He'd turned grim, more silent than his usual self. He loved hearing himself talk, and wouldn't miss an opportunity to speak to save his life. Yet he sat silent, watching, just as Gary did, how the others argued about the ethics of building a chemical weapon for their enemy.

"You're insane! All of you!" Dr. Mallory declared from the bottom of his lungs. "I respect everything I've heard here today, starting from one's duty to survive, and ending with pure, unbridled fear of pain and death, but how does creating a dangerous chemical weapon and putting it in the hands of our enemies make it better? It just delays the issue, while magnifying it! You *will* suffer, and you *will* die, or be forced to see others suffer and die, and know that you're to blame for it!"

"Didn't we agree to release weak formulations?" Dr. Crawford intervened, in a pacifying tone.

"If we create this, no matter how diluted, their scientists will be able to run with it and finalize the research," Dr. Mallory replied. "We can't assume they won't."

"But we can't stall any longer," Dr. Fortuin intervened. "It's been almost three days, and they're growing impatient. We have to make something happen, to prove that we're actually working."

"Three days? Humph," Dr. Mallory scoffed. "This type of research can take years!"

"Agreed," Dr. Fortuin replied, "but they won't hear it!"

Tension crackled among them in the loaded air, and Adenauer didn't intervene. *What's eating him?* Gary wondered. He approached the group slowly.

"We all want the same things," he said gently. "We want to live, and we want to do so while maintaining our code of ethics and our humanity. Why don't we focus on that, instead of going at one another's throats? We're not to blame for this, none of us are." He stopped talking, searching their faces to see if his message made it across to them. They relaxed a little, imperceptibly almost, all except Adenauer. "Good. Then let's build the most harmless chemical compound we can think of, something inherently useless and wrong, and give them something without giving them anything. How's that for a challenge?"

"Huh…interesting," Dr. Crawford chuckled. "I'd go with steroids. Everyone knows their effect, it depends largely on the subject's body mass so it will be unpredictable in results, and it's freely available at the world's gyms anyway. We wouldn't be telling them anything they don't already know."

"How about testosterone?" The feeble voice of Dr. Chevalier rolled the "r" and elongated the words, making her question sound almost musical. "It could work. Studies show that compounds that enhance the production of naturally occurring testosterone, like branch chain amino acids, taurine, or the direct intake testosterone supplements need to be monitored closely. Psychotic breaks and violence are listed as side effects."

"A little too effective for my taste," Dr. Mallory replied. "We need something more benign. Remember, we don't want the compound to work."

"What if we formulate a selective serotonin reuptake enhancer? An enhancer, not an inhibitor. Something like Tianeptine, for example, but without its antidepressant stabilization function. It will effectively and harmlessly deplete the serotonin levels in the synapses, temporarily." Dr. Adenauer spoke, for the first time in more than an hour. "Balanced subjects will get depressed and mildly angry, and depressed subjects will have somewhat stronger symptoms, but they're already used to self-managing those with food, medication, et cetera. Not really a solution they could ever use, but in tests it might work enough to buy us some time."

No one replied, but they seemed encouraged by Adenauer's suggestion.

"Sounds good," Gary summarized. "Let's get to work. While Dr. Adenauer will lead the actual research, I will stall by asking for some more equipment and supplies, and Dr. Bukowsky will attempt to hypnotize our lovely guard."

As they fell silent in approval, a distant quarrel caught their attention.

"Get serious, Lila, is this because I cheated on you?" The pilot's tone was patronizing, annoying.

"How dare you?" Lila yelled. "How dare you even ask me that? You bastard!" Lila pounced and hit him in the chest with her fists, but the pilot didn't budge;

he just chuckled.

"What's going on here?" Gary asked, heading toward them fast, followed closely by the rest of the doctors.

"You wanna know why we're here?" Lila asked, wiping tears off her face with her sleeve. "Ask him!"

"Lila—" the pilot started to say, but Gary interrupted. He never liked the pilot; there was something slimy about him.

"What is this about?" he asked.

The pilot didn't answer. He sat there, in the same corner where he'd spent the past couple of days, staring at his boots.

"Tell them," Lila snapped. "Where's your courage now, you sick son of a bitch!"

Dr. Bukowsky came closer to Lila and gently grabbed her arm. "What's going on, my dear? I'm sure we can help, if you just let us know what happened."

Gary expected to hear about some lovers' quarrel. Regardless of how stereotypical it sounded, pilots and flight attendants got involved romantically more times than not. Probably everyone else had the same expectations, more or less.

Then Lila spoke.

"He brought us here...he's the one who sold us out. And he killed Captain Gibson. He shot him, right there, in his pilot seat, so he could take the plane to Russia." She sniffled and wiped her tears again, then added, "There...now you know who he is."

The pilot looked at her with mean eyes, almost squinting, grinding his teeth, and pursing his lips. "You fucking bitch," he muttered.

"Is that true?" Dr. Adenauer asked, drilling his eyes into the pilot.

The pilot remained silent for a while, then spoke quietly, "Yes."

"Why?" Dr. Adenauer asked quietly.

"This was not supposed to happen," the pilot replied, talking fast in a pleading tone. "You have to believe me. Please."

There was no sympathy for him anywhere in that room. Gary felt a wave of anger clenching his fists and tightening his chest. He could barely breathe.

"Talk," Adenauer commanded.

"They paid me to change direction and land the plane here, that's all. It wasn't supposed to end like this."

"What did you expect, you fucking moron?" Gary snapped, and immediately got stared at by Adenauer, who hated profanity. He didn't care. "Did you expect to get your cash and fly out of here, free as a bird?"

"Y–yes," he stuttered.

"God, you're such an idiot," Gary said, turning his back to the man. He couldn't stand looking at him. Never before in his life had he wanted to kill a man with his bare hands, not before that moment. "You make me sick."

"I've always wondered how we got here," Dr. Crawford said, "but I had assumed it was the other pilot, because we haven't seen him since. Unbelievable."

"There are many chemicals here that can kill you without leaving a trace," Dr. Fortuin said, surprising everyone. The composed, calm Dutch didn't seem like the type to think that. "Most likely, one chemical or another will kill you at the right moment. Count on that."

Fear flickered briefly in the pilot's eyes, quickly replaced by a hint of a superior smile.

"You're forgetting," he said, "that I'm the only one who can fly that 747 out of here."

Alex stood in front of the wall-sized map, staring at the piece of Russian territory shown on it, northeast of China and north of Japan. Where could a plane that size go? Where could it land? With the amount of fuel it carried, it could be anywhere on continental Russia.

She held the fresh cup of coffee close to her nose, inhaling the delicate French Vanilla flavor that filled the room. *Where are you? Where on Earth are you?*

A quick tap on the door, then a bulky man in his sixties entered the war room hesitantly, followed closely by Tom.

"Alex, meet Roger Murphy, former ATC shift supervisor at LAX," Tom said. "Mr. Murphy, this is my associate, Alex Hoffmann."

They shook hands, and the man sat down with a quiet groan, giving the map on the wall a furtive glance. Medium height and heavy set, the man wore thick-rimmed glasses and an untrimmed moustache that had lost its symmetry a long time ago. One edge was hanging lower than the other was, but it wasn't just the hair longer on his left side; his features were slightly lower too; his lips and cheek lopsided. Alex wondered if Roger Murphy was aware that he had probably had a small stroke recently.

"Mr. Murphy, thank you for coming here today," Alex said.

"Yeah, how can I help?" His speech was a little slurred too.

"I need to understand how someone might make a plane disappear in a different spot than it had actually disappeared."

"Huh? What do you mean?"

She backtracked a little. "How would one know where a plane is at a certain moment in time?"

"All commercial planes are equipped with transponders," Murphy replied. "The typical transponder emits an identification signal in response to a received interrogation signal. Radar operations depend on transponder signals to pinpoint aircraft position and altitude with precision."

"How does it work?"

"Secondary radar pings the transponder, then sends what we call an interrogation signal. Upon receipt of this interrogation, the transponder will return its code or altitude information. Some transponders are designed to be used in busy airspace areas, and are compatible with automatic collision avoidance systems. What kind of aircraft are we talking about?"

"Umm…" she hesitated a little, looking at Tom for a split second. "A Boeing 747-400," she replied, causing Murphy to pop his almost bald eyebrows up in an a skewed expression of surprise.

"Oh, then it most likely has best-in-class transponder equipment onboard."

"So how can one grab a 747?"

"What do you mean?" Murphy fidgeted uncomfortably in his seat. His concerned expression showed he was becoming less and less at ease with the direction their conversation was going.

"Let me tell you what this is about," Alex said, thinking she needed him to open up, not hold back. "We're trying to locate flight XA233, and we're thinking that it could have somehow made it to land, but ATC never knew about it."

"Ah…" Murphy said, slouching a little in his chair, more relaxed. "I see where this is going. Yeah, well, I guess you could make the plane disappear if you would just turn the transponder off. Really, that's all it takes."

Unbelievable. Modern aviation in the twenty-first century. Huh…"That's all it takes? No GPS onboard?" Alex probed.

"All aircraft have GPS, but it's for the pilots' use while in flight. It doesn't transmit anything to anyone."

"The pilots do get their info from satellites, right?"

"Yeah, but the airlines aren't equipped to retrieve, interpret, and use that type of information from the satellites. No one is."

"So, if you wanted to grab that 747 and land it here, somewhere," she asked, pointing her laser spot casually at the Russian mainland near the Pacific coast, "how would you do it?"

He stood with difficulty and scratched his balding head. "This is where they were last tracked?" Murphy asked, pointing at one of the red pushpins.

"Yes."

"You could do that two ways, I guess. It depends, really. You could start by dropping altitude, then kill your transponder, do a course change, fly back these few hundred miles, then land."

"Why drop altitude?"

"So that the last transponder ping sees you in distress, losing altitude right before the so-called crash, right?"

"Ah, yes. You're right."

"But there's a small problem with this method. Ideally, you'd want the plane out of the air when the alarm sounds."

"What alarm?"

"When a plane is assumed crashed, all nearby radar stations will start searching everywhere, and everyone starts looking. At that time, you want your hijacked plane to have landed already."

"So how do you pull that off?"

"Easiest way? With another plane, a plane no one will be looking for. You'd bring the second plane really close to the 747, above it or under it would be best. Then you synchronize transponder codes. The Boeing turns its transponder off, at the same time as the other plane turns its transponder on, using the same code. It's programmable from the cockpit, you know. Then the Boeing changes course and heads for the mainland, while the second aircraft continues for a while on the 747's original flight plan, pretending it's the Boeing, then simulates the crash."

"Wow...This way, the 747 lands before anyone even looks for it, right?" Alex confirmed.

"Right."

"What kind of plane does the other one need to be? What would work?"

"Even a personal jet would do. They were out at sea, and radar doesn't have the accuracy you'd expect. It can't distinguish that well between hull sizes. That's why we need transponders. So any jet can do it, as long as it can match the 747's cruise speed and altitude."

"Which is?"

"Speed? 500 miles per hour, maybe 550."

"Which jets can match that?"

"Non-commercial? Cessna jets would do that, a Dassault Falcon 50, Learjet, there are a few."

She exchanged a quick look with Tom, barely able to hide her enthusiasm. If there was a way, there was hope. She refocused.

"Why would you grab a 747? Can you reuse it?" Alex asked.

"I guess I could, if I'd repaint it, strip it of all Universal Air markings, replace its black box, yes, I think I could."

"How much is one of these planes?"

"About 200 million dollars," Murphy replied without hesitating. The man was a walking and slightly slurred talking aviation encyclopedia.

She frowned. This theory didn't make much sense.

"I think there are easier ways to steal 200 mil," she voiced her doubts.

Roger Murphy stood, ready to leave. He showed an uncanny way to know when she'd run out of questions.

"Depends on what you're after," he concluded.

That's right, Alex thought, barely refraining from hugging the man. *That's precisely right. What are you after this time, my dear V?*

Adeline Bernard woke up with a start. Someone moved very close to her, and her senses, hypervigilant, caused her to wake up abruptly. She looked around her, a little dazed, until, within seconds, she remembered her reality.

Captive!

Crammed together with hundreds of others, in what seemed like a large, round industrial area or warehouse, with barely enough room to stand, sit, and lie down, for what seemed now like an eternity. The air, stuffy and heavy with the smell of human waste and sweat, was hard to breathe and brought little oxygen to her thirsty lungs.

Food and water were brought once daily, stale water tasting of swamp and rusted metal, and cabbage or potatoes for food, boiled and tasteless. Prisoners rotated through kitchen duty, having to prepare their own food in precarious conditions. They boiled the cabbage and potatoes in huge pots over an open fire, in a smaller room fitted with a massive stove and a chimney of sorts. Every day, right after the meal was cooked, someone came in and took a large pot of it away. That's how Adeline knew the doctors and Lila were still alive.

The worst of it was not knowing. Not knowing what was going to happen to them. That, and missing Blake. She missed him terribly. Every time she thought of him, her eyes welled up. *Don't give up on me, baby...I'm still alive, and I love you!* The thought of him mourning her death was unbearable. She hugged herself, whimpering, as a tear found its way down her cheek. *Don't give up on me, baby, I'm here!*

They were well-guarded, at least two armed men watching their every move from elevated positions on the sides of the huge atrium. The captives were hundreds, against just a few men, but the Russians had machine guns and didn't hesitate to kill. Probably more would pour in at the first sign of trouble, considering the large number of video cameras hanging from the high ceiling, all with their red LEDs on.

She made an effort to snap out of it and got up. She straightened her dress, thinking how uninspired she had been to wear a dress on that flight. She normally wore pants when she traveled. Pants would have been such a blessing now, when she had to sleep on a cold and dirty cement floor.

She walked around a little, looking at the people near her. They were in bad shape. In the days that had passed, a lot of things had run out, from much-needed medication for some, to hope for almost everyone. But she wasn't giving up. No. She decided to help the best that she could, by talking to some of them.

She saw the Chinese doctor's wife and child a few feet away. The mother leaned against the wall, holding her daughter tightly, and quietly sobbing. Adeline touched her arm gently.

"Can I help?" she asked.

"No," the woman replied with a thick Chinese accent. Her voice was soft and high-pitched, almost like a child's. "I'm—I'm just scared, scared and tired. I'm scared for Wu Shen more than anything."

"Your daughter?"

"No. Wu Shen is my husband. My daughter is Yun Tsai," she replied, a little surprised that Adeline didn't know the difference. "I'm afraid of what he could do, because of us, because he fears for our lives," she said, sniffling a little.

"I see," Adeline whispered. "What about your daughter? How is she holding up with all this?"

"She's running a fever. It's better now. It's Wu Shen I'm worried about…"

Adeline encouraged her a little more, then moved away, aimlessly. She saw the idiot in first class, the one who'd sat in the second row on the flight, and decided to avoid him.

"Two weeks," she heard him say, "two more weeks and none of this would have happened."

Curious, she turned and looked at him inquisitively. "Two weeks?" she asked.

"Yeah, two more weeks, and I take possession of my own jet. Two more weeks, and I would have been absent from this party," he added bitterly, gesturing toward the hundreds of people confined together.

She felt a wave of anger and disgust at the man's selfishness.

"Ah, shut it, for God's sake! How can you live with yourself?"

She walked away, not waiting for his reply, and approached a group of people huddled together, talking.

"Do we know where we are?" a middle-aged, overweight woman was asking.

"Someone said this is an abandoned ICBM silo," a man replied. "Missiles," he added seeing the woman's confusion.

"Oh, my God! Do you think there's radiation here?" the woman asked.

The same conversations, heard over and over again, spoken with different levels of anxiety and desperation. The same questions, asked over and over again, in the illogical hope that they could bring a different answer.

The one question she didn't dare ask concerned their immediate future. On the day of their arrival, while waiting in line to board the trucks, she'd heard a Russian clearly state that they were going to be used as lab rats.

For what?

Vitaliy Myatlev finished reading Dr. Bogdanov's report on his computer, and regretted he didn't read it in printed format. That way he would have had something to tear to pieces, or slam down against the desk.

"Motherfucking idiot!" The man was a moron. Period. In only a few days, he'd managed to lose Faulkner, one of the best researchers in the field, because he just had to punch him in the stomach. How stupid could Bogdanov get?

Myatlev stood abruptly, pushing his desk chair all the way into the wall. He went to the window, opened it, and lit a Dominican cigar, savoring the fresh, heady smoke as it filled his mouth, his nostrils. Better.

Then he read the report again, this time in a calmer state of mind. All right, maybe it wasn't that bad. After all, in just ten days since Myatlev had come up with the idea, he'd hijacked a commercial flight, set up a state-of-the-art lab in the middle of nowhere, and had the best scientists in the world working for him. Not bad!

Yes, they will need a few more days to have the first batch ready, but so what? So fucking what? In the grand scheme of things, it didn't matter. These things normally took years. For him, it would be just days, or maybe a couple of weeks.

Then he would really conquer the world. No one would be able to say no to him anymore. He would be able to manipulate and control everyone in his path, from business opponents to clients to governments. No one would be able to resist.

He poured himself another glass of vodka and slammed a few ice cubes on top of it, sending droplets of clear liquid splashing all around him. He sipped it with reverence, letting it work its miracles in his weary body, and expressing his enjoyment with a loud, satisfied exhalation of air mixed with bluish smoke.

We are slaves to our brain chemistry, all of us, he reflected. *Equally vulnerable. There's no willpower, no intelligence, and no spirit that won't succumb to the right mix of drugs.*

He'd learned that from his friend, President Abramovich, from the stories of his early days in the KGB, when he had worked in punitive psychiatry, learning how to manipulate and defeat people with drugs. After all, why would that wealth of knowledge be limited to Abramovich's use? Or to Russia's? He could definitely use it in his business. Although he'd been on the Global Fortune 50 list for some time now, that wasn't even close to being enough. It was never going to be enough.

After careful planning and precise delivery mechanisms, tested in the field on a vast number of unsuspecting subjects in all kinds of environments, he could rule the world. His business opponents could make some bad decisions, driven by an unexplained surge in one brain chemical or a drop in another, and he'd be there, watching, waiting, ready to reap the benefits. They could feel overly aggressive and competitive in purchasing an asset, paying to the seller—Myatlev, who else—two, three times the fair market value. They could suddenly feel weak and demotivated when bidding against one of Myatlev's many global corporations about contracts worth billions of dollars.

That's why the formulations had to be precise, and work with accuracy. It had to gain him control. Random violence, as they had on the latest failed test, the one that left an entire offshore drilling platform covered in blood, gave him nothing.

Spring in southern California is pure paradise. Not too hot, clear blue sky, and the air is filled with a multitude of scents from flowering bushes and trees, especially from citrus trees that bloom about this time. Tom's backyard had several lemon and orange trees at the peak of their flowering season. Yet somehow, all that serene beauty failed to register in Alex's brain, occupied at full capacity with the search for the impossible.

The thought that the lives of 441 people could be in her hands kept her going on adrenaline, in a desperate race against time and against all odds. It had already been seven days since they'd gone missing. They were definitely in distress, if even still alive. And what progress had they made? Little, if any. She was getting desperate. She stomped her leg impatiently, annoyed at the time she was wasting on food, on the "at least one hot meal a day" rule that the Isaacs had put in place.

"All right, guys, bring your plates," Tom called from near the grill.

Alex jumped from her patio chair and grabbed a plate on her way.

"What's cooking?" she asked.

"Just cheeseburgers, nothing fancy this time," Tom replied. "Claire is bringing some fries."

She liked her burger naked, no bun, but with all the trimmings. She grabbed hers from the grill, paired it with a couple of slices of bacon, and made room for Sam, who'd just arrived.

"So good to have you here, Sam," she said, after hugging him and kissing him on his clean-shaven head. "I need you badly on this case; I need you to keep me true, and give me some more ideas."

"Happy to oblige," Sam replied. "Tom's home looks more and more like a hotel. Sorry for the imposition!"

"Ah, no worries," Tom replied. "Claire and I love a full house. We just wish it could have been under better circumstances, that's all."

Steve was next in line, and grabbed his burger quickly, without saying a word. Blake was last, hesitant, wearing his shoulders hunched forward and his head lowered.

"I'm not really hungry, you know," Blake said. His voice and his entire demeanor showed the turmoil he was going through. Time was slipping by, and little progress was being made. He must have felt desperate, painfully aware of every minute they spent away from the war room, of every minute his wife remained missing.

They took their seats at the table, and Lou brought everyone cold drinks from the fridge.

"OK, we are severely pressed for time," Alex said between bites, "so I will ask you to make this a working lunch."

Everyone nodded or mumbled approvals, so she continued.

"Why would I hijack a plane? We sort of talked through that; I don't think any new ideas have surfaced. But *where* would I take it? I think if we can answer that question, we have a better chance to find it. A 747-400 is a huge plane. Mr. Murphy told me it needs two miles of runway to land or take off. That is not easy to find outside of commercial airports. Thoughts?"

Sam wiped his mouth quickly and set his napkin down on the glass patio table.

"There are strategic highways out there. Many countries have them, including ours. These are stretches of straight highway with removable median barriers. Most of us have driven on these strategic highways and thought nothing of it. But, if need be, that median barrier goes away, and the highway becomes a landing strip for aircraft of any size."

She felt frustration take over. With this case, whenever she thought she had a way to zero in on that plane's location, someone would say something, or something would happen to kill every bit of hope.

"You're frowning at your burger," Tom said. "It can't be that bad, I hope."

"No, the burger's fine, Tom, I'm just frustrated, that's all. I thought we had a way to find potential landing sites, and, apparently we don't."

Blake's eyes clouded a little more.

"How? How were you thinking to find those landing sites?" Steve asked.

"By satellite. These things you can see through satellite imagery. By the way, why aren't the airlines using satellites to find the missing planes?"

"Satellites are most often already spoken for, and hugely expensive," Lou replied. "There's little-to-no satellite bandwidth available for such searches, which could be very demanding on resources. Airlines should have their own satellites they could reroute and search, but they don't. However, don't despair. Your idea is still good. Very few highways outside of the United States have such long stretches of straight, double-lane highways. You could spot those easily from above. I think I could code something that would scan imagery to find that. All we need is relatively new imagery, and I think we're set there, with Google

Maps."

"Those images could be years old," Alex said. "But that's a great idea, Lou!"

"Maybe not so old. I read somewhere that most images on Google Maps are less than three years old. Not ideal, I know, but it's there, readily available, ripe for scanning and comparing. I'll put something together after lunch, see what kind of image-pattern recognition software I can find and adapt. Maybe the boys have written something recently that we could use," he added, referring to his group of white-hat hackers and close friends.

"Jeez, I feel old and obsolete," Sam said toward Tom. "These kids are talking mumbo-jumbo again. I can barely keep up."

Tom nodded and replied, "I know exactly how you feel, my friend."

"We're just saying we could scan existing satellite imagery to find stretches of highway, that's all," Alex clarified. "If the imagery is not older than a couple of years, we could hope to capture 90 percent or so of the potential landing strips out there that could land a Boeing."

"What will that do for us?" Blake asked. "What are you hoping to achieve?"

The answer seemed fairly obvious, but she saw more in Blake's question.

"I'm hoping to eliminate where the plane can't be," she replied in a gentle tone of voice. "Sometimes, when you can't find out directly where things are, you can apply a process of elimination."

"Where would you start looking?" Blake asked again.

"We know what kind of fuel reserves this plane had when it took off. That allows us to calculate a range, and apply that circular range over the map, centered in Tokyo. Essentially, we draw a circle on the map with a radius equal to the plane's range, and eliminate everything blue water."

"Why centered in Tokyo?" Sam asked. "They flew due northeast for a few hours toward San Francisco before falling off the radar."

"Yes, but Mr. Murphy, the expert who came in yesterday to answer some questions for us, told us that you can pull off this type of hijacking by switching transponder codes between two aircraft. We have no way of knowing where or when that happened, so we're going with the most conservative scenario, expanding our search area inland by several hundred miles."

Blake covered his face with his hands and whispered, "This is a needle in a haystack!"

Alex sprung from her chair and went over to him, touching his shoulder. "Don't despair. Please. I know it's hard. It's already been a week since they disappeared, I know, but guess what? The more we work on this, the more I see hijacking as a viable possibility, as opposed to a mid-ocean crash. There's hope, Blake. We will find her, I promise."

She searched her soul a little after making the promise. Did she really believe they could find the plane everyone else assumed had crashed at sea? Yes, she did.

It was crazy, illogical, and yet she knew in her gut that V was somehow behind it. Why? She still didn't know.

The fact that everyone avoided mentioning was that any chance to find Adeline alive dropped dramatically with every day, with every hour that went by. They all knew that, but never spoke of it. They all worked around the clock, living mostly off coffee and burgers, in a desperate race against time. Time was in the hands of her unseen enemy, a massive advantage on his part—441 lives…

She refocused on Blake, whose desperation and sadness were engulfing him like a shroud.

"I wanted to ask you, do you know of anyone who'd want to harm you or Adeline?"

"I don't know…there could be."

"Motivated enough to pull this off? With means to pull this off?"

"I–I don't know. I don't think so."

"Have we heard anything about any ransom or political demands? I guess not," she continued. "Which makes scenario three the most plausible, and Sam, that's why I needed you here."

"Scenario three?" Sam asked.

"Yes. I am thinking V might be behind this. I don't know why, but it just feels right. After all, if that plane is anywhere other than the bottom of the ocean, then it's in Russia."

Silence fell around the patio table covered with half-empty plates.

"What's he after?" Sam asked quietly.

"Don't know yet, and don't think I haven't been trying to figure that out," she replied angrily, almost snapping at him and instantly regretting it. "But if V is indeed behind this, prepare yourselves." She paused a little, in an effort to calm herself. After all, it wasn't Sam's fault for asking. Whenever she thought of V, she just got angry—angry at herself for not being able to nail that sick bastard, angry at her own ineffectiveness, her failure.

She took a deep breath, and then continued, "Lou is still processing deep backgrounds on all passengers. My guess is that will tell us what he's trying to pull this time."

"And satellite imagery analysis?" Blake said, with a shred of panic in his voice. "When can you do that?"

"Backgrounds are processing as we speak," Lou answered in a pacifying tone. "I wrote some code that does that. It should finish running by late tonight or tomorrow morning, all 441 people onboard that aircraft. We'll know everything, from call and data usage patterns, to financials, professional information, family issues, everything."

"But don't worry, we will proceed with all three scenarios," Alex added, causing Sam to frown a little. "There's something else, guys. We need to figure out how to get our hands on some satellite time. Images that are a couple of years old might be a good start, but I need fresh imagery. I'm thinking that if we look real hard from the satellite, with one of Lou's pattern-recognition modules running, we could find the actual plane."

Dr. Adenauer's mind wandered back to the place of his birth, and the disappeared loved ones in his family. He was born in 1963 in rural West Germany, in a small town called Marl, close enough to Dusseldorf to be modern, remote enough to be picturesque and serene. The youngest in a family still recovering from the wounds of war, and still mourning its dead and missing, Theo had very little to be joyful about in his early years. But the most poignant of memories, the one still haunting his thoughts and nightmares, was the memory of his sister, Helga.

Ten years his senior, Helga entered the whirlwind of bipolar affective disorder with the onset of puberty, just when Theo was starting to be old enough to understand and remember. Of course, there was little to understand at first, when he was just a pre-teen, and Helga's mood swings left him crying and confused, unable to comprehend why his big sister, playful and fun just the day before, could turn into an angry monster, lashing out with words that hurt worse than fist blows.

With time, his parents explained what was going on. They told him that her mean words, crying spells, and bad behavior were not her fault; she was sick. Theo understood, and became committed to helping her. He suddenly realized, about the time that he entered puberty, what he was meant to do with his life. He would become a doctor, a great one, who could cure his sister and end the constant suffering of his family.

He studied hard, and worked desperately to understand everything that he could about the human brain. Since high school, he'd started devouring any book or medical publication he could get his hands on, absorbing, learning, analyzing.

He was admitted to the Universität Düsseldorf in 1981, and his grades gave him recognition from the dean and from his professors. Some took an interest in the highly motivated young man who had the most interesting questions about brain chemistry, about chemical imbalances in the brain, and about understanding the deep synergies among complex psychotropic drugs used in controlled combinations.

He still had a few weeks left before graduation when Helga jumped in front of a train, ending her desperation-filled days just before Theo could return home and help her.

He went home to Marl and mourned with his grief-stricken parents, not in the least concerned about the classes he was missing, or about the risk of being expelled. His guilt was tormenting him, eating at him from within. It was his fault that Helga died. He didn't find the cure fast enough, didn't graduate quickly enough.

The dean called one morning, when Theo was still spending his time staring into emptiness, at the home of his and Helga's childhood, and somehow talked him into returning to school. He graduated a couple of months later, and immediately began the research work that had been his mission ever since he could remember.

His academic record brought him a choice of research engagements, and he chose the path that led him closest to what he wanted to do: heal the invisible wounds of the suffering brain. It was too late for Helga, but there were others just like her, others he could still save.

Achievement after achievement, conference after conference, and award after award, his career soared. But he never stopped, and never slowed down. The most remarkable of his achievements, a drug that reduced the risk of suicide by 90 percent in clinically depressed and bipolar patients, had brought him a nomination for the Nobel Prize. He almost missed the news; that was the year his parents died, within a few months of each other.

Sometimes he wondered if he was indeed arrogant, as many had said about him. He didn't think so. He'd taken hard looks at himself many times, probing for signs of narcissism or other personality disorders, but, in his case, there was no foundation for such concern. It was just value, pure value. His record of achievement supported that, and he was well aware of his own worth. If that happened to come across as arrogance, well, that was unfortunate, but it wasn't something he was willing to change. His career was nothing to be humble about.

It had been years since he'd wandered down memory lane, remembering Helga, and the things he held most dear in his heart. His commitment to help people. His entire life dedicated to ease the suffering of the chemically imbalanced brain. And now? What was he going to do? Let some terrorists, because that's what they were, use him to gain access to a weapon meant to *bring* chemical imbalance to the brain? Then how could he live with himself?

Yet there was no easy choice. He could pretend to comply, and deliver weak formulations, as harmless as possible, stalling for as long as he could in the hope that something would eventually happen to free them from their hell. Or he could resist, refuse to deliver, and endanger the lives of hundreds of people.

This wasn't really a choice.

May God have mercy on my soul...

He stood from his lab chair and rubbed his creased forehead for a little while.

"We're ready," he said, showing the other doctors two small containers with capsules.

They gathered around him quickly. Drs. Davis, Fortuin, and Chevalier, who had worked side by side with him, pulled their chairs closer.

"The red ones are a modified, diluted selective serotonin reuptake enhancer. We will tell them they need time to absorb and become effective, to preemptively account for the ineffectiveness of the compound. The green ones are equally diluted SSRIs. They're just modified, low-dose Prozac essentially."

He stopped talking and searched their eyes. Many reflected the same anguish he was feeling. Others, only deep sadness for what they were about to do.

"All right," he said, taking a deep breath, "let's call them."

A few minutes after they had informed their omnipresent guard, Dr. Bogdanov entered the lab and took the two containers. Then he switched on a couple of monitors, image feeds from an empty room.

The doctors stood there, watching in silence the screens showing the empty room from different angles. Then the Russians started bringing in the test subjects, ten of them. One by one, they were dragged in there, screaming, pleading, sobbing, manhandled brutally by the guards. One by one, they had their mouths forced open and the capsules shoved down their throats. One by one, they choked, fought, scratched at the strong arms holding them down, and had no option but to swallow the drugs. Then one by one, they settled down, sobbing quietly, fear and desperation engraved deeply on their weary faces.

Vitaliy Myatlev finished his vodka-enhanced coffee and flicked the butt of his cigar out the window. It had rained that morning, bringing a luscious tint to all spring greenery, and cleaning the air of the constant stink of Moscow's pollution. But rain also brought joint pain to his left shoulder and also to his lower back, making him irritable. He wanted to go home and get in bed, but he still had to be there, in his goddamned office at the Ministry of Defense. There were days when he just hated his life, but, for as long as Abramovich held the supreme position in the Kremlin, he had to walk the line.

"Anything else?" Myatlev asked Ivan, seeing how his aide and bodyguard shifted his weight from one foot to the other, hesitant to leave.

"Umm...if I may, I was thinking that now everything is in place at the lab and everyone's working nicely, we should tie up all loose ends. Leave no trace."

Myatlev rubbed his shoulder furiously, trying to make the pain go away.

"What the hell do you mean, Ivan? Stop fucking around and get to the point."

"The plane, boss. We should destroy it. It's evidence we don't want to leave behind."

Myatlev rolled his eyes and let out a sigh of frustration. People can be so stupid, even the smart ones.

"Where's the plane now?"

"In a hangar, buried in the side of a hill. It's an old, abandoned facility near a decommissioned airbase and ICBM site. Middle of nowhere, really."

Then why destroy it? No one would ever find it hidden in there.

Myatlev resisted the urge to yell at his aide. Ivan had been his most trusted, loyal employee, and he valued that. He also knew he couldn't afford to risk losing the loyalty of the man who knew so much about him. He tempered himself, bringing his anger down to a quiet simmer.

"Don't destroy a 747, for God's sake. We might need that sometime. Just strip it of all markings and recognizable features, and have it sealed and guarded around the clock. And get me a masseuse."

Ivan frowned and hesitated a little before acknowledging. "Yes, sir."

Alex stood in the doorway, watching Blake from a distance. He'd been up since before dawn, skipping breakfast and avoiding company. He sat on the edge of a lounge chair, hunched forward, clasping his hands absently. He rocked back and forth, almost imperceptibly, and probably wasn't even aware he was doing it. He must have been sick with worry, and she couldn't make it better, not yet anyway.

She approached him quietly, and gently touched his shoulder.

"Blake?"

He turned toward her, watching her intently with sunken, bloodshot eyes surrounded by black circles.

"I need your help," she continued. "We tried...we tried anything we could think of, to gain access to newer satellite imagery. We reached out to several satellite operators. We even tried hacking into one. Then we tried leasing a damn satellite. Nothing worked, so we need you to step in."

"Me? What can I do?" He stood with difficulty, strained to straighten his back, and then rubbed his eyes furiously.

"Bring in the big bucks and that influence of yours. Can you get us satellite time? Do you know anyone who has a few? And, if not, can you buy us a couple?" Alex spilled her questions in rapid fire, not giving him the chance to answer.

He stood quietly for a couple of seconds, his eyes drilling into hers with increasing force, radiating strength, determination, and confidence. Then he spoke, "Consider it done."

"Blake, it's 55 million dollars apiece, these things," she added hesitantly.

"Then let's see how soon we can get a couple up there."

He took out his cell phone and speed-dialed a number from the phone's memory.

"Yeah, get me the earliest appointment with SatX's CEO. We've met. Yeah, today, now, ASAP. Then set up, right after that, a conference call with DigiWorld." He listened for a moment to what his personal assistant had to say, then continued, "No, I don't care about their calendars. It has to be today."

She smiled. That was the Blake Bernard she remembered: powerful, decisive, aggressive, going through walls when he had to. Together, they'd find that plane, no matter where on Earth it was hidden, and they'd find the 441 souls onboard. Together, they'd find Adeline.

Dr. Wu Shen Teng watched the screens with deep concern ridging his forehead. The source of his worries was different from what the other doctors shared. The others obsessed about the ethics of their actions. They debated, under the dire circumstances they were facing, whether they should take actions that led to drug experimentation on human subjects, or risk everyone's lives by saying no. However, Dr. Teng was concerned with the ineffectiveness of the compound they were testing.

The others didn't have their families with them; they could afford to be concerned with ethics, the Hippocratic Oath, and the core issues of preserving their humanity in the face of hardship. They could do that all they wanted, while their families were safe, somewhere in the United States, Germany, France, or wherever. *His* wife and child were locked in a dungeon, hopefully still breathing, and most likely scared out of their minds.

So far, they'd managed to persuade the Russians that the first test subjects were supposed to be men, for the drug tests to be relevant. Women would be useful later, Dr. Davis had said, when they were going to add a hormonal component to the drug mix. Some scientific mumbo-jumbo had made the case sound plausible, when in fact the doctors were trying to protect the women and children. That Dr. Davis could lie like a son of a bitch, not a blink in his eye.

Wu Shen Teng stared at the screens, troubled by what he was seeing. Mostly nothing was going on with the test subjects. Some of the men had gotten into an argument; some were shoving, and cursing took place, but no real violence. The two men who had taken the antidote sat quietly on the floor, leaning against the wall, a little spaced out. The rest paced the room impatiently, or mumbled oaths under their breaths.

How long would it take the Russians to figure out they were being played? How long before they started shooting people? How long before they'd kill his family, just to teach the doctors a lesson?

The doctors were pushing it too far. There should have been some significant effects. This lame result was ridiculous. This was dangerous. Stupid bleeding hearts were endangering everyone.

The lab door unlatched noisily, giving Wu Shen a start. Dr. Bogdanov walked in, followed by one of the fiercest looking Russian goons, a monster they had dubbed Death. Just like King Cobra, his nickname had originated from one of the man's ink jobs. His entire back was tattooed with a twisted image depicting death holding a child in the same manner that Mary held baby Jesus in the well-known depictions of Madonna and child seen on church walls.

Death closed the lab door and remained watch in front of it, holding his machine gun with both his hands, ready to engage.

"This," Dr. Bogdanov yelled without any preamble, pointing at the monitors, "this is ridiculous. This is *der'mo,* this is crap! This is not the drug you have promised me. This is not what I expected after a week of work!" Bogdanov spat on the floor angrily. "This is shit! Lame shit!"

The doctors stood flocked together, watching Bogdanov grow angrier with every word he spoke.

Wu Shen felt the grip of fear taking a fistful of his guts and twisting it. He could barely breathe. What was going to happen to them?

"Make no mistake," Bogdanov continued. "If you don't give me what I want, I will start again. With others, who can give me what I want. The way I brought you here, I will bring others, as soon as I'm done waiting for you to deliver and I kill you all. That's an easy job."

Bogdanov looked at them with a threatening glare, then said, "Be ready for another test batch tomorrow. And make sure it works this time."

Then he turned and headed for the exit, as Death opened the massive door.

Wu Shen didn't think much. He just reacted, his intestines still knotted with fear. He jumped ahead and caught up with Bogdanov, and grabbed his sleeve, just as Death shoved the barrel of a Kalashnikov in his chest.

"Can I please speak with you, sir?" Wu Shen asked humbly, keeping his head down and his spine bowed, in typical Chinese mannerism to show utmost respect and deference in front of a superior. "In private?"

Wu Shen Teng followed Bogdanov quietly, not daring to look at more than the man's feet, waiting for the opportunity to speak. His heart pounded in his chest, and he felt sweat drops forming at the roots of his hair. *What am I going to say?*

He heard the lab door latch close behind him, and then Bogdanov stopped abruptly.

"What do you want?" he asked harshly.

"Doctor, please," Wu Shen Teng pleaded, clasping his palms together. "I–I have my family here. Please promise me they'll be safe...Please."

"Humph," Bodganov scoffed. "Take him back," he told Death.

"No!" Wu Shen Teng said in a high-pitched, piercing tone. "No, please! Promise me they'll be safe and I'll—I'll tell you things."

"What things?"

He'd caught Bogdanov's attention.

"Things...things you need to know."

"Like what?" Bogdanov was starting to lose his patience, and sounded threatening.

"They're stalling. They're keeping drug concentrations low on purpose. That kind of thing I can tell you, if you promise me they'll be safe. Please!"

Bogdanov reached out and grabbed Wu Shen Teng by the lapels of his lab coat, easily lifting the thin man a few inches off the ground.

"You have your family here, you say?" he growled. "How interesting! Keep me informed, or your family dies. Is that understood, you little piece of shit?"

Wu Shen Teng nodded his compliance vigorously, and Bogdanov shoved him toward the lab door. As Death opened the massive door, Bogdanov shoved Wu Shen Teng violently into the lab, and cursed behind him.

"*Tvoyu mat!*"

Wu Shen Teng fell hard from the shove and rolled on the concrete floor, then curled up on his side, sobbing hard.

Dr. Davis rushed to his side, and kneeled right next to him.

"What happened? What did you tell him?"

"I begged him to let me see my family," Wu Shen Teng managed to articulate between uncontrollable sobs. "He won't let me see them."

"This must be hard for you," Davis tried to comfort him. "Hang in there, I'm sure they'll be all right."

"You don't understand," Wu Shen Teng said, trying to stifle his sobs. "Until now, he didn't know they existed. He didn't know I had a family in there. Now he does."

Oh, God, what have I done?

"There's nothing I hate more than sitting idle and doing nothing, just waiting," Sam said, getting off his chair and starting to pace the living room, impatiently, his hands stuck deep in his pockets. "Makes me feel old."

"The kids are working as hard as they can," Tom said. "We just need to give them time to do their thing."

Blake looked at them both, and said nothing. For him, waiting must have been the hardest.

Lou stuck his head through the open door and said, "Come on over, guys, we have passenger manifest analysis data ready."

They all followed Lou into the den, where Alex and Steve were talking satellite deployment.

"One of the satellites is a loaner, it's already launched, it just needs to be redeployed to that area," Alex said, pointing at the map, right above the Russia–North Korea border, a tiny sliver of black line perpendicular to the coast of the Sea of Japan. "The other one is being launched tomorrow at 4:00AM local time. It will need a few hours to deploy. By tomorrow afternoon, they should be both operational and scanning. We're looking to secure a third loaner today, leased from CNC News. We'll see how that goes."

"Do you have deployment patterns figured out?" Lou asked.

"Not yet. We'll work on that right after this. What do you have?"

Everyone had taken a seat, except Steve, who leaned against the back wall of the room.

Lou searched everyone's eyes, a little hesitant in saying what he needed to say. Alex felt a chill down her spine, but nodded an encouragement to Lou. Whatever it was, they needed to know, so they could deal with it.

"The passenger manifest deep background analysis is completed, and you're not going to like it." He cleared his throat a little, and then continued. "There's a prevalence of accountants and salespeople on that flight, but somehow I doubt that the hijacking was about sales or taxes. A relatively large number of scientists who were onboard XA233, nine to be precise, represents the third most significant data cluster in this analysis. The scientists were on their way back from a pharma conference, the biggest one in the industry. They are a varied group of researchers—neuroscientists, neurologists, psychiatrists, a psychopharmacologist—all touching the field of neuropharmacology."

They all fell silent for a little while, processing what they had just heard.

"Oh, my God…" Alex whispered.

"You might have been right about your third scenario," Lou said. "This could be about chemical weapons."

"What are you saying?" Blake asked in a high-pitched, trembling voice.

There was no way she could sugarcoat that. Alex looked him straight in the eye and replied, "Some kind of nerve agent."

The days were getting longer, and the air was filled with the summer warmth, making it a lovely afternoon to hunt bear. Clear sky, calm wind, and a balmy temperature, just perfect. *Now let's hope we find and kill the damn bear fast, so we can all go home and call it a night,* Myatlev thought, grabbing his rifle from Ivan. His back and stomach still hurt, but if Abramovich wanted to hunt bear with his best friends, he got to hunt bear with his best friends. *Goddamned food chain and distribution of power in this world...*

Myatlev joined Dimitrov and Abramovich near the cars, and exchanged hugs and traditional kisses on the cheeks with the other two. They had quite the entourage trailing behind them. They all had at least two bodyguards, dog handlers holding hounds on six-foot leashes, drivers, and aides. Abramovich even brought his personal chef, and a small team to prepare a hot meal, if finding a bear proved challenging.

God, I hope that won't be necessary, Myatlev thought, giving the confused chef a critical glare.

Abramovich's aide waited for the three of them to get ready, offering a tray with vodka on ice in small, cut crystal glasses, and bite-sized snacks: pâté de foie gras on thin toast, and tiny cheese crackers.

"Ura!" Abramovich cheered, raising his glass.

"Ura!" Myatlev and Dimitrov responded, meeting their glasses with his.

They gulped the vodka, then put the glasses back on the tray, and started walking toward the forest.

"Show me what you have there," Abramovich said, pointing at Myatlev's gun.

"Ha!" Dimitrov laughed. "That's why I don't like hunting with this bozo anymore. He always humiliates me with his fancy hardware. I've been hunting with the same rifle for the past five years."

"That's your way of admitting that mine is bigger than yours?" Myatlev quipped.

Abramovich laughed. "Good one, Vitya, you tell him," he said.

Myatlev showed his rifle to Abramovich, offering it to him as if on a tray, held horizontally with both his hands.

"Here you go," he said. "Try it out. It's a Holland & Holland bolt action magazine rifle, a .375."

Abramovich handed his own rifle to his aide, and took Myatlev's Holland & Holland. He handled it expertly, aimed at a virtual target, then let out a whistle of appreciation.

"I still have the Cottonmouth you gave me last year," Abramovich said, with a hint of regret in his voice. "Great rifle."

"I'll trade you if you'd like," Myatlev offered. "I'll hunt with the Cottonmouth, and you can take the H&H. Keep it, if you like it."

Abramovich's face lit up. One of the most powerful men in the world, and he was so susceptible to gifts and bribery it was pathetic. Yet Myatlev was grateful for knowing which buttons to push with the highly unstable Russian president. Any advantage when dealing with that lunatic was a gift from God.

Abramovich came to Myatlev and hugged him, then added an enthusiastic smooch on his cheek. "You know how to make your friend happy. Thank you!"

Dimitrov threw Myatlev a discrete, all-knowing smirk, while the president was busy playing with his new gun.

They continued walking toward the forest, as the light became heavier with the hues of dusk.

Suddenly, Abramovich ordered their aides to fall behind with a quick gesture.

"What's new with Division Seven?" he asked, as soon as the other men were out of earshot.

"We're making progress," Myatlev replied, and Dimitrov nodded. "We have deployed several key assets in the field, and they're recruiting left and right with the help of a newly formed cyber unit."

"I see…" Abramovich sounded unconvinced, impatient, and frowned a little. Not good.

"We are grabbing all kind of intel from our enemy. Soon we'll be caught up with the latest military technologies, weapons, systems, everything we need."

"Ah…this is nothing," Abramovich replied, making a dismissive gesture with his hand. "Give me something concrete, something I can sink my teeth into, and see the doom of our enemies coming."

Myatlev hesitated a little, thinking. Maybe it wasn't too soon to share this with him, despite a worried, warning glance Dimitrov had just shot his way.

"All right, how's this? I've formed a research unit in the far east, to develop controlled violent behavior."

"That's interesting," Abramovich replied, turning toward Myatlev. "Tell me, what do you use? Drugs?"

"Yes, drugs, and I knew you'd be interested, knowing your background with psy ops. I have a team of researchers, some of the best in the world, working on the perfect drug mix to induce and control violent behaviors."

"To do what?" Abramovich asked, frowning a little.

"Just imagine, controlling the forces from within our enemy's most sacrosanct organizations, the ones they trust the most, they depend on the most. Controlling how they react, how aggressive they are, when they start killing, and when they stop."

The president still wore a frown on his face. Myatlev stopped talking, a little worried with his reaction.

"These researchers, who are they? How come they're working for us?"

Myatlev swallowed hard, clenching his jaws, while thinking of the best way to explain it to the unpredictable Abramovich.

"Nine top-notch researchers were on their way back from a conference. They boarded their flight more than a week ago, but never made it to their destination. That was flight XA233."

He stopped talking, letting Abramovich process what he'd just heard.

"What?" he growled. "You took flight XA233? *You?*"

Abramovich drilled him with his stare.

"Y–yes, that was me, us."

Abramovich stared silently at Myatlev, making him wonder if he was going to survive the day. The Russian president had made people disappear in the depths of Siberia for far lesser offenses.

Unexpectedly, Abramovich grabbed Myatlev by the shoulders and kissed him on his cheeks, three times, in customary Russian style.

"You got balls the size of trucks, Vitya, but you're a reckless idiot," he finally said. "Did you stop to consider the consequences of what you have done?"

Myatlev shrugged, speechless. He didn't know what to say. He looked at Dimitrov for some guidance, but Dimitrov only shrugged.

"Jesus Christ, Vitya, if the world finds out about that plane, they could completely blockade us, roll out full sanctions. Hell, they could even invade us! You reckless fool! Genius, but reckless," he ended his tirade signaling his aide for drinks.

"Since when do you care about what the world has to say, Petya?" Myatlev asked, mustering his courage. "We're patriots, we're mercenaries in the service of Mother Russia, and we have no other supreme goal than to see her glorious and victorious again!"

Myatlev swallowed hard; tension was still crackling in the air.

The aide brought their shots, then disappeared discreetly.

They grabbed their glasses and raised them, but before they could clink them together, Abramovich said, "Yes, be bold, my friend, but don't be stupid.

Where the hell is that plane now?" he asked, then gulped down the alcohol without the usual cheers.

Myatlev frowned slightly.

"It's hidden, buried under a hill, at an abandoned air base in the east."

"Put some PVV explosive on it and blow it to hell. It never existed. Never happened. And those people can never be found, you understand me? None of them can ever see the light of day again. Once they finish what you have them do..."

He ended his phrase making a gesture with his hand, running the tip of his fingers against his neck, in the centuries-old gesture that signified decapitation.

"Not a single one, you hear me?"

"Da, *gospodin prezident*," Myatlev replied, turning formal all of a sudden to illustrate his commitment.

They resumed walking quietly toward the forest. No sign of any bear anywhere, and the dogs were barking playfully thirty yards behind them.

"You know, all I really want is my war," Abramovich suddenly said, a cloud of concern shadowing his eyes. "Neither of you are delivering that to me. You keep coming up with these crazy ideas, most of them don't even work, when all I want is to drop a nuke over New York, another one over San Francisco, then watch the Americans squirm. Why can't I have that? It would be simple, clean. They'd go into a nuclear winter so deep and dark, they'd beg me for food and aid for decades. That's what I want. To see them begging, defeated."

"That's not that easy to do, gospodin prezident," Dimitrov finally spoke. "We can't just shoot missiles toward those cities; their early detection systems would catch anything we throw their way. Even if we do nuke them, then what? We annihilate the entire planet. You see, that's the real problem with nuclear war. Once radiation is out there, it can go anywhere, and a simple change in the wind direction could kill more Russians than Americans. We need to be smart about it. That's what we're trying to do."

Abramovich looked at them both with an expression of deep disappointment.

"Neither of you has the balls for what I need," he finally spoke. "Was I so wrong about you?"

They had stopped walking, and stood facing each other in a small circle, all engulfed in their conversation.

"I will give you what you want," Myatlev said, "we both will. We just need a little more time to finish what we've started building. You want them to pay for the sanctions, for their arrogance? They will, I swear to you, here where I stand, on my life! If it's a nuclear attack you want, that's what you'll get, but we have to be smart. They can't see us coming, and they have to be weakened from within first. Controlled. By us."

Abramovich nodded, pursing his lips, probably wondering what to believe, what to expect. Myatlev fell quiet, giving him time to think.

The voices of their aides sounded louder now, and he could almost distinguish a yell. He looked back at them, and saw them gesturing desperately and running toward them with their guns drawn. Then he turned toward the forest and saw it.

A brown bear, huge, was forging ahead, running fast, and approaching them in big leaps.

"Bear," he screamed, and readied his rifle.

But Abramovich had already fired, his bullet grazing the bear's right shoulder, making it roar as it stood on its hind legs. The bear's roar was deafening, echoing strangely in the silence of the forest. Slobber dripped heavily from its open mouth, its teeth bared, and lips curled with anger. Then it fell back on all fours and resumed its attack, not even limping from the bullet wound.

Dimitrov had sprung to the left and was fumbling with his weapon, unable to fire.

"Jammed," he yelled, then started running farther, still holding his useless weapon.

As in a dream, Myatlev took a few steps to the right, leaving Abramovich alone on the path of the charging bear. Calmly, he readied his Venom tactical Cottonmouth, feeling a hint of recognition handling the exquisite weapon that used to be his.

Abramovich, who had taken his second shot but missed, walked backward, as in slow motion, unable to take his eyes off the attacking monster. The hounds had caught up with them and charged the bear from all directions, but they didn't slow its attack.

The bear was thirty feet away from Abramovich, advancing in big leaps, roaring, and baring his formidable fangs. Then Myatlev fired one shot, calmly reloaded, and fired another.

Both shots hit their target, one entering the bear's massive skull through its ear canal, and the other hitting it in the neck. The bear fell heavily, its dying groan terrifying, the momentum pushing its lifeless body farther on its path. As it fell, it took Abramovich down with it, landing with its massive head and front paws on the president's legs.

Myatlev approached calmly and extended his hand to the pale, round-eyed Abramovich, as his aides moved the bear's head and paws away from the president's body. Abramovich grabbed his hand with gratitude, grasping it firmly.

"And this, my dear Petya," Myatlev said while pulling the president off the ground, "is how you get your enemy. You attack where he least expects, where he doesn't see it coming."

There he was again, sitting sideways on his favorite lounge chair, head bowed, hands clasped tightly together, as he rocked almost imperceptibly back and forth.

Alex cringed thinking how Blake must have felt. Ten days since XA233 had fallen off the radar, ten days of anguish, not knowing if his wife was still alive. No, she corrected herself, he *knew* she was still alive. Blake believed that to be true with every fiber in his body, and he wanted her back.

She approached him and touched his shoulder gently. He turned to her, letting her see the pain written on his face. Hollow eyes surrounded by black circles, a creased brow, and an unshaven face. She could barely recognize him; he was falling apart right under their eyes.

"Alex, thank goodness," he said, taking both her hands into his. "Please help me," he continued, almost sobbing. "I can't—I can't sit like this and do nothing. What if she...Do something, please!"

She stood silent, unsure what she could say. They were all working round the clock, doing the best they could think of.

"Let's go, let's just get out there," he continued his plea. "I—I have every bit of confidence in what you say, and if you say the plane's in Russia, then let's just go there, now!" He was squeezing her hands tightly, his tight clasp conveying the same pleading urgency his words did.

"Blake, listen," she spoke softly. "Russia is a big place...where would we go? Plus, it's not exactly a tourist resort, you know. We have to be careful. Here, we have equipment, access to the Internet, to technology, to people who own satellites and are willing to share them with you. We have contacts, and we have access to resources."

His creased brow relaxed a little, as he processed what she was saying. He was, ultimately, a rational man driven by logic, regardless of the all-consuming pain and worry he must have felt.

"But I promise you this," she added, "The moment I have even the slightest idea of where that plane would have landed, it's wheels-up for this team. We're going out there, we're going to find them, and we're going to bring them back. That's a promise."

He let go of her hands, a little embarrassed for his moment of weakness, and stood, his back still hunched. Then he started pacing the patio slowly, pensively, rubbing his forehead with one hand, the other stuck firmly in his pocket.

"I can only imagine how hard this is for you," Alex said, "but don't give up hope. You have to try…we're making progress. I know it's hard for you to see that, when you'd like us to go out there guns blazing, but we have so much information now. We have a working theory, and in my line of work, that's what makes a case."

He nodded silently.

"OK, let's go inside," she summoned him, putting a little more energy in her voice. "The team's waiting for us. We need to explore this neuroagent scenario, see where it leads us."

She turned and walked in, heading to the war room, followed closely by Blake. He'd straightened his back and seemed calmer, more hopeful, recomposed. Good!

Tom was making coffee at the small machine in the corner, taking drink orders and delivering them. Lou had just received a cup of Hawaiian blend from his hands, a little uncomfortable having his boss serve him coffee. He needed to relax a little more; probably his military background was driving behaviors in him that would never go away. After all, he still called Alex, "boss." When she objected, he always said, "Once a SEAL, always a SEAL, ma'am!" and saluted, making them all laugh hard.

They all took seats around the table, except Alex. She remained standing, pacing slowly in a weak attempt to remain calm and focused. Her blood was boiling with every second that passed.

"OK, so let's talk the chemical warfare scenario," she said, sounding more confident than she actually felt. What did she know about chemical warfare? Almost nothing, plus a few hours' worth of Internet research. "Thoughts? I think this could change things a little."

"Totally," Lou said. "This could be a national security threat. We need to call people."

"I agree," Alex replied, "but who would believe us? When the entire world is looking for this plane at the bottom of the ocean?"

"Exactly," Blake intervened. "I know, because I tried really hard, using all my influence. And they didn't even want to hear me out."

"Unfortunately, I have to agree," Sam added, putting his already empty coffee cup on the table with a hint of regret. "They'd probably consider us some loony conspiracy theorists and discard us in an instant."

"Let's play this out," Tom said. "Why would they discard our theory that fast?"

"Well, let's say we call the feds in on this, right?" Sam started explaining. "They give us a few minutes, not more, and that's even after us having to explain how we got our hands on deep-level background information for 441 people."

Lou cleared his throat and gulped a little coffee, swallowing hard, then wrung his hands together. "Oh, boy…" he muttered, "not good."

"Then, they'd call the airline and ask if it's even remotely possible for that plane to have landed hundreds of miles from where the airline's searching for it, right?" Sam searched their faces with his scrutinizing eyes, one by one. They all agreed. "What do you think the airline would say? Do you think it would admit that, essentially, it has no clue where the aircraft really is once it takes off? Or would the airline swear that XA233 simply has to be on the bottom of the ocean somewhere?"

They all remained quiet, watching Sam intently.

"Yes, I'd have to agree, it would be a waste of time," he ended his argument. "The satellites are going operational later today; I'd say let's keep going on our own. Until we have some solid evidence, we don't have a case with any one of the law enforcement agencies. Let's keep in mind that 441 people are out there, and we're their only hope. We don't have time to bet on the government. God only knows what's happening to them right now, or how many are still alive."

A long, shuddering breath came out of Blake's chest.

"Blake, man, I'm so sorry," Sam said, hopping off his chair and squeezing Blake's shoulder. "We'll find her, I promise you. I'm such an idiot, jeez…"

Blake looked up and spoke softly, yet firmly, "You can't keep apologizing, or constantly censoring your communication, trying to shield me. You're right, you're her only hope, so please stay focused on finding all of them, and don't worry about me. I can handle it."

Steve watched the interaction quietly, but then asked, disrupting the uncomfortable silence that ensued, "Could someone please explain to me what you're thinking, jumping from an apparently coincidental group of scientists on a return flight from a conference, all the way to chemical warfare and nerve agents? I must be missing something."

"We had previously established means," Alex replied, "when we figured out how it could have been done. We still don't have a confirmed UNSUB identity connected to those means, but at least we've established it was possible to hijack a plane like that. But we were missing motive. Why would someone grab a 747 mid-flight? If you recall, we explored the scenarios of a financially, or politically motivated hijacking, but no calls were made that we know of, asking for any trade in return for the plane and its occupants. We were unable to answer the *why* question until now, especially why XA233, and not any other commercial flight."

She looked at Steve, but he still looked a little confused. She continued, "But what if you'd like to conduct ultra-secret research on chemical warfare, specifically on neuroagents? What better way than to hijack the plane carrying the world's leading experts in neurochemistry, and force them to work for you?"

"Oh, I see...What do you think they're making, what kind of nerve agent?"

"No way of knowing," she replied.

Silence engulfed the war room again, equally uncomfortable.

"That's why you think V is behind this then?" Steve asked.

"Yes," Alex replied. "It fits."

"But—" Steve started to say, but she immediately interrupted him.

"Yeah, yeah, I know. I have no proof; I have nothing, no hard evidence to back me up. But, to me, it feels right. I *know* it's him."

"You're saying no one else could pull this off?" Sam asked.

She threw him an angry, disappointed glare. Sam doubted her too.

"You did ask me to keep you true, remember?" Sam added.

She cooled off a little. Sam was right to ask questions.

"Yeah, I did, didn't I? But you know how these things are sometimes. You just have to follow your gut. Both of you taught me that," she said, swaying her index finger from Tom to Sam and back.

"Correct," Tom admitted. "I also taught you to keep an open mind."

"But I am—" Alex said, in a high-pitched tone showing her growing anger.

"We all trust you, Alex," Steve said conciliatorily, "it's not about that."

"Then what?" she snapped, turning toward him. He'd been the first to distrust her, to lose confidence in her reasoning. The first to betray her, to cross the line that had forever changed their relationship.

Steve remained silent for a second, visibly uncomfortable with what he was about to say.

"It's about your determination with finding V. We don't want you to have that determination cloud your judgment, that's all. I guess we're just a bunch of concerned, overprotective men, that's all," he ended with a shy smile.

She couldn't contain the chuckle that dissolved all her anger in a split second.

"Are you, now? So let me get this straight, I am being sexually discriminated in my place of employment?"

"Oh, no, no, no," Tom said, "we are so not going down that path. I would really like to retire before getting sued for any type of workplace issue," he stated somberly, but with a smile in his eyes.

Alex looked at them, feeling a forgotten warmth take over her heart. They were on her side, all of them, despite all their questions. Smart people ask questions and want to see proof for everything.

"Look, guys, I know how this looks, especially considering how obsessed I'd become with catching V, the bastard." She spoke in a softer voice, dropping all her defensiveness. "I am painfully aware that there's no real evidence, and I'm even more aware that we might end up finding the plane and its passengers, yet still find no evidence of V, or who the real UNSUB mastermind behind this hijacking was. But the clock is ticking, and we only have a few hours before we need to submit our search grids to DigiWorld to deploy the satellite search patterns."

They fidgeted a little, turning their attention to the map. Sam used the opportunity to grab another cup of coffee, and filled the small room with a strong, dark-roast aroma.

"Let's organize the search grids for now, thinking of two satellites, not three. The third hasn't been confirmed yet. Do we think China is worth searching? It's in the neighborhood," she asked.

"Why not Iran? Libya?" Sam asked. "Anyone could have taken that plane. It could have landed on a commercial airport for all we know."

"No, definitely not on a commercial airport," Alex replied. "Too many witnesses. As for China, Iran, or Libya? I don't know...I honestly don't. But it just doesn't *feel* like it's any of them. It feels like Russians. To me, this is V's handiwork, but I am keeping my options open."

A moment of silence followed, while they looked at one another, unsure what to say.

"We need to make a call, guys, that's all," she added, "I am very open-minded right now, conceding the fact that it might not have been V behind this, or not directly. What do you think?"

"It's your call, kiddo," Sam said.

"Agree," Blake confirmed.

Lou saluted, his typical way of saying that he'll follow her lead, and Steve nodded.

"Godspeed," Tom concluded.

"Then Russia it is," Alex decided firmly. "No China, or anyone else for now."

She took a marker and drew a circle sector on the map, centered on Tokyo, and interrupted at Russia's borders.

"I'd suggest one satellite scans east-to-west from the north, and the other one starts the same search pattern coming from the south. We could break this down in swatches of about 300 miles in width, before having to reposition the satellites. I think this is the fastest way to get results. It makes sense to me they'd start from the coastline, not from inland. That's how I'd go about it."

"Makes sense," Lou said.

She turned on the TV and projected some images from her laptop.

"We've found several strips where the plane could have landed. Airfields, potentially strategic highways. There are quite a few within range, and far apart.

This is not actionable info, I'm afraid. There's no way to tell where they'd have landed just based on this."

"Why?" Blake asked, a new wave of pallor hitting his face.

"We were hoping there would only be two or three landing strips within range, but we found more than forty. We can't go into the field and investigate them one by one. They're many and far apart, most of them isolated. It would take us weeks."

"What are you saying?" Blake continued.

"I'm saying that satellites are our best bet, maybe our only one."

She reached for the coffee cup to relieve her dry throat, but it was empty. She put it back on the table with a frustrated sigh.

They all remained silent, concern showing on their faces in different ways. Blake had resumed staring at the floor. Lou's lips were pursed and his jaws clenched, and he was stomping his foot rhythmically, impatiently. Steve had a rarely seen frown clouding his brow, and Tom had clasped his hands together, probably struggling with this kind of powerlessness. Sam seemed unfazed, looking confident, but she knew him better than to fall for that appearance.

"What are we talking about here, in terms of time?" Sam asked.

"About 36 hours, maybe 48. That's all it will take, and we'll finally know. That's all it takes for the satellites to screen that area at high resolution," she replied, pointing at the circle drawn on the map. "If there's a Boeing 747-400 out there, in those woods, they'll find it."

"How?" Steve asked, hesitantly. "What if there's no direct visibility, how will the satellites see the plane?"

"Oh, we've thought of that," she said, displaying a colorful image on the screen. "In recent years, technologies have been developed to use satellites for mining and mineral prospecting. Our satellites will use those orbital prospecting technologies, more precisely infrared scanning, advanced space-borne thermal emissions, and reflection radiometer scanning. Just like how satellites would find metal buried in the ground, they can find the plane, no matter how deep it's buried or hidden in the forest."

"How would infrared work, in this case?" Lou asked. "That's more for weather applications, right?"

"Right," Alex confirmed. "Keep in mind the specific heat of metal is lower than the heat of the forest, or any surrounding natural surface materials, like rocks, vegetation, and dirt. It would stand out simply because it's colder."

She looked at everyone in the room, feeling a little overwhelmed again. There were 441 lives, all depending on her judgment calls. *Oh, God… please help me be right about this.*

She shook her doubt away, straightening her back, and raising her head with a confidence she forced herself to feel.

"Guys, we're almost there. One more day and we'll know where to go."

"Great," Lou said, "it's about time. I'm dying to go out there and shoot the sons of bitches who thought this shit up."

Dr. Davis looked up from the gas chromatograph's screen, searching for the source of the annoying little buzzing sound. There it was… a mosquito had just landed on the tile-covered lab table. He slammed his palm hard, killing it, and making some test tubes rattle in their stands. He also gave Dr. Chevalier a start. She was sitting at the microscope just a few feet away and looked at him disapprovingly.

"I apologize, Marie-Elise, it was just reflex," he said in a gentle tone of voice.

Instantly, her eyes welled up, and a silent tear started rolling on her cheek.

He pushed his chair closer to her.

"What's going on, huh? Would you like to tell me about it? Maybe I can help…"

She sniffled, a little embarrassed, keeping her eyes pinned to the floor and her shoulders forward, seeming small and vulnerable. She hugged herself tightly.

"It's—it's my husband. He had a heart attack just a month ago," she said, her voice strangled by tears. "I don't even know if he's still alive. We might never get out of here, you know?"

"Marie-Elise," Gary whispered, "you have to hold on to hope. You have to—"

The sound of the massive door springing open silenced him. Everyone watched silently as an enraged Bogdanov walked through the door, followed closely by Death and One-Eye, both carrying their automatic weapons.

Without any provocation, One-Eye grabbed Dr. Mallory, who was closest to the door, and shoved him hard on the floor at Bogdanov's feet. Declan Mallory fell hard and stayed down, probably dazed, too shocked to react. The quiet, composed Brit didn't have an aggressive bone in his body.

Gary gasped, then covered his mouth. He grabbed Marie-Elise's hand and squeezed it tightly. Like threatened animals in the wild when predators are near, they all huddled closely together, finding some comfort in one another's presence.

He heard Wu Shen Teng's stifled sobs somewhere behind him. He turned and looked at him, trying to offer an encouraging look. For some reason, what he'd intended as comfort had the opposite effect on Wu Shen Teng, who covered his mouth with both his hands to silence the sound of his renewed sobbing.

Bogdanov reached down and grabbed a fistful of Mallory's hair, forcing him to his knees.

"If I don't have a successful test in 48 hours, he will die," Bogdanov said in a quiet voice, a threatening, growling whisper. He looked at them with eyes filled with hate, then spat on the floor.

They all stood quietly, huddled together closely, holding their breaths. Gary felt the urge to step forward and do something; he wasn't sure what. He took half a step forward, but Marie-Elise clutched his hand tightly and whispered, "No!"

Then Bogdanov spoke again.

"You've been sabotaging this from the first day," he said, surprising Gary, and probably the rest of the doctors.

How the hell did they know? They'd been careful, keeping their voices down whenever they spoke, and taking turns keeping their guards busy and discreetly supervised. They thought they had a way to buy themselves some time. They'd been wrong all this time. *Fuck!*

"You think you're smart, *da?*" Bogdanov continued, his voice filling with contempt. "You think you can stall us, and we're just dumb Russians and we won't know? We know everything!" he shouted, punctuating his statement with a boot kick to Declan Mallory's stomach.

Declan curled up on the floor, groaning and writhing with pain, trying to breathe, gasping for air.

Marie-Elise's grasp on Gary's hand tightened, as anticipating what he was thinking of doing. But he didn't have time to act.

"You do that again and you will die, one by one," Bogdanov added, drilling his eyes into theirs. "From shock," he continued, his menacing voice dropping to a whisper again. "I will break every bone in your body, one by one, slowly, until your body gives up on you. That's my promise to all of you lying cunts."

Bogdanov nodded toward One-Eye, who brought the stock of his Kalashnikov brutally down on Mallory's rib cage. They all stood there, paralyzed, hearing the bones cracking and Declan scream. Gary felt a wave of nausea hit him.

"This is your final warning," Bogdanov added, then left briskly, followed by his men.

The early morning air pushed through the open window, helped by a scented breeze heavy with spring blooms. The aroma of freshly brewed coffee almost covered that, as one after another, cups filled at the machine, and the team members took their seats around the small table, steaming cups in front of them.

"OK, so we find the plane," Alex said, jumping right to the heart of things, "then what? Call the feds?"

"I don't think that would be an option, even if we find it," Blake replied. "I'd still rather have us continue on our own. They'd have to go through channels; it would take a long time."

"Sam?" Alex prompted.

"I tend to agree with Blake. We're looking at getting the feds, or maybe the CIA in this case, more likely, to orchestrate an op in a foreign country, based on some disputable satellite imagery and our stories. I don't think they're gonna do it. Not fast enough, anyway."

She stood and started pacing the little space she had available, between the table and the wall where the map was pinned. She rubbed the back of her neck nervously, grinding her teeth.

"OK, let's talk extraction scenarios, then," she conceded, silencing the self-doubt she was feeling. She wasn't special ops material; she felt overwhelmed at the immense responsibility hanging on her decisions, her actions, and her judgment. "Lou? You're the closest thing we have to a special ops expert; I think you should lead the extraction discussions."

"Sure, boss, I'd be happy to," he replied, then went to the whiteboard with a marker in his hand. "We have two tactical issues," he continued, writing as he spoke. "One, we're assuming that the people are still with the plane, and they might not be. In fact, why would they be? Whoever holds them needs to feed them and house them, no matter how precariously. That takes space and resources."

"Oh, God..." Blake said, "you're right. We might find the plane, but they could be long gone from there."

"Long gone, but not very far, I'd think it's safe to assume," Alex intervened.

"Why?" Lou asked.

"This is not some random hijacking under the spur of the moment. This was a well-planned op, and, most likely, if they're housing the people at a certain location, they would have taken them by plane there, or as close as possible—441 people are a lot of individuals to be moving from point A to point B."

"Agreed," Lou said, "sounds reasonable. But that means once we find the plane, we'll have to go there and find them. This is our first tactical issue," he specified, writing the number one in a circle on the whiteboard, under the phrase, "Unknown hostage location."

"And second?" Blake asked.

"Having 441 people means a lot of exfiltration," Lou replied, "a lot of exfil to handle from behind enemy lines, under potential fire. Some might be hurt, weak, or sick. I think the best bet remains the plane. Get them out of there exactly as they came in."

"Makes sense," Alex said, smiling for the first time in days. "We'd need a pilot though. One of the 747's pilots had a Russian name; let's assume him hostile. We can't count on him. I'd rather count on Blake's pilot. And we're also assuming that the 747 can still be used."

"Yes," Lou agreed, "we're assuming that the Boeing is still airworthy, and has enough fuel to get everyone back to Japan. But we need firepower, serious firepower."

"Why?" Blake asked.

"The UNSUB has enough people to control 441 hostages," Lou replied. "We're talking about anything up to potentially fifty armed forces, maybe even more. They could have air support, heavy weaponry, surveillance, advanced recon, who knows? We have to be prepared."

Alex fidgeted uncomfortably, shifting her weight from one foot to the other.

"Umm…and I'm not…I can't be counted on, you know, I'm no special ops material," she struggled to say, feeling uncomfortable and embarrassed. "I am coming with you, of course, but I'm not that great in a battle. I've never been in one."

"Nope, that's not true," Sam said. "I've seen you in action. You're cool under pressure, you keep your head well-bolted to your shoulders, and you don't hesitate. I'd have you watch my six anytime."

"Same here," Lou said. "I've trained you and I've seen you in simulations. I've also seen you in the field; you're a great shot. Just remember your training, and you'll do fine."

She looked at them both, then took in a deep breath and said, "Then we're set. But we're still not enough, the three of us. We need some serious help."

"Four," Blake said. "I'm coming too."

"Blake, that's not a good idea," Alex replied. "We can't watch over you while we're out there. You're better off waiting for us here, where it's safe."

"I won't need you to watch over me. I'm a damn good shot, and a Desert Storm veteran. Give me some credit, will you? I can't stand waiting one more second, so I'm coming with you. That's decided."

Sam nodded, and Lou whispered, "Welcome to the exfil team then."

"I'm repeating myself here," Alex said. "We need help, serious help. Where do we find it?"

"I'm thinking mercs," Lou replied, "military hired help."

"I'll make some calls," Blake offered.

"No, not this time," Lou replied. "Let me make the calls, I'll know better what to ask for." He paused a little, gathering his thoughts. "We can't hire them in the States, though."

"Why?" Blake asked.

"They'll need to bring a lot of gear with them, including choppers. We're pretty sure we're gonna find that plane, only we don't exactly know where and when we'll find the passengers. I'd rather have the four of us do the initial groundwork, stealth. With a dozen mercs or so in tow, and their equipment, they'll see us coming from miles away."

"Then they'll need to be located in Japan," Alex said. "It's the only friendly area that's close enough to our op zone."

"See? What did I tell you?" Sam asked with a chuckle. "You're already mastering this game. The only thing, just don't call them mercs; they hate that. Even if they are guns for hire, that doesn't mean they don't have principles and a code of honor."

"Oh...What should I call them, then?"

"Military contractors is better."

"All right, let's find us some Japan-based military contractors to help us."

Myatlev gave his half-smoked cigar a disappointed, frustrated look, as he rolled it between his thumb and index finger. A wave of humid heat had taken over Moscow, and the polluted, stinking haze ruined his smoking enjoyment, bringing a faint smell of gasoline exhaust to the otherwise perfect Arturo Fuente cigar.

He flicked the cigar over the terrace railing and leaned back in his lounge chair, thinking, letting his mind wonder, reliving the bear attack. He could have delayed taking that shot just a few seconds, and it could have been no more Abramovich. No more unstable, moody, arrogant bastard to order him around and tell him what he could and couldn't do. No more having to go to work in his office at the Ministry of Defense. No more fear of having the president's favor turn into persecution, and no more threat of Siberia looming over his head. It would have been an easy, clean kill, brought to him as a peace offering from destiny itself. Abramovich's life, offered to him on a silver plate, and he chose to save that life.

Yet, in the heat of the moment, he'd chosen to pull that trigger and save the bastard, and he didn't regret it. Despite his unpredictable stubbornness, Abramovich was worth more to Myatlev alive than dead. The possibilities were endless, his to explore, materialize, and reap benefits from.

Even if that meant, every now and then, yielding to the bastard's will and doing what he was told.

"*Tvoyu mat,*" he muttered under his breath, then called out, "Ivan!"

Ivan instantly appeared out of nowhere.

"Da?"

"Blow up that 747, Ivan, and do it soon," he said, feeling his jaws clenching at the thought of it. Such a waste...a senseless, stupid, cowardly waste. But blatantly disobeying a direct order from Abramovich and irritating him wasn't an option.

"Sir?"

"Yes, yes, you heard me," Myatlev confirmed. "And you heard Abramovich yesterday. It has to get done. "

Myatlev stood up, straining, feeling a pinch under the right side of his ribcage. Maybe it was time to give his liver a checkup. So much stress wasn't good for anyone, and the vodka didn't help, but he wasn't going to stop living before actually dying.

"Send someone you trust, Ivan," he continued. "Tell him to pack it with C4 and blow it up."

"Yes, sir," Ivan acknowledged. "Consider it done."

"Route a satellite over it and record the explosion, in case Abramovich wants to see some proof."

Ivan nodded, getting ready to leave.

A cunning smile appeared on Myatlev's lips. "Tell your man to collect some of the plane's debris after the explosion, and take that out to sea. Tell him to throw that debris in the water near where they said it crashed. This way they'll stop looking."

Ivan smiled widely.

"Consider it done," he repeated before leaving.

A feverish sense of anticipation anxiety crept up on all of them, as they watched the hours slip by and counted each hour obsessively, waiting for DigiWorld's call to come in with a possible location. They responded to that anxiety in different ways, suited to their individual personalities.

Sam smoked, playing with the smoke as it left his lungs, at times competing with Steve in the art of blowing the perfect smoke ring. Was cigarette smoke better than cigar smoke when it came to smoke rings? They debated that for almost forty minutes, driving Alex crazy.

Blake analyzed the news, as he did with every chance he got, looking to the media for any new information about the missing plane. By the bleak look on his face, there was nothing new in the press.

Tom had started heating up the grill, too late for breakfast and too early for lunch, but that was Tom's stress relief; he liked to cook.

Alex had nothing to do, just paced back and forth on the patio, occasionally biting on her right index fingernail, so unsettled she couldn't even sit down. How much longer would they have to wait? Were they still going to find the passengers alive? Or just piled up in a superficial mass grave somewhere? If the UNSUB had taken the plane to get a hold of nine neuroscientists, what about the rest of the people? What had become of them? If satellite scans failed, what other means would she have to find the missing XA233? Has she been wrong all this time, focusing on Russia? Had she been wasting time and people's lives on her obsession with V? Damn waiting...There were too many questions and not enough answers, and it pissing her off. *I hate this powerlessness shit,* she thought. *Now I'm almost like Lou, I just wanna shoot whoever took that damn plane.*

"Hey, I got us a crew," Lou said cheerfully, coming out in the backyard with some papers in his hand.

They gathered around him hastily. Finally, some damn news.

"OK, here it is," Lou said, showing them his notes. "We have a crew of fourteen standing by, with two choppers, ready to fly in when we call them. They didn't seem overly preoccupied with operating behind the Russian border."

"American?" Alex asked. "Or Japanese?"

"American. There's an American military base in Wakkanai, at the northern tip of the Japanese islands. These guys, Dark Ravens they're called, are a contractor with troops over there. Starting tomorrow morning at 0600 they're on the clock, and that's costing us $160,000 a day, whether we use them or not."

"Whoa," Alex said.

"Doesn't matter," Blake dismissed her reaction to the cost of the operation. "I just wish we knew where to tell them to go."

"Will fourteen be enough?" Alex asked, thinking of Lou's estimation of potentially fifty armed forces working for the UNSUB.

After a quick moment of silence, he frowned a little, and then replied, "They'll have to be."

Dr. Adenauer sat on a lab stool, hunched over the tile-covered table, rubbing his forehead obsessively. He couldn't do what they asked; yet he had to. There was no way out. All these people were there, enduring captivity because of him, so if his soul was going to burn in the hell of his conscience, then so be it.

He stood and walked toward the cot where Declan Mallory lay, breathing shallowly and sweating profusely. The heat was unbearable; it was getting hotter from one day to the next, and that made it even worse for Mallory. Every breath he took must have been excruciatingly painful, regardless of the improvised pain medication they'd been able to offer. Luckily, so far there didn't seem to be any evidence of internal bleeding, a common side effect of the type of trauma he'd been subjected to.

Dr. Adenauer summoned everyone to join him around Dr. Mallory's cot.

"There's no other option," he spoke, his voice heavy with the burden of conscience. "We have to increase the strength of the compound."

"No, you can't do that!" Gary Davis said. "They're people, for God's sake; you can't test that on people! You could kill them!"

Dr. Adenauer rubbed his creased forehead again.

"Don't you think I know that?" he snapped. "I haven't been able to think of anything else. But what you fail to understand is that if they decide we're worthless to their...their quest for this drug, they will kill us all. All of us, including the hundreds of others who were on that plane. Everybody."

His words fell heavy, bringing deafening silence with them. He knew he was right, and he knew he was the one who needed to make the difficult decisions the rest couldn't stomach.

"Can't we at least find a way to test safely?" Gary Davis insisted. "Can we ask for lab rats?"

That made sense; Adenauer had to admit, although the precise dosing of the compound in their makeshift lab would probably pose some issues. It did make sense, nevertheless.

He approached King Cobra, who was watching them from a distance, with his eyes half closed, succumbed to the heat.

"Tell your boss we need lab rats," Adenauer said firmly, "and by that I mean rodents, not people."

Despite the very late hour, none of them felt anything but eager anticipation. Alex had been so anxious to get there after receiving the call, that she didn't even replenish her coffee. She'd just grabbed her jacket and left, waiting for Blake and Lou with her engine running, muttering "C'mon, c'mon," every ten seconds.

Now the three of them stood in front of DigiWorld's huge screens, squinting hard and trying to see what the operator was saying.

"We've brought you here," the operator said, "because we've captured an image, a ghost as we call it. See? It's right here."

They stared some more, but were unable to discern anything.

"It's a faint haze, almost thin as clouds, but the haze shown on the image is displayed in a pattern compatible with that of a plane," the operator clarified. She looked very young for her job, but seemed sure of herself.

"Where?" Alex asked.

The operator moved her mouse and circled a certain area on the huge screen that showed a stretch of forested land with small puddles of water, maybe a swamp.

"Right here, see? This is where we think we have what we call a ghost pattern."

"Meaning what?"

"Meaning that while it's not really the discernible image of a plane, this haze has a few points in common with the plane's shape. It's almost as if we captured the ghost of the plane...that's why we call these types of images ghost patterns. They look like wisps of thin cloud. Umm...they look just like how ghosts are shown in the movies, but match the pattern, the shape of our search subject, the 747-400."

She touched a few keys and grabbed the image of a 747-400 from a library of images. Then she rotated it a little around the horizontal and vertical axes, positioning it at a certain angle, then overlapped it on top of the ghost pattern she was seeing.

The screen flickered green dots where the two images matched. There were twelve green dots on the screen, blinking.

Blake was holding his breath. "What does this mean?" he asked, pointing at the screen.

"It means we've found your plane, Mr. Bernard. It's hidden under something, it's shallow, not buried deep, yet still hidden somehow. Because the plane itself is hollow, not solid, the resonance scanner sees it as a ghost pattern rather than a solid, well-contoured shape. But it's there."

"Bring the satellite to focus on that area, as close and high-res as possible," Alex said. "Give me maximum zoom; let's see what we can learn about that place. Lou," she turned toward him, "can you see if there are any drones in Japan we could use? Maybe that military base has some?"

"I'm on it, boss," he replied, yanking his cell phone out of his pocket and taking a few steps away to make his call without disturbing anyone. "If I remember correctly, NanoLance had a testing program in place in Japan, a dual research project on fully automated UCAVs. I happen to know some people," he added with a wink, "I'll make some calls."

"Where exactly is this place?" Alex asked.

The operator zoomed out, the ghost pattern turning into a tiny red dot on the map.

"It's in Russia, 200 miles inland from the Sea of Japan coastline, near a small town called Mayak. It's an abandoned airbase. Has an airstrip too."

"Get me high-resolution angular shots," Alex asked the operator. "Let's see who and what's down there. Prepare for a long night."

Dr. Adenauer finished injecting the third rat with the compound, then picked up a second syringe, and gave the squirming little animal a second shot.

"This is the antidote," he explained to the small group in attendance.

The group included Gary Davis, Marie-Elise Chevalier, Klaas Fortuin, and Wu Shen Teng. One-Eye was also observing, any attempt to keep him away or distracted having failed miserably, yielding only angry grunts from the taciturn gorilla.

Dr. Adenauer finished injecting the antidote, then marked the rat with a touch of methylene blue on its white coat, making it easy to identify from the others. Then he placed the rat in the same cage with the other two he had injected earlier.

Minutes passed in silence, while nothing remarkable happened in the rat cage. The test subjects behaved like normal rats, sniffing, chewing on the occasional speck of dirt, moving around in the cage, but ignoring one another.

Then suddenly one rat jumped at another, making a barely audible growl. It attacked the other animal fiercely, plunging its teeth in the other's throat, while its front claws tore at the victim's belly. The other rat fought back as hard as it could, tearing pieces of the attacker's coat with its claws, gurgling sounds coming out of its throat as the attacker squeezed its jaws tighter, killing it. The rat bearing a blue mark on the back of its neck stood trembling in the corner of the cage, watching the fight with big, round, beady eyes.

Within seconds, the fight was over, leaving one dead rat in a pool of blood, another one heaving and dying from a deep laceration that had cut open its abdomen, and a third, alive, unharmed, but paralyzed with fear.

"May God forgive us all," Dr. Chevalier said quietly, holding her hand over her mouth, as if to smother a scream of horror.

"He won't," Dr. Adenauer replied through clenched teeth.

"Great job," One-Eye spoke. "I will tell my boss," he added, then left the room.

They stared at the scene in front of them, unable to move or react. Dr. Adenauer picked up some gauze, soaked it in alcohol, and began cleaning the spray of blood that had stained the table around the cage.

"The dose was too concentrated," Bogdanov spoke, startling everyone. He had entered the lab unheard and unseen, while they were only paying attention to the horrible aftermath of their test. "We want them aggressive, but not like this. We want control. We want the rage to appear natural; I've told you that. What are you going to do?"

He was actually waiting for an answer, making sure they understood they had to deliver.

Theo Adenauer cleared his throat, still choked after he'd watched the experiment, and offered a plan.

"We could try slow-release capsules next, to see if it's the strength of the compound, or the delivery mechanism that allows the best control."

"We need the compound aerosolized," Bogdanov replied. "How are slow-release capsules going to help with that? Reduce the concentration and try again. What are you using?"

"SSREs," Adenauer replied, surprised. It was the first time Bogdanov had asked any technical question about their work.

"Decrease the strength, but add some steroids, maybe it will help," Bogdanov replied. "You're supposed to know that. Is this rat the one injected with the antidote?" he asked, pointing at the survivor.

"Y–yes," Adenauer hesitated, unsure where he was going with that.

"They need to attack the non-violent test subjects, not each other. Fix that."

"How?" Adenauer asked, surprised at the request.

"You world-famous researchers figure it out. You have 24 hours, or else he starts dying," Bogdanov replied, pointing toward the cot where Declan Mallory lay on his back. "I think I have already taken care of a few ribs, yes? Only 24 hours, that's it. Then I continue breaking his bones, one at a time."

Alex stormed out of the DigiWorld building followed closely by Blake and Lou. They had gathered all possible imagery about the plane's location, and she felt the exhilaration that only hope can give. Hope that she'd been right, that they'd make it in time to save all those people. Hope that they'd found the right plane.

She stopped abruptly and asked, "Blake, does your plane fly that far?"

"Yes, it does. It will take us about fifteen hours to get there, including refueling stops."

"All right, let's get ready. Wheels up in two hours."

"I need to make a quick detour," Lou said. "Boss, can you please pack me an overnight bag? I'll meet you on the tarmac."

"Where are you going?" Alex asked.

"Shopping."

The annoying voice of Dr. Bogdanov filled the room as Myatlev took his call hands-free. He was going on and on about what they were doing over there, giving too few specifics, and wasting his time.

"So, you don't have it yet, that's what I'm hearing, right?" Myatlev interrupted him. "After two weeks, you have nothing?"

"Sir, if you allow me, progress is being made," Bogdanov replied with a little more insecurity seeping into his voice. "They are adjusting the levels of active compound to get the desired results. There is a precise dosage that will work, requiring many rounds of testing and fine-tuning."

Myatlev restrained himself with difficulty. This moron wasn't going to get him what he wanted. But it was too late to turn back now.

"I want them controllable, you hear me?" Myatlev told Bogdanov for the fifth time. "What we need to do will not work without precise control, and calculated levels of aggression. Do you understand?"

"Y–yes, sir."

Myatlev hung up, letting out a long sigh of frustration. Bogdanov was probably going to fail; he had heard the uncertainty in his voice. Maybe what he wanted couldn't be achieved after all. He wanted a level of precision and control over the aggression of his test subjects that could enable him to play them like puppets on a string. After all, it would be a disaster if a business opponent started killing people instead of signing the wrong paperwork, bidding too high, or taking too much risk. However, having the test subjects turn homicidal lined up well with his other motivation, the official one. He wanted to seed violence in the heart of the enemy's law enforcement, making them turn against the people they were sworn to protect. Such senseless, apparently random violence would be ripping through America from within its own structures, like a cancer destroying the body it had invaded.

But it might have been the time to consider plan B. Abramovich was not going to settle for another failure, if this plan wasn't going to work. He walked slowly to the office next to his, and entered after a quick tap on the door.

"Mishka," he greeted Dimitrov as he came into his office. The air was stale and the curtains were half-shut, defending the room from the scorching heat outside. Dimitrov hated air conditioning, and preferred it turned off. He said cold air gave him migraines. *I bet it's this stuffiness that gives him the migraines,* Myatlev thought, eager to finish the business he was there for, and get back to the breathable habitat of his own office.

"Vitya," Dimitrov replied. "What news are you bringing?"

"Nothing good, I'm afraid. Not yet." He paused for a little while, almost afraid to speak his mind. It was a big step he was about to take, a big step on a road with no return. "They can't fully control the effects, not yet, anyway," he added, shrugging apologetically. "I think we need to be prepared for attack in a different way, and give Petya what he wants, what he always wanted."

Dimitrov took off his thick-rimmed glasses and set them down on the desk slowly, massaging the bridge of his nose with his thumb and index.

"What are you saying, Vitya?"

Maybe there could be a way to prosper in a post-nuclear world. Or maybe he could do something to manage Abramovich's belligerence and ensure the prosperity of his business empire at the same time. Maybe he could just be prepared, but not act, just to have a plausible excuse in case the shit would hit the fan with their beloved president. Maybe he could invest in food futures; in the post-nuclear world, clean, radiation-free food supplies would become very expensive. His investments could yield three-digit, even four-digit returns.

"Can you make me some small nukes?" Myatlev finally asked, just a hint of hesitation tinting his voice. "They'd have to fit in a small backpack, nothing big."

Dimitrov's jaw dropped, then he replied quietly, "How many?"

"Fifteen or so. Not sure yet...I'm still thinking," Myatlev replied, lost in thought.

Or maybe I should have let that bear finish its business before killing it.

Dr. Gary Davis watched closely as Adenauer's elegant hands mixed the compound ingredients quickly, after measuring them on the digital micro-scale. Every step he took in preparing the compound he documented clearly in a notebook, each step listed in detail under the heading "Compound 11." It was the eleventh formulation they were trying. *If I were to see him out of context,* Gary thought, *it would seem like he's in his own lab in Germany.*

Then Adenauer started preparing the capsules. He made ten of them, putting them in a small jar.

"Why so many?" Gary asked.

"I can be more precise mixing a larger quantity of compound, you know that," Adenauer replied, visibly irritated to be challenged.

"I only want to test on two subjects, that's it," Gary stated firmly.

"No, we'll need more. We'll raise suspicions if we test only two," Dr. Teng intervened.

"I'll handle the suspicions," Gary replied, sounding more confident than he felt. "If we could at least attempt like we're talking about human beings here, that would be great," he snapped, sarcasm cutting through his voice and glinting in his eyes.

"Do you think I can ever forget that?" Adenauer said, keeping his voice low but loaded with anger. "Who do you think I am?"

Under Gary's surprised eyes, Adenauer's angry glare turned to immense sadness.

"I'm ready to die right here, today, if that removes a single other human being from harm's way," Adenauer continued somberly. "Next time they want to kill someone to make a point, I will volunteer. I am ready."

"Theo!" Marie-Elise exclaimed, getting One-Eye to lift his eyes and scrutinize their small group. "You can't do that!" she continued. "We need you! We all need one another!"

"It's pointless," Adenauer replied calmly. "My decision has been made." His eyes stared somewhere in the distance, looking past them, toward the back of the lab. "No one will come for us…we're all doomed. I will die anyway, so I've made up my mind to die before loading my conscience with more harm done to these innocent people. I can't live with that."

"None of us can," Gary replied, "but we have to. Have you considered what will happen to the other passengers if we give up and they no longer need them, or us?"

No one replied. Gary looked at Adenauer encouragingly. "Come on, Adenauer," he said, "let's put our heads together and figure out how to survive, while causing the minimum amount of damage possible."

"What if I'm wrong?" Adenauer asked. "What if this is wrong, what if it's deadly? How would I live with myself then?" he added, pointing at the jar holding the ten capsules.

"It's a risk we have to take," Gary replied. "The fact that we're trying keeps them alive, don't forget that."

Yet Gary could see Adenauer's point, and, for the most part, he felt the same way. How much longer could they resist, and to what end? Was there any shred of logical hope left? What scenario made sense? They were buried underground, in an abandoned bunker, most likely being exposed to some form of residual radiation, hidden someplace so deep and so remote that no one could ever find them. He couldn't think of any scenario, any theory that made a rescue even remotely likely to happen.

As for an escape, they weren't even close. They were empty-handed in front of thugs wielding machine guns and flaunting their lack of conscience. The pilot had no idea where the plane was. That sack of shit had told them they'd landed in the middle of a forested swamp, so remote from any city that they could be walking for tens, maybe hundreds of miles before finding help. And what help? More Russians? Nope, they didn't have a single card in this game.

Yet for the Phoenix, Arizona-born, Gary Davis, former Boy Scout and Afghanistan veteran, losing was not an option. Neither was captivity. He would think of something, he'd find a way. Until then, regardless of the cold, bare facts, he couldn't afford to spiral into depression and hopelessness.

He made an effort to gather his strength, then approached One-Eye and said, "We need two test subjects, male. Give them these," he added, handing him two capsules with the newest formulation.

"Why two? We have hundreds," One-Eye asked in heavily accented, barely understandable English.

"We need to run aerosolized tests, and for those we'll need more people. We can't waste them. Do you understand what aerosolized means?"

One-Eye grunted and left the lab, taking the capsules with him.

Gary sighed and clenched his fists, shoving them in his pockets. There was nothing else he could do… not at that point, anyway. He went back to the table and turned on the monitors.

There was no sound, so they couldn't hear the two men screaming and grunting as they fought the guards who quickly overpowered them. One of the Russians would grab them from behind, immobilizing their arms, while the other would grab them by the nose and force their mouths open, then shove the capsule down their throats. Then they'd force their mouths shut and their heads tilted back, so they would have no other option but to swallow the pill or choke to death. It wasn't a fair fight; the passengers were no match for the guards, whose physical builds were testimonials to years of lifting weights and popping steroids.

Bogdanov joined them in the lab, watching the monitors intently. Gary had a hard time keeping a straight face in the presence of so-called Dr. Bogdanov. What kind of doctor was he? But then again, even Josef Mengele, the infamous "Angel of Death" at Auschwitz had been a properly licensed physician.

For a few long minutes, nothing happened. The two men stood almost immobile, leaning against the walls of their cell. Then, slowly, they started to move, and the people watching the monitors could see them talking to each other, although they couldn't hear what was being said.

The two men starting moving, almost in circles, around each other, while their postures changed from neutral to aggressive. Their upper bodies leaned forward, their arms held at a distance from their bodies, half-bent, ready to strike, their knees slightly flexed.

Then suddenly, violence erupted. The two men jumped at each other's throats, trying to strangle while kicking each other. One, dressed in a dirty, blue shirt, was visibly larger than the other, and was gaining ground rapidly in the unfair fight. He slammed his opponent, who couldn't have been more than five feet, seven inches, and 175 pounds, against the wall, then strangled him with one hand, while with the other he pummeled his stomach repeatedly. The other one's face turned a dark shade of red, and his powerless hands tried to fight off the suffocating grip of his assailant.

"Let's stop this," Gary yelled, taking a few steps toward the Russian. "Bogdanov!"

One-Eye shoved his machine gun barrel into Gary's side, forcing him to back off.

"Please, let's stop them, we have what we need," Adenauer pleaded.

"No," Bodganov replied. "Let the test run its course. I have a report to write."

The hangar, buried in the side of a hill, was engulfed in thick darkness and an eerily silent atmosphere. Not a leaf moved; thick cloud cover prevented moonlight from casting any light on the ground, and the hangar stood there, barely visible even to the trained eye. Only the hangar door was accessible; the rest of the structure had been excavated into the side of the hill, making the grassy hill act as the perfect camouflage for the facility.

Two guards, busy chatting and smoking, sat huddled together on a nearby tree trunk, not paying any attention to the hangar door. By the slight bluish glare on their faces, they bunched over a mobile phone, most likely looking at pictures or playing a game. Nothing else one could do with a phone in those parts of the world; there wasn't a cell tower for miles.

The man, dressed completely in black, knew exactly where to go. He approached the structure, sneaking silently, and opened the small access door next to the main hangar doors. He walked inside, closing the door behind him, then stopped for a while, listening.

There wasn't a single sound coming from inside the hangar. Outside, swamp toads had resumed their concert, briefly interrupted by his arrival. Feeling comfortable with the silence, the man switched on a small LED flashlight, and allowed his eyes to become accustomed to the light.

There it was...the massive jet stood there, completely dark and immobile. The man walked around its huge landing gear, looking for the best location to place the explosives. With minimum effort, he climbed on top of one of the wheels, then inside the landing gear compartment.

He then opened the backpack he was carrying, and placed the plastic explosive charges carefully on one of the gear struts, securing it in place with duct tape. Then he placed the timer and detonation pins, inserting the pins slowly, carefully, into the putty-like explosive.

Then he checked his watch and set the timer, allowing enough time for the cleanup team to arrive, to pick up the debris, and take it out to sea.

At that point, he switched the timer on, and watched for a few seconds how the timer counted down in red LED digits, glowing in the darkness of the landing-gear compartment.

Satisfied, he hopped off the wheel, exited the hangar, and disappeared into the night, unseen and unheard.

Alex listened to the Phenom's engines revving with a pleasant sound that seemed surreal under the circumstances. Everything looked so peaceful, so perfect, and yet, at their destination, somewhere halfway around the globe, things were bound to be drastically different.

Blake's pilot, an old acquaintance of hers, was wrapping up his preflight, getting ready to taxi. Alex took a deep breath of crisp morning air, and climbed the five steps to board the elegant aircraft. *Yep, this is it...better have it together, girl,* she encouraged herself.

She'd packed her small duffel bag in a hurry, taking the bare necessities: spare socks, a sweat suit, a couple of Ts, and her toothbrush. Normally, she wouldn't have gone anywhere without her makeup kit and hair spray, but this time she doubted any of that stuff would make a difference out there, in the depths of hostile Russia.

"Here you are," Lou said. "Let me give you your stuff."

He handed everyone SatSleeves.

"What are these?" Blake asked.

"This device fits on your cell phone and turns it into a satellite phone. No matter where you are, it just works. It will come in handy, believe me. Give one to your pilot," he said, handing Blake an extra SatSleeve.

"Dylan?" Blake called.

The pilot came into the cabin.

"Alex, Sam, Lou, meet Dylan Bishop. He's been my pilot for seven years, I think, right?"

The men shook hands. Alex simply said, "Hey, Dylan," then added for the rest of them, "We've met before. He hauled me out of India one time...I owe him a big one."

"Ah, yes, that's right, me too!" Sam added and shook Dylan's hand again. "Thanks for doing this; we appreciate it."

"All right, let's focus," Lou said, as Dylan resumed his role in prepping the jet for takeoff. "Radios. We have encrypted, long-range radios equipped with ear buds and laryngophones, which you wear like this," he demonstrated, putting on a collar that held a throat microphone. "These radios integrate with our cell phones. When you receive a call, you have the option to patch the call into our radio environment, and allow everyone with an encrypted receiver to hear or participate in the communication."

"Wow," Alex said, "I didn't know you could do that."

"For a lot of money, you can do anything," Lou replied, smiling. "Weapons."

He opened a large, khaki-colored duffel bag filled with guns, and started handing them out. "I have Tavor automatic weapons for everyone, handguns, and tactical knives. I brought tactical vests, night-vision goggles, handheld GPS, the encrypted radios I was telling you about, and survival kits that will hold us up to 72 hours."

"What's this other stuff?" Alex asked, seeing how there was a lot more hardware left in the duffel bag.

"Just some grenades, an AK47 for Sam, in case he misses the old days, and a CornerShot that will fit your handgun. I've brought some ammo too."

"Wow...I've heard of these, but never used one. How does it work?" Alex took the CornerShot from Lou, examining it closely.

"It's the best accessory to have in urban combat," Lou said. "You attach your handgun to it like this," he demonstrated with Alex's Walther, after removing all its ammo, "Then you aim through this pop-out LCD screen, giving you visibility around the corner without any exposure to the enemy. When ready, you pull the trigger, also from a covered position."

"I see you have a preference for Israeli weapons," Sam commented.

"There's a valid reason for that, you know," Lou replied. "Take these, for example. The Tavor is compact, precise, low-recoil, configurable, the perfect choice for our mission."

Sam took the Tavor from Lou's hand and checked it out thoroughly.

"I'll pass on the AK47, thank you very much," he added, holding the Tavor.

"Lou, you mentioned urban combat, yet we're flying in the middle of nowhere, a forested swamp," Blake intervened. "How come?"

"These weapons will do nicely in open terrain, but we also have to be ready to storm that airbase, or whatever facility they are using to hold the passengers. Most likely, close-quarters weapons and tactics would be valuable there," Lou explained.

Blake nodded, frowning a little. He looked worried, but resolute.

"All right," Lou spoke louder, getting everyone to listen. "Everyone, please pay attention. We have a long flight ahead of us, and some new guns to get used to. I have personally checked each gun, and made sure they're unloaded; I will check them again. Please get to know them during this flight. Become familiar with how they feel, how they handle. Simulate loading and unloading until you're lightning fast; I will provide empty clips for practice, simulate targeting, and firing your weapon. Don't load your weapons until we're on final approach at our destination; let's try not to put holes in this plane, if possible. When we're close to landing, I will hand you your ammo clips and everything else you need. We good?"

"We are solid," Alex replied, feeling tension in her shoulders, as the perspective of going to battle became more and more real.

"Golden," Sam replied.

Through the open door of the cockpit, they heard Dylan call San Diego ATC.

"Good morning, San Diego Tower, this is flight November Sierra 1413 ready for takeoff, runway 2-7."

"November Sierra 1413, winds two six zero at fifteen, cleared for takeoff."

They buckled up quietly as the plane started to pick up speed, immersed in their thoughts.

"We can't do this anymore, we just can't," Dr. Adenauer said, unable to hide the pain in his voice. "Not anymore. I won't stand for it."

"Please don't say that, think about my family," Wu Shen Teng pleaded, tears flooding his eyes.

"I *am* thinking about your family," Dr. Adenauer replied. "How would you like them to die, like that?" he thundered, pointing at the monitors that had been switched off the day before, right after the test had ended with the loss of an innocent man's life.

"Theo," Marie-Elise said, "don't say that. Maybe there's hope."

"You're a fool, Adenauer," Gary Davis said. "What do you think will happen?"

Dr. Teng stood there, paralyzed, tears streaking his cheeks as he stared at the dark monitors.

Bogdanov entered the lab and slammed the huge door behind him.

"Are you ready to run the aerosolized test? The same formulation should be good."

They fidgeted uncomfortably, and a deathly silence engulfed the lab.

"No, we are not," Adenauer spoke calmly. "We will not be proceeding with the tests anymore." He cleared his voice, drew a deep breath, and then continued, "I stand behind my decision with my life."

Bogdanov stared at Adenauer, who didn't flinch. Then he turned and said something in Russian to King Cobra. Cobra left.

Now that he'd said it, Adenauer felt better, calmer. *Man can only die once*, he thought. He remembered something he'd once heard someone say. "Life is wondrous, death is peaceful, it's the transition that's troublesome." He wasn't sure those were the exact words, and he couldn't remember for sure who'd said it; maybe it was Isaac Asimov? In any case, for some reason, his mind found solace in those words at that moment. He was ready to die. He couldn't bear to be responsible for another human being's demise.

Cobra came back, dragging with him a middle-aged woman, her upper arm held tightly in his grasp, yanking her at every step as he walked. She sobbed loudly, pleading with him in what sounded like Swedish, but Cobra didn't care. He threw the woman on her knees in front of Bogdanov. She curled up in a ball, hugging her knees, and sobbing hard.

"So, you are willing to stand by your decision with your life, yes?" Bogdanov asked calmly.

Adenauer felt his gut churn with fear. *Oh, no! Please, God, no!*

"Are you willing to stand by your decision with her life too?" Bogdanov asked.

Before he could answer, Bogdanov drew his sidearm and shot the woman in the head. Her sobs instantly quieted, as she fell to the floor with a thump. Blood began draining from her wound, pooling at Adenauer's feet. He took a step back, staring in disbelief, his jaw dropped, feeling his ice-cold blood draining from his head.

"That was your last warning," Bogdanov said. "You have 24 hours."

Alex watched the vast expanse of forested Russian territory draw closer, as the Phenom started its descent.

"All right, guys, this is it," Lou said. "We'll touch down in a few minutes. We all know what to do. Lock 'em, load 'em, and get ready."

The Phenom landed smoothly on a poorly maintained runway, then taxied slowly to the end of the terminal.

As soon as the plane slowed down, they all snapped out of their seat belts and closed the window blinds on both sides.

"I'll go get us a hangar somewhere," Blake said, grabbing a wad of cash from the duffel bag. "US dollars still work here?"

"Better than ever," Sam replied, grabbing a fistful of hundred-dollar bills for himself and shoving them in his pocket. "I'll go get us a car; we're some 45 miles away from the hangar coordinates. We need transpo."

"How on earth are you gonna get a car?" Blake asked. "This place doesn't look like it has Enterprise."

"Ah...the old spy way," Sam winked, then opened the aircraft door and hopped off in a couple of steps. Blake followed.

"Let's gear up," Lou said. "Start with the vest first, just like I showed you."

"Yes, boss," she replied, unable to contain a tension-loaded smile.

She strapped her tactical vest on. It was black, rigid, and had a lot of pockets, making her look bulky. She felt her abdomen through the harsh fabric, then traced her waistline and her hips, barely noticeable under the tactical vest. She groaned.

"You gotta be kidding me," Lou said humorously. "Really?"

"Hey, a girl's gotta be careful about how she looks, all right?" she replied. "G.I. Jane wasn't exactly sexy, you know." A nervous chuckle showed her real state of mind.

"No, but she was effective, deadly. And so are you. You'll do fine," Lou added, softening his voice. "Trust me."

"Yeah," she replied, still tense.

*Oh, boy…*Her first real gunfight, behind enemy lines no less. Yet it was more than just pre-battle jitters that kept her on her toes and put tension in her heart. She just wanted to know if she'd been right. Would they find the missing plane? Would they find Adeline and the passengers? Most of all, would she find V? Would she be proven wrong about V's involvement in this? Or right? She had no evidence, no real reason to suspect a connection, but she believed there was one. She believed that with all her heart. She just had to find it, then she'd learn V's identity and finally nail the brilliant, evil son of a bitch.

She checked her Walther's ammo clip before putting it back in its holster. Then she strapped the tactical knife's holster to her thigh, and loaded her pockets with the gear Lou was handing her, verifying each item as she took possession of it.

Radio equipment with ear buds and laryngophone, twenty-five-mile range, connected with the cellphone, encrypted, checked, turned on.

Handheld GPS, on.

Sat phone, working, full battery, on.

Battery life extender, full.

Three ammo clips for the Walther PPK.

Night-vision goggles, battery full, turned off.

Three ammo clips for the Tavor, going in her cargo pants side pockets.

Two small grenades.

One smoke pop.

A first-aid kit.

A food ration.

"Lou, I can barely move!" she whined, taking a few steps, trying to see how everything felt as she paced the aircraft's narrow aisle.

"Get used to it," he replied dryly, as he finished loading his gear. "You'll need all this stuff."

Blake hopped back on the plane, then instructed his pilot where to go.

"We got us hangar space, discreet and off the record," Blake said proudly. "They think I'm here to see my mistress, and I have to keep my visit a secret."

"Hey, whatever works, my man," Lou replied, extending a high five to Blake. "Gear up!"

Alex noticed Blake spoke with the same nervous chuckle in his voice that she had. They were all nervous, all looking forward to see what they would find. Excited, yet afraid at the same time. Would they find the plane where DigiWorld had said? How about the people, how would they find them? How about Adeline, was she still alive? She didn't even stop for a minute to worry about her own safety, or what would happen if the Russians captured them; that concern didn't even register with her. However, they all felt the tension, the anticipation anxiety, and the excitement, what Lou called the pre-battle high.

The aircraft resumed a slow-speed taxi and soon entered a small, decrepit hangar, lit poorly by a single, yellowish light bulb hanging from the rusted ceiling.

A few minutes later, the sound of a car engine got their attention. Sam hopped out of a dirty, dark brown SUV, bearing an unknown logo, and pointed cheerfully at the vehicle.

"Ta-da! How do you like it? It's a Vaz, the best I could do under the circumstances. Let's get going," he said.

Alex stopped at the top of the aircraft's steps to take a deep breath. Hot, humid air, buzzing with tiny insects and mosquitoes. The slight smell of jet exhaust and a more pervasive smell of bog water. *So this is Russia,* she thought, hopping down two steps at a time and climbing in the front passenger seat of the SUV.

Sam climbed aboard the Phenom and reappeared within two minutes, wearing all his tactical gear. He took the driver's seat and started the engine. Blake seemed at ease, handling his weapon comfortably, as if he did nothing else all day long. Lou was the last to join them, carrying a small duffel bag that he put in the trunk of the Vaz.

"Some more ammo, explosives, and other stuff," he explained, seeing the inquisitive look Alex threw his way.

"Coordinates set," Sam said, grinding the gears a little when shifting the manual transmission. "We should get there in less than an hour."

They drove silently for a while; there was little left to say. Alex watched the forested landscape, finding she somewhat enjoyed the drive. *If the circumstances were different, I would probably even like it,* she thought—curving, single-lane road stretching for miles in the thick, lush forest, small lakes here and there, sunny, warm, and peaceful atmosphere. *How deceiving appearances can be...If we're right about this, 441 people are going through hell somewhere in the middle of this beautiful, deceivingly serene forest.*

"All right, guys, this is where we leave the car and start walking," Sam said.

"How long?" Alex asked.

"About three miles that way," he replied, pointing in a direction perpendicular to the road.

"Through the swamp?" Alex protested. "Are you sure?"

"He's sure," Lou confirmed. "This is what the GPS is telling us. Keep in mind an airbase would be hidden, not really a freeway stop, you know."

"I get it, but it would still have a road that leads to it, right?"

"And this one has a road too, only it doesn't start from here. Trust me, walking is our best shot. We should be there within the hour. By foot, no one will hear us coming. We're assuming the place is guarded."

"OK, I got it," she said. "Get the car out of sight. We shouldn't raise suspicions."

Sam smiled. "Sure. Told ya', you're a natural."

They walked with difficulty, their boots sinking in the mud every few steps. They trailed single file, Lou leading the pack, and Alex found she was grateful for the Army boots Lou had provided.

Suddenly, Lou stopped, lifting his right arm with his fist clenched, military code for "stop." They froze in their tracks and waited, listening and looking around them. Then Lou pointed two fingers at his own eyes, then pointed them in the direction of what looked like a grassy hill or mound.

Yes, that was it! It looked just like the satellite images they'd seen on the DigiWorld screens, a metallic structure buried in the side of a hill. The structure was large, at least 250 feet wide by at least 100 feet tall, and had huge doors, big enough to allow a 747 to enter snugly. An old road, overtaken by weeds growing out of every one of its cracks and potholes led to its door, extended in the opposite direction as far as they could see. If they followed that road, they'd probably find an airstrip at the end of it somewhere. She checked her GPS and confirmed her theory. There was an airstrip at the end of that road, a 2.5-mile long airstrip. A little short for a 747 landing…a short, tight, maybe even rough, yet doable landing.

Two armed men guarded the structure leisurely, leaning against a tree trunk, smoking and chatting. Their Kalashnikovs hung on their shoulders by their straps. *Shit,* Alex thought, *this could get ugly. Who knows how many more Russians could be inside that hangar.*

Lou signaled Sam, and they engaged in a quick exchange in military sign language. Still hidden by the thick forest brush, and watching every step they made, they approached the two guards silently, unseen and unheard.

They fell behind them and swiftly Sam stabbed one guard in the neck, while Lou grabbed the other one in a tight chokehold, then broke his neck with a quick side twist. They grabbed their weapons and checked the surroundings quickly, then gave Blake and Alex the signal to approach.

Close together, keeping a low profile, they approached the small entrance in the hangar, a side door almost completely covered in rust. Sam opened it slowly, and then followed Lou inside. A few seconds later, they cleared Alex and Blake to come in.

They entered the hangar and Alex gasped. A wave of excitement resonated through her entire body. They'd found it! Above her head, the tail of a huge 747 extended all the way to the doors, almost touching them. In the dim light coming from the open door, the plane looked surreal.

They continued to walk quietly, carefully listening and watching. Not a sound coming from anywhere. Except for the huge plane, the hangar was completely deserted.

"Oh, no..." Blake exclaimed.

"What's wrong?" Alex whispered.

"It's not her plane," Blake said with desperation in his voice. "This one has no markings. All Universal Air flights have the XA logo on their tails."

She looked at the tail, rising eight stories high in the air, and wondered why she'd missed that. She wanted it to be the XA233 so badly, that she didn't see the evidence in front of her.

She stared intently at the disappointingly white tail, scrutinizing it inch by inch, looking for some detail, some hint. Then she grabbed her LED flashlight and scanned the white tail again, squinting.

"Wait a second...there!" she exclaimed, pointing the flashlight at a certain spot on the plane's tail. "Blake, what do you see?"

Sam and Lou lit their flashlights and pointed them at the same area.

"See?" Alex said. "They peeled off the logo and markings, but there's a trace left, where the paint was dulled by the adhesive material of the logo. The curvy X? You see?"

Blake nodded, unable to speak for a few seconds, choked, while tears pooled in his eyes.

"I knew it," he whispered. "I know she's alive!"

Alex grinned widely and side-hugged him, not taking her eyes from the markings on the plane's white tail. They were right; they had a chance.

"Now let's find her," she said, walking briskly toward the aircraft door, still fitted with mobile stairs. Let's see what we can find inside, maybe there's something we can use.

"Right," Lou said, and joined her.

As she walked past the huge landing gear, she looked up, intrigued to see it up close. She'd never been so close to a commercial airliner before. She slowed her pace a little, observing the double sets of wheels, the shock absorbers, the gear mechanism. Deep inside the gear compartment, a red glint caught the corner of her eye as she turned to leave.

She froze. Feeling her blood instantly turn to ice, she looked up, searching for the source of the elusive red glint, the eerily familiar flicker. Then she found it. A timer, counting down, with only nine seconds left to go.

"Oh, shit," she said, then screamed from the bottom of her lungs, "run! Run!"

She ran as fast as she could, her tactical vest and all her gear rattling on her and slowing her down. Everyone ran without looking back, following her lead. They exited the hangar running, but she didn't stop there. She continued toward the forest line, running as fast as she could.

The sound of the explosion reached them first, and then, within milliseconds, the shockwave hit them hard, smashing them to the ground and covering them with smoldering debris.

Ivan hated to be the one who had to wake Myatlev up in the morning. Eternally hung over, sullen, and grumpy as can be, Myatlev was not easy to deal with in the early hours of the day. Entering his bedroom usually turned Ivan's stomach. He clenched his teeth and winced just thinking about it. The stink of metabolized alcohol and sweat, combined with stale cigar smoke and, sometimes, just to make it worse, the smell of bodily fluids exchanged freely during his boss's sexual encounters, made it almost unbreathable, even for the hardcore ex-Spetsnaz that he was.

Regardless, he had no choice but to wake him, and with bad news on top of it. Ivan stopped in front of Myatlev's bedroom door, rapping his fingers against it and waiting no more than two seconds before entering.

There he was, butt-naked, lying flat on his back, his morning wood still impressive for his age and state of physical decay, his snores roaring louder than a tank engine climbing a steep hill. At the far end of the bed, a young girl, not much older than sixteen, crouched shivering. Wrapped tightly in sweaty sheets and trying to take as little space as possible, she stared at him with big, round, pleading eyes.

Ivan waved the girl away, and she was quick to disappear, grabbing her things on her way out. Then, taking a deep breath, he approached Myatlev and cleared his throat to wake him up. Nothing. No throat clearing was going to cover that snoring. He touched Myatlev's shoulder, and said, speaking louder and louder with each word.

"Boss? Boss? Good morning. Boss?"

Myatlev finally opened his eyes, groaned, and licked his dry lips.

"What the fuck is it?"

Ivan handed him a glass of sparkling water and a couple of rehydrating pills, to help with his obvious hangover.

"We blew up the plane, as you said," Ivan replied, unperturbed. "We recorded the explosion via satellite."

"Good."

"But there's a problem," Ivan continued. "You'll have to see."

He pulled open the laptop he had brought along, and pulled the recorded satellite view of the hangar. The recording started a few minutes before the explosion, showing four people approaching the hangar, taking out the two sentries, commando-style, then sneaking inside the hangar, only to come out of there running for their lives just seconds before everything blew up in a huge blaze of fire.

"What the hell?" Myatlev said, suddenly awake. "Who are they?"

"Unknown," Ivan replied. "But my man is still in the area. He'll find out."

Alex landed hard face down, the shock knocking the air out of her lungs. All the hardware she carried in her vest pockets crushed her flesh when she'd smashed into the ground. She breathed shallow, feeling a sharp pain at the left of her sternum with each breath, but managed to put her hands on top of her head, trying to protect herself from the flying, smoldering debris. She looked to her left and saw Sam squinting and cussing under his breath. She couldn't make out what he was saying; the sound of the explosion still rang in her ears. It didn't matter though. It mattered he was still alive.

To her right, Lou and Blake were starting to move tentatively, as to figure out if there was anything broken. *Good, we're four for four, excellent score,* she thought, trying to encourage herself to get up.

The falling debris let up, only smaller pieces of lighter materials, ash, and embers still coming down on them. She stood slowly, checking every limb carefully, mindful of all aches and pains, ruling them out one by one as non-critical. A cut on her forehead dripped blood in her right eye, and she wiped it off with the back of her hand. It wasn't deep; she was OK. She turned toward Blake, who also stood, a little dazed, but in one piece. Sam got back on his feet with a little more difficulty, continuing to mutter oaths at every step, pallor appearing on his stained face. He wiped his shaved head with his sleeve, and walked a little crooked, dragging his left leg.

"What happened?" Alex asked.

"Nothing," he replied, barely audible over the persistent ringing in her ears. "I'll be fine, don't worry. Let's take care of that," he said, pulling out his first-aid kit and extracting a butterfly bandage. "There," he said, applying it gently to her forehead.

"I lost the spare ammo," Lou said bitterly. "It's gone. It was near the hangar door."

"It's all right," Alex said. "We're all carrying spare clips, we should be OK." She turned toward Blake, who continued to look dazed, standing, yet appearing as if he was about to collapse. "Blake, you OK?"

"We got nothing," he replied, sounding sad and defeated. "We have no proof, nothing. It's all gone."

"No," Alex replied enthusiastically, "that's not the case. Now we *know* you were right. We've all seen that plane with our own eyes. We don't need to prove that to anyone to know what to do next. *We* know it, and that's enough. Now we know she's alive."

Blake looked at her with renewed hope.

"Yeah, but where?" Lou asked. "They could be anywhere."

"Ah...don't worry," Sam replied, "we'll find out."

Blake looked at Sam with hopeful, intrigued eyes. "How?" he asked.

"The old way, the spy way," he replied with a faint smile on his pale lips.

They looked at him intently, waiting for him to explain what he meant. This time, he wasn't going to get away with his coined phrase that implied he was just going to work some miracle and make it all happen.

"When nearly 500 people are moved through a place so small, without major population density, someone is bound to have noticed something. Anything. And we'll start from there," he said, his cryptic smile continuing to flutter on his lips. "Trust me," he added and winked, creasing his soot and mud-stained face.

"What next?" Alex asked.

"I'd recommend we get the hell out of here," Lou said. "There might be a cleanup crew coming, and we should take cover. Let's head back into the woods, and find us a place where we can wait for Sam to work his magic and get us some field intel."

"Sounds like a plan," Alex said. Then she approached Lou and grabbed his forearm. "Don't let him go alone, Lou," she whispered in his ear, "he's badly hurt."

"And you?"

"I'll be fine. I have Blake, and we have guns. We'll hide somewhere and hang tight until you get back."

Lou nodded his agreement, and then spoke louder, for everyone to hear. "It's time to call in the support team. We have a confirmed scenario, and we'll need help the moment we have the final location."

"Agreed," Alex replied. "How long before they get here?"

"They're coming from Sapporo, on Hokkaido Island, that's about 200 miles out," Lou replied. "Shouldn't take them more than sixty, at most ninety, minutes by chopper. They'll have to fly low and slow to avoid radar."

Alex took in a gulp of hot, humid air and bit her lip. *This is it...it's about to get real, as real as it gets,* she thought, bracing herself. *Unsanctioned paramilitary action on another country's sovereign territory, behind an unofficial enemy's lines. We better be damn right about everything we're doing.*

"Let's not waste time, then," she said, sounding confident. "Send them the coordinates."

Gary Davis struggled to breathe, to stay calm. Anger took the best of him, controlling his every thought and every move. By now, he could be sure his blood pressure was through the roof, and no way to measure it. The silent killer...damn!

He'd never been too good controlling his frustration. Quick and impatient in nature, a determined, ambitious, motivated go-getter and an ex-Marine, Gary's time in captivity ate him from within like a disease. It infuriated him, scorned him on a level that he'd never thought possible. There had to be something they could do...they couldn't just obey their captors and let themselves be used like that, then be killed. They had to find a way out.

He'd been weaving daydreams of vengeance and escape ever since they'd been taken to that god-forsaken place. He'd been running escape scenarios in his mind, thinking that maybe he could, through some unspecified yet absolutely necessary miracle, grab the Kalashnikov away from Death, or One-Eye, or whomever. Then what? Then he'd figure something out.

He finished mixing a new formulation, grunting with frustration at every step and hating himself, and loaded the test sample in the gas chromatograph. He was almost done with mixing one active compound and one antidote. Red capsules...green capsules...

He wiped his sweaty forehead with his sleeve. There was something gnawing at the edges of his mind, like an idea he couldn't yet grasp or formulate. The heat and the omnipresent stench didn't help either. Days were getting hotter, and the absence of showers had become everyone's curse. Little mosquitoes had made it through whatever filtration system still stopped the larger ones, but the small ones that had reached the lab were growing fast, stinging them constantly, and making their restless sleep even worse.

The talented Dr. Fortuin had mixed up an antihistamine gel to control the itching, and had produced enough for all of them to use generously and gratefully. Just like table salt, oil, and vinegar, Fortuin's little miracles of applied chemistry had made their lives a little more bearable.

Yet they were in shambles. Two of them were bedridden. Declan Mallory was almost constantly sedated; his crushed ribs were not healing. Gary also suspected some slow oozing internal hemorrhage, where the sharp edges of his broken ribs might have lacerated his spleen, maybe his left lung.

Dr. Jane Crawford, unable to stabilize her blood sugar in the absence of the right mix of rapid-acting and long-acting insulin shots, maintained good spirits, but hardly ever left her cot anymore.

Dr. Adenauer hadn't eaten anything since the lead terrorist, Bogdanov, had shot that poor woman just to make his point. For some reason, Adenauer thought he was to blame for everything that was going on, including their presence in the hot, humid hell they were currently sharing.

Gary wished there could be something he could say, something he could tell them to make them feel better. No words came to mind. He repressed a long sigh and returned his focus to the gas chromatograph screen and the capsules he was preparing.

Red capsules...green capsules...What was he missing? Why were these two colors tugging at his mind?

Red. In his own color code, red meant something bad. Red capsules contained the formulation they were trying to produce for their captors, the formulation that was going to increase aggression in the exposed subjects in a controlled manner.

Green. Green stood for something good. Green capsules contained the antidote, the formulation that would reverse the effect of the red capsules, or, if used as a prophylactic, prevent the red capsules to have any effect.

Red capsules...green capsules...

Then he finally saw it, the elusive idea that had been driving him crazy.

"My God," he exclaimed, almost cheerfully. "We should have thought of this a long time ago," he continued, slamming his palms together and rubbing them excitedly.

Death lifted his eyes and stared at him inquisitively for a second, then lost interest.

"What are you talking about?" Adenauer asked, startled from his thoughts.

Gary signaled them to huddle up, and led them out of Death's earshot, near Dr. Crawford's cot.

"What if we mixed a strong sedative instead, one that would have a very fast effect when aerosolized, and drop Death dead over there?" Gary explained in an excited whisper. "We'd be taking green pills ahead of time and we'd do fine."

"I already thought of that," Adenauer replied sullenly. "I thought of that since the first day we got here. But what good is that going to do us, huh? You take one man's gun, then what? Are you going to storm out the door, in a shooting match against God knows how many Russians? How many people are you willing to sacrifice in the crossfire?"

Gary stood silent, disarmed by the cold logic presented by Adenauer. Yes, then what?

"We—we haven't seen too many Russians, right?" Gary insisted. "Here, guarding us, or coming with Bogdanov, we've only seen three. King Cobra, Death, and One-Eye," he counted on his fingers.

"Four," Marie-Elise said. There was this other Russian on the first day, the one with a beard, remember him?

"Yes," Gary said. "I remember him. And there were definitely more at the trucks, when we got here."

"You have to assume that there are quite a few more, guarding the others," Fortuin added calmly, as if the entire dialogue was academic in nature. "You'd have to assume at least twenty Russians or so, all trained sociopathic killers."

"So we have nothing," Gary said, feeling blood boil in his veins. "That's what you're saying? That we have nothing, no way out of here? That we're gonna die in this rotting hell without even trying to put up a fight?"

Without even realizing it, he had grabbed Fortuin by the lapels and was shaking him, pushing him against the wall.

"Gary," Jane Crawford spoke quietly, sitting up against her pillow. "Knock it off and get your shit together, what the hell?"

Somehow, hearing her voice, the American accent reminding him of home, of who he was, calmed him instantly. He immediately let go of Fortuin's lapels.

"I–I am so sorry, Dr. Fortuin, I don't know what got into me," he apologized, feeling ashamed.

"Well, I guess it's all right," Fortuin replied with cold dignity, straightening his clothing and running his fingers through his silver hair. "We're all frustrated and desperate, son, don't let it get the best of you."

"I know, you're right," he admitted, feeling his cheeks burn. "I just wish there was something we could do. If we could only get more of them in here at the same time, not just one, then my plan would work."

"Umm...maybe we could," Dr. Teng spoke tentatively, keeping his gaze riveted to the ground.

Gary turned toward the thin, frail man, surprised.

"How?" he asked.

Wu Shen Teng's back bowed a little more, and his head hung low.

"I–I have...I have been telling Bogdanov things, in exchange for my family's safety."

"You what?" Gary reacted, grinding his teeth and barely keeping his voice under control. "You...betrayed us?" He couldn't even find his words, suffocated by anger.

"Yes," Dr. Teng replied, his voice choked and trembling. "I thought I was protecting my family. I was wrong, terribly wrong." He clasped his hands together in a pleading gesture, not lifting his eyes from the ground. "Please, forgive me."

Marie-Elise closed her eyes in a silent gesture of disappointment, and Adenauer muttered something in German.

"Unbelievable," Gary replied. "Absolutely unbelievable."

"Oh, no, it's believable, Gary, trust me." Jane Crawford spoke. "Just put yourself in his place, for Christ's sake. You'd do anything."

"Let's stay focused, please," Dr. Fortuin said. "Dr. Teng, you're saying you could bring more of them in here?"

"I think I could," he replied. "I think I know what to say."

"Keep in mind we're not combatants," Adenauer said. "Some of us can't even shoot a slingshot."

"I'll handle the shooting," Gary said. "Bukowsky can help."

"Sure, I can do that, I'm a decent shot," Bukowsky replied.

"I can too," Jane Crawford added. "I used to shoot clay pigeons for sport."

"Works for me," Gary said with a wide smile. "Dr. Teng, you have to get them in here and get them to stay for a few minutes. Even if we use aerosolized anesthetics, we can't get them to drop to the floor instantly. We have to consider what solution concentrations we can risk exposing ourselves to, and it would take the aerosol a little while to work."

Wu Shen Teng nodded.

Gary started pacing slowly, clasping and unclasping his hands, running the plan details in his mind. It could work...There was definite risk involved, of course. The compounds would need to be precisely titred, the aerosol effect localized, and the antidotes powerful enough to resist a strong, fast-acting sedative without harming them. If the sedation effect was too slow, the Russians would have the time to react and shoot people before falling flat. If it was too fast, it would pose risk to the very people they were trying to save. The doctors would risk becoming drowsy when they needed to stay fast, sharp, and quick on their feet. Not easy, but definitely worth trying.

"There is some risk," Gary said after a little while, "but I think it's well worth it. I, for one, don't want to die in this shithole." He searched their faces, and, satisfied with what he saw, he added, "Then let's get to work!"

Myatlev finished reading another one of Bogdanov's reports, and rubbed the back of his neck, thinking. Maybe it was going to work after all. The latest test had been promising, and Bogdanov had cranked up the heat on those doctors, getting them to take their situation more seriously and start producing some real results.

He sighed and leaned back in his chair, then checked the time. He should grab some lunch, but before going out to eat, he wanted another shot.

Ivan barged in through the door before Myatlev had a chance to call him. That's what he liked about his right hand; he was always there, reading his mind, giving him everything he needed.

This time Ivan carried a piece of paper instead of the shot he'd been craving. He groaned with disappointment.

"What is it, Ivan?"

"My man in the field looked everywhere for the four people we saw on satellite running from the hangar, and nothing. No one's seen anything or heard anything. The only unusual thing he found was that an American private jet, a Phenom 300 had just landed there, at Khabarovsk Airport, just a few hours earlier. Four passengers and a pilot. That could be it."

"Who are they?"

"We have no idea," Ivan said, hesitantly. "The flight was unregistered, and didn't even go through customs. Someone bribed someone, that's for sure. We have no way to find out who they are and what they want."

"Ivan, you disappoint me," Myatlev said bitterly, getting up from his massive leather chair and going to the window to light another cigar. "It's time to think for yourself, not wait for me to think in your place, and feed you everything you need to do piece by piece, da?" He sounded clipped and impatient.

Ivan shifted his weight uncomfortably, but remained silent.

"Well, what will you do next?" Myatlev prompted.

"Track the plane?" Ivan asked, unsure.

"Yes, track the damn plane, Ivan! A Phenom has got to have an owner. Get the tail number, find out who owns it, where the flight originated from, and get video from their place of departure. Cyber Division will help you get all that really quickly. Then ask someone to pull their backgrounds."

"Understood," Ivan confirmed, looking ashamed.

Myatlev softened a little. Not everyone had it in them to think globally, considering all the assets at their discretion. After all, Ivan was his bodyguard more than his assistant, and Myatlev had selected him for his combat skills and his loyalty, and little else.

Myatlev's irritation stemmed mostly from learning that someone had come so close to the most secret of his operations. This secret, if exposed, could bring everyone down, including President Abramovich. There was no way Russia could ever be able to explain the hijacking of a commercial flight. That was an act of terrorism. Those four people, regardless of who they were, needed to be dead and buried before they could compromise him.

"OK," he concluded, lighting his cigar. "Find out who the hell they are and why they're messing with me."

He breathed in the rewarding scent of the Arturo Fuente cigar, letting the aroma soothe his stretched nerves. These days he did little more than smoke, drink, and worry. He was stressed out, and his entire body felt it and screamed its pain. No wonder he was coming apart at the seams, with gastritis, liver pain, back pain, the whole nine yards of a stressful life.

This operation, instead of being the quick success it should have been, was turning into yet another one of those cases where it seemed like fate was toying with him. It felt like an unseen enemy knew precisely what he was trying to do, and that enemy was doing everything possible to foil his best-laid plans. No matter how hidden. No matter how elusive. How was it possible?

He felt paranoid again, and hated it. He liked being lucid and cool in the face of an imminent threat, and didn't like feeling hunted and harassed. But that's exactly how it felt, and it wasn't the first time. What if there was, indeed, someone who was out to get him?

Alex fidgeted a little, trying to find a more comfortable position. She sat at the root of a tree, leaning against the wide trunk that had her back covered, and kept her eyes scanning the horizon line constantly. Blake sat across from her, watching in the opposite direction, both of them keeping their Tavors clutched tightly, ready to fire.

They'd found a small clearing in the woods, somewhere near Mayak, a small town lost in the swampy expanses of forest. Every minute or so, she checked the time, impatiently waiting for Sam and Lou to be back with some news. They'd been gone for a while; she was getting worried.

A snapped twig made her heart stop for a second, and a wave of adrenaline surged through her body. She sprung to her feet, wincing. The sudden move brought a sharp pain to her ribs, right next to her sternum. She positioned her weapon, ready to fire, and listened intently. The sounds of rustling, wet leaves were getting closer, clearer, and more discernible. Someone was coming.

She signaled to Blake, who hopped to his feet, silent as a feline, and lifted his Tavor in a shooting stance. She couldn't see anyone, and, judging by how Blake scanned the forest, neither did he.

They appeared from behind a tree close by, Lou supporting Sam in his unstable, limping walk. Relieved, she lowered her weapon, but Lou frowned the second she did that. Surprised and worried, she asked Lou a silent question, raising her eyebrows. His reply came in the form of a silent gesture that meant, "They're everywhere."

Great.

They huddled together, and while Lou kept guard, Sam briefed them in a choppy, labored whisper.

"We have a lead," he said, still out of breath. "There's an abandoned ICBM site only twenty klicks from here, that way," he added, pointing northeast. "No one's used it in many years, not since '89, when the arms race slowed down."

"That's it?" Alex asked, a little disappointed. "An abandoned missile silo doesn't seem like much of a lead, Sam."

"So, then why are there trucks loaded with food and supplies going in there every couple of days?"

"That's more like it," she whispered, letting a wide grin appear on her face. "Let's get going."

"Gotta be careful, we already ran into a couple of trucks filled with armed men heading back toward the hangar. I'm thinking cleanup team. Keep your eyeballs peeled."

"Let me get precise coordinates," Lou said.

He took out his SatSleeve-equipped phone, wrote a quick message to DigiWorld, describing what they were looking for, then sent it together with a screenshot of the map view with their current GPS location. Within two minutes, a discrete vibration alerted him and he confirmed with a thumbs-up to the rest of the team that he had the coordinates.

He showed Alex his phone. DigiWorld had sent maps, routing, terrain views, and infrared scans of their target location. Infrared scans showed several clustered heat signatures. Their only lead looked better and better by the minute.

Lou signaled them to start moving.

"I think we should call for extraction at this time," Sam said, leaning into the support offered by Lou's arm.

"What if they're not there?" Alex replied. "What if it's not them? And I think CIA would need a couple of days to organize an extraction, right?"

"A few days? In this hell hole?" Blake asked. "Not acceptable...sorry. We can't wait. Who knows what could happen in a couple of days. We need to move now."

"Affirmative," she replied. "It's only twenty klicks. Let's go there, see what we find. Then we'll figure out options," she added, briefly looking at Blake, then averting her eyes.

What she wouldn't say was, "Let's see how many are still alive."

They worked feverishly, almost without even speaking to one another. Each of them knew exactly what they had to do, and, for the first time since they had arrived, felt a little excitement and hope. Focused and careful, Gary Davis checked the results of the analysis delivered by the gas chromatograph.

"How sure are you?" Adenauer asked. "We have to be very precise, or else we'll die," he insisted, sounding parental.

"I know that," Gary replied, a little irritation seeping in his voice.

Dr. Fortuin was in charge of aerosolizing the compound, and was running some tests a couple of tables away. Even he, against his typical Dutch coolness, was rhythmically bouncing his left foot, synchronizing it to the beat of his internal anxiety.

Jane Crawford had left her cot, volunteering to handle the final test on the remaining three lab rodents. She petted the rodents one by one, holding them in the palm of one hand, and scratching behind their ears with another. Then she placed them back in their cage and covered it with the clear Plexiglas casing, to verify the containment of the aerosol delivery environment. The clear casing was fitted with a small tube that could be hooked to the aerosol canister. The tube was taped to the hole, ensuring perfect containment of the tested gasses. Satisfied, she removed the casing, allowing the rodents unrestricted access to air for a while, and then rubbed her hands together, smiling. She was ready to test.

Marie-Elise approached Gary, curious, carefully eyeing King Cobra, who sat close to the entrance, flipping through a dirty magazine printed in faded colors on cheap, yellowish paper.

"Have you decided what to use?" she asked, keeping her tone low, almost inaudible, although King Cobra didn't have the knowledge to understand what they talked about, and he obviously wasn't paying any attention.

"For sedation?" Gary asked.

Fortuin rolled his chair closer to them, to listen in.

Marie-Elise nodded vigorously, smiling shyly.

"I've decided to go with a mix of anesthetics after all. I've mixed thiopental, for fast induction, with fentanyl and desflurane. I know, I know," he added, seeing how worried Marie-Elise and Fortuin suddenly looked. "It's untested, never before attempted, and two of these drugs aren't typically delivered via aerosol. They're injected, so we don't even know how effective they'll be. No need to tell me that, I know what you're thinking. But we're out of options and we're desperate; I guess you'd have to agree to that statement."

Fortuin pursed his lips, and Marie-Elise gave him a reassuring nod.

"Try your best, you two," she added, including Adenauer. He had worked diligently by Gary's side, not stepping away for even a minute.

"We will, we are," Gary replied, a frown creasing his brow.

There was significant risk involved in what they were trying to do. They would be in the same space with the Russians when the aerosol was going to be released. They needed to stay lucid, with their motor functions and judgment sharp and quick, and two of those anesthetics didn't even have an antidote known to science.

"It will work," Adenauer said resolutely. "It has to. I've measured and calculated everything carefully. I even took into account their average weight and their obviously increased metabolic rate, and the high likelihood that they're steroid users. I've considered our group's average weight, age, and metabolic rates in formulating the antidote. It will work, I promise you."

He sounded so sure of himself, so authoritative. Gary envied that composure, that grip the scientist had on the facts, the data, and his own emotions. The man was a rock. An arrogant, slightly unnerving one, yet a rock, and a real asset to any scientific team, especially one in distress.

"How about the antidote?" Marie-Elise continued to probe. "What will we take?"

"Well, considering what we had to work with," Gary disclaimed before enumerating, "we're going to use naloxone as an opioid antagonist, methylphenidate, better known to us all as Ritalin, to give us the equivalent of an adrenalin shot to the brain, and caffeine. With this mix, I am hoping we'll survive the anesthetic gas cloud bright-eyed and bushy-tailed."

Silence fell heavy for a minute or so.

"There is nothing in that mix to counteract the desflurane, is there?" Jane asked.

"There is nothing known to man to counteract desflurane," Adenauer announced pedantically.

"Then why do we want to use it? It also happens to stink like shit," Jane continued, her choice of language bringing disapproval in both Adenauer and Fortuin's eyes.

"Desflurane is the only anesthetic with proven aerosol delivery effectiveness that we happen to have in this joint," Gary replied. "We have no idea how effective fentanyl and thiopental will be if inhaled; I don't think it was documented anywhere, and we can't really browse the Internet and do research right now. Both can be lethal if injected in high doses, but I have never seen them used in aerosolized form, without a mask. So pardon me if I wanted some reassurance that they're gonna hit the deck face down and quickly," he clarified, gesturing vaguely in King Cobra's direction.

No one argued with that logic; there was little that could be said.

"I do think I have a way to minimize our exposure to desflurane," Gary added, "but it's tricky."

Adenauer lifted his eyes from the micro-scale's screen.

"Let's play through this, all right?" Gary started explaining. "Let's assume Teng goes out there and persuades them to come in here by the hordes. Five, six, who knows how many? They can only enter through there, right?"

He pointed at the huge, rusty door, the only access point to their makeshift lab, and continued. "Then they'd climb down those few steps and, at least for a moment, stop there, around that first table. I'm thinking we could move these other two tables to cut their direct access to the back of the lab, and sort of keep them near that first table. See my point? They'd stay together, waiting on Bogdanov's direction, for at least ten, maybe twenty seconds. If we release the aerosol right there and then, we'd have a better chance to floor them quickly. As for us, we could huddle toward the far end of those tables. Let's say we move the lab rats back over there and run a test, give us an excuse to be huddled over there. Declan can stay on his cot; he's far enough as it is."

"What's the catch?" Jane asked, reading the hesitation in Gary's voice correctly.

"Well, we need someone to volunteer to deliver the aerosolized mix at the precise moment they come through that door. We can't control the time they'd burst in through there, so we have to have someone manually start the release."

"I'll do it," Adenauer offered. "I'm the most massive of the entire group. My body mass will work in my favor."

"I was offering to do that," Gary objected. "I'm younger; I can hold my breath for longer, and I should be able to recover easily after I stop breathing it in."

"Nonsense," Adenauer pushed back. "You're one of our very few combatants. You need to be able to shoot those guns. I can't do that; I've never fired a weapon in my life. It's decided. I'll release the gas."

Gary shoved his hands in his jeans pockets. Stubborn, arrogant, old fool...there was no point in arguing with him.

"All right, then, let's move that table over there, just say we need to have more space for another centrifuge. As soon as the gas mix is ready and pressurized, we'll tuck the canister between the two centrifuges and the chromatograph. They won't see it." He stared at Adenauer with concerned eyes.

"You release, and you step back toward where we'll be, understood? The compound is very strong. Don't take any stupid risks, Theo. You could die." He bit his lip, then explained further. "We were willing to err on the side of speed rather than caution, so the anesthetic mix is a bit strong," he added apologetically.

"I know precisely just how strong it is," Adenauer replied. "I'll be fine."

"OK, then, we're set. Let's test the compound on the rodents first."

Jane fed one rodent a capsule, returned it to the cage, and let it sit a few seconds to take effect. Then she released a small burst of gas through the tube leading to the transparent case. Within seconds, the two other rats fell to the ground, apparently lifeless. The third rat still stood, fidgeting and sniffing around, doing fine, even if a little agitated.

"A bit strong," Jane said, while extending a high five to Gary.

"Let the assholes bite the dust," Gary replied. This time, his profanity elicited a smile instead of an eye roll from Dr. Adenauer.

The rusty door was shoved open with a startling noise, and Bogdanov approached their group with big steps.

"What's going on?" he asked, looking at the cage.

"Just another failed test," Gary replied impassively. "Only the antidote rodent survived the test."

"*Blyad!* You're a lame bunch of incompetent idiots! You have one hour, then I will start killing one of you bastards every hour until you give me what I need."

Myatlev had given up going out for lunch; his appetite had vanished, swallowed by the wave of paranoid thoughts taking over his mind, replacing his typical logical thinking with anxiety-driven, nonsensical thoughts.

He didn't feel hungry anymore, but there was a persistent, annoying pain in the pit of his stomach, gnawing at him, spewing hissing jets of acid, making him miserable. With a long, frustrated sigh, he called his admin and asked for a cup of chamomile tea, making her raise an eyebrow and ask whether he liked anything stronger added to the tea. That was unprecedented; he never drank tea, but he hoped the warm, soothing liquid would dilute the burning acid in his stomach and take away the pain nested in there.

Ivan walked in right behind his obliging assistant who brought his tea. He looked worried, a deep frown ridging his brow.

"Ah, you're back already," Myatlev said. "Good. What have you found out?"

"Umm...the plane belongs to a financier, a very rich and quite famous banker, Blake Bernard, the head of Global Transactions."

"Bernard? I think I met him once. Interesting..." Myatlev commented, forgetting all about the tea and lighting another cigar. What the hell was Bernard doing, visiting the backyard of his secret operation? "What else?"

"He's traveling with a retired CIA operative now in his sixties, a former Navy SEAL, and a technology consultant—a woman."

"That can't be it, Ivan, these people are a business team, not a commando unit. Keep looking. Although," Myatlev added, suddenly aware of an indefinite uneasiness tugging at his gut, "they sound a little too military for a business team." He ran his fingers through his thinning, buzz-cut hair and swallowed a sigh, then continued, "Huh...maybe Bernard and the woman are the actual business team, and the other two are there to protect them from the scary Russians," he chuckled and lounged back in his immense leather chair. That must have been it; he just needed to relax. "I wonder what Bernard's after in this part of the world."

Ivan cleared his throat, continuing to frown.

"Boss, there's more." He sounded concerned, and he rarely was.

Myatlev's expression changed, all his features expressing alertness and vigilance. With a quick nod, he encouraged Ivan to continue. He leaned forward in his chair, feeling tension knotting in his shoulders, driving knives of sharp pain in his neck.

"Cyber ran their full backgrounds, and they're all clean. Too clean, almost. But Cyber also ran international travel history for them, and one thing caught my attention."

"Go on," Myatlev prompted.

"The woman was in India at the same time ERamSys Corporation worked on your elections project."

"What?"

Myatlev sprung to his feet and started pacing the office furiously, like an enraged caged animal, while a fresh, all-consuming wave of paranoia played a number on his brain, shifting it into overdrive. In his line of work, coincidences didn't exist.

"Let me see her face," he growled, seizing the file from Ivan's hands and scattering all the papers on his desk. He found the picture of the woman, extracted from her photo ID most likely, and picked it up, staring intently at the eyes locking with his from the blurry, magnified printout.

Could it be true? Could his worst nightmare actually be reality? Maybe it wasn't his paranoia talking when he thought there was someone out there set to get him. Maybe it was his gut, telling him to watch out. That gut of his had saved his life and fortune more times than he cared to remember. When he looked at that stranger's face, he felt his gut twisting, ringing all kinds of alarm bells. Why? What interest could there possibly be for a technology consultant, an American woman he'd never met, to want to hunt him down?

"What's her name?" Myatlev whispered his question between clenched teeth, continuing to stare at the woman's picture.

"Alex Hoffmann."

Whom was she working for? That was the real question. Someone was using her to get to him; that was for sure. Women don't just hunt people like him. Women aren't hunters; women do as they're told. Behind this American woman there had to be a powerful man, a motivated enemy with access to information, to the secrets in his life. A ghost from his past, maybe from his days in the KGB? Or maybe a business enemy, a competitor who wanted him destroyed.

So many theories…yet all converged to the same focal point. Someone close to him had betrayed him. Myatlev felt a pang of fear hit his gut, as he realized just how few people had access to information about his most secret of operations. Ivan…but Ivan didn't have the resources, the acumen to orchestrate something like this. If Ivan were ever motivated to take him down, he could expect an honest knife in the heart from him, nothing more.

Dimitrov, the Russian minister of defense, was another man privy to his darkest secrets...But first, Dimitrov was on his side; he believed that with all his heart. Dimitrov was also too soft, not the kind to weave plans of great magnitude, involving people in other countries. He was a brilliant military strategist, implicitly not covert in his nature. No, it couldn't have been Dimitrov.

Then who? A thought froze the blood in his veins. It could have been Abramovich. The sick son of a bitch had everything: a devious mind, tremendous resources, and an appetite for playing mind-fucking games. Abramovich could have very well decided that Myatlev had outlived his usefulness, and decided to play a game before eliminating him. Maybe Abramovich wanted to make him pay for who knows what real or imaginary offense he couldn't even think of.

Myatlev felt a wave of nausea contemplating that scenario and his own paranoia. Well, if that was the case, he wasn't going to go down without a fight. Better said, he wasn't going to go down at all.

He'd had enemies before, and yet here he was, still alive, and more powerful than ever. He'd just find out who was pulling that woman's strings, and kill them, and everyone around them.

He looked at Ivan with a changed expression. All anxiety had disappeared from his eyes, replaced with cold determination and a vengeful lust for blood.

"Find out everything there is to know about this woman," he said. "Leave no stone unturned. Ask Cyber to look at everything she's ever touched and everyone she's ever cared about. I want everything, you hear me?"

Ivan continued to stand, waiting for his boss to finish.

"Now, Ivan, now!" Myatlev snapped impatiently. "And call Bogdanov. Tell that idiot to expect trouble and bring in more firepower."

Wu Shen Teng watched them closely, hoping that at least one of them would make eye contact with him, or speak to him. But what was he expecting? He had betrayed these people, and *he* couldn't bring himself to look them in the eye. Maybe the part he was planning to play in their escape could redeem him in some small measure. In *their* eyes…As for his own conscience, he'd have to live the rest of his life remembering how he failed cowardly and dishonorably, jeopardizing the lives of his family, and the lives of everyone else. Unforgivable.

Teng watched them getting ready, their faces somber and determined, reminding him of ancient Xia dynasty warriors preparing for battle. He took a deep breath and approached the group, feeling the blood chill in his veins.

Dr. Davis handed each of them a green capsule, discreetly, making sure King Cobra didn't catch on to what they were doing.

"I've made a few extras, you'll find them here." He placed the small container with the remaining capsules inconspicuously near the liquid dosimeter. "Don't take more than one unless really needed, and absolutely not more than two."

"How about Declan, Gary?" Jane Crawford asked.

"I'm thinking of putting an oxygen mask on him," Dr. Davis replied. "He might be better off sleeping through all this." He rubbed his chin, thinking a little before continuing his argument. "We've kept him sedated and loaded with painkillers. I'm concerned that if we wake him and expose him to all this, we'd only be shocking his system for no good reason."

"Agreed," Adenauer replied.

"I've given a pill to Lila, and instructed her to stay by the back wall," Dr. Davis added. "We're ready."

Teng extended his trembling hand, and Gary Davis placed a green capsule in his palm.

"Don't worry, Teng, you'll be OK," Davis encouraged him. "Just focus on your part, we'll handle the rest."

He couldn't bring himself to speak; he just nodded, keeping his eyes firmly stuck to the ground.

Jane Crawford stared a little at the green capsule in her hand, and then tucked it in the chest pocket of her shirt. A crooked smile fluttered for a second on Gary's lips.

"What are you smiling about, Cheshire Cat?" Bukowsky asked Davis.

"Can you imagine all of us meeting at next year's conference? The things that only we will know? Having survived all this?" Davis replied, still grinning, making an all-encompassing gesture with his hand.

"You're really that sure we'll survive all this and meet next year? *C'est vrai*?" Marie-Elise asked with a timid smile.

"Marie-Elise, for the first time since a screwed-up destiny brought us all here, yes, I am sure. I'm betting my life on it."

She reached and took Gary's hand with both hers, and Adenauer placed his hand on top of theirs. One by one, they joined hands together, as one, silently, yet the effervescence of their hope and determination sent crackles through the air like static electricity.

"Teng, you too," Davis invited him.

Hesitantly, Teng put his hand on top of everyone's joined hands, daring to lift his eyes from the ground. He didn't see anyone's glance judging or despising him; he saw everyone counting on him to do his part. He wasn't going to let them down.

"I'm ready," Teng said.

"All right, let's play ball," Gary Davis replied. "Take positions, stay focused."

Teng locked eyes with Davis, who nodded encouragingly. He approached King Cobra and said, "I need to speak with Dr. Bogdanov. Now, please; it's urgent."

King Cobra grunted, then stood, shoving Teng up the steps that led to the massive door. He unlatched the door and stepped outside, speaking into his radio. Then he slammed the door behind them, locking it with a rusty squeak.

Bogdanov appeared within seconds, frowning impatiently as he approached, walking briskly on the long, curved hallway.

"What?" he snapped.

Teng kept his eyes lowered.

"Please," he whispered, "you said you're going to start shooting people. Please don't start with my family, please!"

"Why the hell not?" Bogdanov shouted. "You haven't given me anything. You're worthless to me, and so is your family."

"No, no, please," Teng pleaded, feeling chills down his spine and fear prickling at his gut. "I can maybe…maybe tell you something now?"

Bogdanov waved his hand impatiently.

"They're planning to jump the guard," Teng continued in a low whisper. "They're going to try to disarm him and break free."

King Cobra scoffed, probably amused at the thought. Teng ignored him, and focused on Bogdanov.

"You shouldn't send him alone in there," he continued, pointing briefly at King Cobra. "They're not as harmless as they seem, you know. One of them used to be a boxing champion. Another one is a black belt in martial arts. And they do have knives, scalpels."

Bogdanov clenched his jaws and pursed his lips angrily, then spoke something into his radio. Static crackled for a second, then a husky voice replied in Russian.

King Cobra grabbed Teng's arm, almost lifting him off the ground, and shoved him back into the lab. He couldn't regain his footing at the top of the stairs and fell, rolling off the steps and landing on the dirty concrete floor. Then King Cobra disappeared, slamming and bolting the door behind him.

Adenauer, in position near the entrance, helped Teng get back on his feet and join the others, at the far end of the lab tables.

Teng signaled to them he'd done his part.

"And?" Gary Davis asked in a whisper.

"I don't know," Teng replied. "It should work. They spoke on the radio and left. I'm not sure, but it should work."

Alex unscrewed her canteen and gulped down a mouthful of water, after swishing it in her mouth a little, to trick her brain into thinking she drank more than that. The humid heat had let down a little after sunset, but she was still sweating profusely under all the heavy-duty clothing and weight she was carrying. Mosquitoes were an enemy force of their own, biting her viciously despite the thick layer of bug repellent cream she'd applied on every exposed inch of skin.

She refrained from slapping herself where a mosquito just stung her; afraid the slap would cause too much noise in the deathly quiet forest. The few crickets that still chirped were far away, barely audible.

Darkness worked a little in their favor, keeping them hidden as they waited, only five klicks away from the missile silo. They sat scrunched down against tree trunks near the edge of the forest, at the established rendezvous point with the contracted backup team.

She was worried their arrival might get the attention of the Russian Coast Guard, very active in that area. Lou, an artist at his special ops trade, had researched the terrain a little and had instructed them to fly in following the river, an old route for caviar smugglers, and one of the very few loopholes in Russian border defense.

A low hum at first, the sound of the approaching helo grew to slightly higher levels, as the lights of the AW101 became visible. Its rotor blades made a distinctive noise, a lower pitch and choppy, with an unexpectedly quiet whoosh. Lou turned his laser spot on, marking the center of the clearing, and then spoke into his radio.

"Inbound, inbound, this is Lima, green marks the spot. Go dark. Do you copy?"

"Copy, Lima. Ready to deploy."

The chopper cut its lights, hovering forty feet above ground shrouded in darkness, as the mercenaries dropped to the ground on ropes. As soon as their feet touched the ground, they took off toward the edge of the forest, guided by

Lou's laser spot.

Alex turned on her night-vision goggles, and took in the unfamiliar green-hued imagery. The device had the option to use infrared on one eye, or on both. She tried it both ways, to see which was better. With both eyes, she had an eerie feeling of surreal imagery, but she had balance and depth perspective. Single-eye option gave her the benefit of infrared vision, but kept her other eye accustomed to seeing and perceiving her environment the usual way. Either case, night vision took some getting used to.

The helo lifted higher in the air and departed, turning its lights back on after a couple of seconds.

She stood, a little dazed, hoping that her brain would adjust faster to the new way to see the surroundings, and walked toward the huddled armed men. Four had already taken positions, weapons ready, covering the perimeter.

She tripped on a tree branch and almost fell. She felt a strong grip on her right arm, steadying her, helping her regain her balance.

"Shit," she muttered, then looked sheepishly at the man holding her arm and whispered, "I mean thanks."

The man grinned, his teeth glistening against his camouflage-painted face.

Alex reached the group as Lou wrapped up his briefing.

"We're five klicks from target. We're expecting 20 to 50 hostiles, and more than 400 hostages."

"Copy," a man replied. "Comms?"

"We have encrypted radios patched into sat phones."

"Weapons?"

"Tavors, handguns, CornerShot, grenades, limited ammo. We've been at this for a while," Lou clarified. "We have one wounded and two civilians."

"Out of how many?"

"Out of four," Lou replied dryly.

"Understood," the man said, after a split second of silence.

"This civilian is ready to fight. You can count me in," Blake said, stepping up toward the man. "Blake Bernard," he introduced himself, extending his hand.

"Call me Martin, I'm the team lead." The man shook Blake's hand vigorously, not hiding his surprise. "*The* Blake Bernard?"

"Uh-huh," Blake replied.

One of the men whistled appreciatively.

"It will be an honor to go to battle with you, sir," the man added, ending his statement with a firm salute.

"Alex Hoffmann," she introduced herself. "Also ready, but not nearly as famous."

Martin shook her hand just as vigorously.

"One question," she said, "how do we call you? Your men?"

"Just call us Bravos. We like anonymity in our line of work; I hope you understand. We're your backup team. Bravo stands for backup."

"OK, got it," she replied, then turned her attention to Lou.

"There's a single entry point to the silo that we can see here," Lou continued his briefing, showing the men his phone screen with the imagery received from DigiWorld. "There are guards here and here," he continued, pointing at the screen, "and there's a hangar or carport of sorts to the side, where some trucks are parked. Those are guarded too."

"Copy," Martin confirmed. "Bravo teams, move out."

Gary counted every minute since Teng had returned to the lab. Would it work? Did Teng keep his side of the deal? Or had he caved under pressure, ratting on them again? *Come on, already,* he encouraged the Russians in his mind. *Come to Papa for a restful sleep, guaranteed to last forever.*

He verified for the tenth time that everyone was in position and ready. Adenauer stood tall, his backbone stiff, and his face carved in stone, right next to the lab table nearest the door. The aerosol canister containing the anesthetic mix was inches away from his hand, tucked discreetly between the two centrifuges and the chromatograph.

Declan Mallory had an oxygen mask on, and slept sedated, undisturbed, unaware of anything. It was better for him that way.

As for the rest of them, they huddled near the far end of the lab tables, pretending to be working on various equipment, and ready to spring into action at the earliest opportunity.

Clamor outside the door caught his attention. Multiple men treaded heavily and noisily approaching the lab, then the rusty bolt was pulled, and the door shoved open forcefully.

"This is it, guys," he whispered, "Godspeed."

Adenauer swallowed his antidote, then turned to face the door.

Four armed men barged in, followed by Bogdanov. Gary recognized King Cobra, Death, and One-Eye, but the fourth was a new face, a huge man wearing a long, monastic beard, and holding a Kalashnikov with ease, as if it were a toy. Bogdanov's face was contorted in anger, his eyes glinting with pure hatred.

Gary saw Adenauer hesitate to release the gas, and he followed his gaze to see Marie-Elise staring at the floor, where she'd dropped her antidote capsule. Gary signaled her almost imperceptibly to leave it. Picking it up would be risky; could get the Russians' attention. She leaned against the back wall, pale, and nodded discreetly to Adenauer, encouraging him to proceed.

Unseen, Gary popped his capsule in his mouth, then swallowed it immediately. Behind him, Jane, Teng, Fortuin, and Bukowsky took their pills, while Marie-Elise let herself slide to the floor, hidden from view by a storage cabinet. Good. This way, if she fainted she wouldn't risk hurting herself in the fall.

He turned to watch the Russians near the lab entrance, and saw Adenauer releasing the canister valve and stepping back.

"You are dead, all of you, you fucking cunts!" Bogdanov thundered.

He pulled his gun and released the safety, pointing it at Adenauer's head. Adenauer stood firmly, calm, brave, and dignified, unfazed by Bogdanov, and taking shallow, infrequent breaths.

"*Kak der'mo,*" King Cobra said, disgust showing on his face. "What is this smell?"

"This is nothing to worry about," Adenauer said, almost smiling. "We work with chemicals here, so that can happen. But see? I am breathing it too. If you take deep breaths, like this, you won't feel it anymore." He demonstrated with his hands, encouraging them to breathe in the stink of desflurane.

God, I hope he's faking it, Gary thought.

Bogdanov pointed his gun at Gary next, then back to Adenauer, his hand shaking just a little.

"What's going on? What are you doing?" he yelled. "I will kill all of you, you hear me?"

Why the hell isn't it working? Gary thought, sweat bursting at the roots of his hair. *It has to work! It has to!*

Then he noticed One-Eye lean against the back wall, and Death running his hand against his forehead and shaking his head, as if to rid himself of a dizzy spell and regain focus.

It *was* working; they just needed a little more time.

Reading his mind, or just being the pure genius that he was, Adenauer started explaining to the men how the sense of smell worked, and how the nose protects itself by blocking the sensory information of a strong smell after a few inhalations, to maintain the capacity of discerning new smells despite the prevalence of a stronger, pervasive scent. Pedantic and calm, he took his time going through lots of trivial details about the wondrous human olfactory system. Bogdanov probably already knew most of that, and the rest of the men didn't really care, but Adenauer's speech kept them busy inhaling some more aerosolized anesthetic.

Then Gary noticed how Adenauer had placed a hand firmly against the surface of the lab table, to help support his weight. He was starting to feel weak, despite the antidote. *Damn...*

Bogdanov was the first to collapse, probably because of his smaller body mass. As he fell, he fired his gun twice. Both bullets strayed and hit the wall above their heads.

Death took two steps forward to catch Bogdanov as he fell, but he never got that far. He collapsed on one knee, then buckled to the side, his head hitting the concrete floor with a loud thud. One-Eye collapsed right where he stood, leaning against the wall. King Cobra was next, and the bearded giant was last, falling forward while trying to fire his Kalashnikov.

"Now!" Gary yelled, and leapt forward, opening a metallic case stocked with chloroform on gauze. Grabbing a couple, he ran and placed one on Bogdanov's nose, and one on Death's, holding them firmly in place for a few good seconds.

Bukowsky was right behind him, taking care of the other men. He placed gauze soaked in chloroform on the noses of One-Eye and King Cobra, and then struggled to flip the bearded thug on his back.

Gary helped roll the man over and took his weapon, while Bukowsky gave him his due dose of chloroform. Then he helped Adenauer move to the back of the lab to breathe cleaner air, and offered him a second antidote.

Jane and Fortuin picked up Marie-Elise and put her on a cot. Fortuin held her head up and opened her mouth, while Jane opened one of the capsules and spread the powder under Marie-Elise's tongue, to speed up the absorption and get it in her blood stream without risking her choking on the capsule. Within seconds, she started fluttering her eyelids and mumbling. She was going to be OK.

Gary and Bukowsky snapped a few power cords from some lab equipment, and used it to tie the Russians' hands. They took their weapons and shared them among themselves. Bukowsky, Gary, and Jane each took a Kalashnikov and a pistol, leaving the rest of the weapons in Fortuin's charge. Jane fumbled a little with the Kalashnikov, but soon figured out how to replace the clip, set the gun on semi-auto, and remove its safety.

"Watch them carefully," Gary said to Fortuin and Adenauer, pointing at the unconscious men lying on the floor. "The slightest move, and you give them more chloroform. Don't hesitate...better safe than sorry, all right? No one's gonna miss them if they never wake up again."

"Yes, yes, understood," Adenauer replied. "Good luck!"

He offered his hand and Gary took it, giving it a firm shake and looking the German in the eye.

"Thank you," Gary said warmly, surprised at the emotion he suddenly felt for the self-sacrificing man he'd always thought too arrogant to tolerate. "For everything."

Then he turned to Bukowsky and Jane.

"OK, let's go kill us some Russians now, so we can all go home."

Myatlev took small pieces of toast covered with pâté de foie gras and chewed them slowly. His mouth felt dry, like sand, and he couldn't even feel the taste of the exquisite delicacy. His thoughts revolved around the same bothersome, life-or-death questions. Why? Who was that woman? Why was she after him? How much did she know? Why was he still alive?

He pushed away his plate, an expression of disgust contorting his lips. Ivan jumped to his feet.

"Was there something wrong with it, boss? I'll have them—"

"Nah..." He dismissed Ivan's concern with a wave of his hand, then stood with a groan, holding his stomach, and released one notch in his belt. Then he started pacing the office slowly. His brows, creased firmly, were ridging his forehead, and somehow made the dark circles underneath his eyes seem more prominent.

He stopped his slow pacing and turned to face Ivan, who waited patiently near the coffee table, ready to pour him another shot.

"What's going on at the lab? Did you call him?"

"Bogdanov? Yes. I told him to pull in some reinforcements, and be ready for an attack."

"Everything all right there?"

"I heard nothing more. But clouds are thick over there; we lost satellite feed."

"Argh...fuck!" Myatlev snapped. Even goddamn nature was against him on this one.

He took a mouthful of cold chamomile tea and winced at the stale, unpalatable taste, then wiped his mouth with his sleeve.

"Goddamn shit...Send in reinforcements. Send the troops we have stationed on Sakhalin."

"But...I thought—"

"Yes, Ivan?" he snapped impatiently.

"You said the lab was above top secret, that no one can know about it. If we bring the troops from Sakhalin, how are we going to keep everyone quiet about the lab?"

Myatlev gave Ivan a long stare, making him lower his eyes and shift his weight from one foot to the other. Sometimes he just couldn't believe how naïve Ivan could be. He knew better than to ask that stupid question. But Ivan was just hired muscle, after all. What did he expect?

"The usual way, Ivan, what the hell? Let them do their job and keep the lab safe. Then, they'll disappear."

Ivan remained quiet, a hint of surprise showing on his face. He'd been loyal, docile, and dedicated all those years, taking out everyone who had the misfortune to stand in Myatlev's path, and had never hesitated in getting his job done. This time though, Myatlev was asking a bit much; the Sakhalin contingent was one hundred and fifty strong, all Russians, all soldiers who deserved better. He understood Ivan's hesitation. He was asking for a massacre...*For the higher purpose,* Myatlev reminded himself, *it's all for the higher purpose.*

"Understood?" Myatlev reinforced his point with Ivan.

"Yes, sir," he replied deferentially.

"And blow up that Phenom. They won't be going anywhere, those fucks."

They walked in single file, in a start-and-stop dynamic dictated by Martin, the contractor team lead who led the way. Two of his men were the advanced recon team, marching ahead of everyone else by a couple hundred yards, making sure they didn't walk into an ambush. Alex had learned how to walk in the green-hued darkness of the forest without stumbling at every step. She lifted her feet higher, then set them down almost vertically, carefully, stepping on branches rather than tripping on them.

Behind her, Lou supported Sam, whose pallor had accentuated in the past hour. He leaned more and more on Lou, and groaned quietly every few steps. Every time she searched his face with worried eyes, Sam smiled weakly, trying to reassure her. It wasn't working. The blast must have caused him an internal hemorrhage or more severe damage than she had estimated. He needed a hospital, as soon as possible. But what was really possible where they were? Nothing much. Where would they go? *Please hold on, Sam,* she thought, *we'll find a way, we always do.*

Stepping carefully not to make noise, and almost mechanically putting one foot in front of the other, she let her mind wander. What would they find at the abandoned silo? Would they find the four hundred people they were looking for? Would they find bodies? Would they find V? If he were indeed the architect of this bold plane hijacking, would he be there, taking care of business? Or would he be hiding someplace distant and safe, letting others get their hands dirty, like the master puppeteer that he was? Would she finally get the chance to find out who he was?

She'd stopped talking to her team about her scenarios. She could see it in their eyes that they didn't believe her anymore. Not even Sam. They must have all thought she'd become irrationally obsessed with her elusive terrorist. Yet she was sure; she knew, deep in her gut, that it was V, the mysterious Russian mastermind, who had the vision and the global strategic brilliance to orchestrate such a bold plan. Terrorists like that weren't born every day. And when they were, they made history in a significant way.

A drop of water hit her cheek, bringing her focus back to reality. Light rain had started to fall, further reducing the visibility, but there was a distant trace of light coming from somewhere. She took off her night-vision goggles.

At the front of their line, Martin suddenly froze, raising his left fist in the air, in a silent command to stop. Then he silently gestured that he saw the enemy, and they should remain behind, under the cover of the dark forest.

They had arrived.

Alex took cover behind a tree trunk and carefully peeked to see. The silo was right there, eighty yards or so from the tree line. It was a massive cupola-covered circular structure, not taller than twenty feet. Probably the rest of the structure continued underground.

The structure seemed to have a single point of entry, a large metallic door. It had been originally painted in military green, but that had faded under the sustained attack of the elements, and was stained by rust.

Two armed Russians stood watch in front of it. They carried their Kalashnikovs loosely; they were not expecting trouble. They wore a strange mix of mismatching old military uniform parts, as if they were outfitted by a World War II Russian Army surplus store. They were not the official Russian Army. *Interesting, and it's yet another argument in favor of my theory.* Alex felt a wave of excitement at the thought. She was getting close to catching the bastard after all.

At the left side of the main building, just like they'd seen in the satellite imagery, there was an open hangar that housed several military trucks, guarded by two armed sentries. From that distance, Alex could see they also had machine guns, but didn't have any night-vision equipment.

Several light sources illuminated the area. A couple of larger spotlights covered the main entrance and the hangar access. Five floodlights covered the piece of asphalt road that connected the two structures, and several tens of feet of the road leading to the silo. The advantage presented by darkness was gone.

Martin signaled his men, and three of the military contractors joined him near the tree line. A rapid sequence of hand signals followed, then they split into two teams. All four men had holstered their weapons and carried their tactical knives in their hands, ready to strike. The rest of the fighters spread out behind the tree line, getting ready to charge.

Alex felt her heart pounding in her chest. She tightened the grip on her Tavor, her finger hovering above the safety lever, but not releasing it. She felt her spine tingling, and adrenaline hitting her gut. This was it…she better be ready.

She felt Lou's touch on her shoulder.

"This is an SS-19 Stiletto base," he whispered quietly, barely audible.

"And?" That bit of information didn't mean anything to her. She felt a wave of irritation at her own lack of knowledge. *Here I am, the clueless soldier. Absolutely great!*

"That means it goes deep underground."

They kept their eyes on the two teams, as they made a silent and slow approach toward the two sentry groups. The team approaching on the right side, targeting the main silo entrance, had the forest line cover them for most of the way, then the silo's wall curvature was going to work in their favor, keeping them hidden from view as they advanced.

The team headed for the truck hangar had it a little rougher; they had to cross thirty feet of open, well-lit field. Martin saw them hesitating to leave the cover of the tree line, and ordered them to stop by extending his arm with his palm facing up and outward. Then Martin and his companion made their move toward the silo entrance.

Alex held her breath, feeling her heart pounding. *Oh, we better be right about this,* she thought. *Otherwise, we're all going away for a long, long time, and I'm not even sure which country will sentence us to death first.* She felt a wave of nauseous anxiety at the thought that she had brought all these people here, in harm's way, based on her theories. She quickly revisited her deductions, and inspected her logic. She hadn't taken any wrong turns in her investigation, or cut any corners. She was sure. The passengers of flight XA233 were there, just a few yards away. They had to be. She felt her anxiety dissipate and she took a long, refreshing breath.

Martin and his companion had approached the sentries, crawling single file against the wall. When they were just a few feet away, they pounced silently and deadly. Martin got the one on the left. With one hand, he covered his mouth keeping him quiet, while the other, holding the tactical knife, stabbed the Russian in the throat, an inch below his ear, slicing deep into his brain. His companion decided to grab his target's head and quickly break his neck with a swift rotating move. He then slowly eased the dead man down to the ground, making sure his fall was noiseless.

They dragged the two bodies a few yards along the wall toward the back, getting them out of sight. Martin signaled the other team to be ready, then whistled loudly, enough to be heard by the other two Russians. The sentries perked their heads and started approaching fast, turning their backs toward the forest line, where the second team waited for the right opportunity to attack. The second team made its move, and within seconds, both Russians were dead.

Martin gave the "clear" signal, and the rest of the support team advanced to his location, followed by Alex, Blake, and Lou. Sam declined wearily, seeming unable to stand, and signaled them to go ahead without him.

They approached the silo door walking briskly, almost running. Martin placed a couple of his men on watch duty, and opened the massive door. It creaked loudly, causing them to freeze in their tracks and clasp their weapons, listening intently.

They entered the structure cautiously, their weapons ready. A long, curved corridor extended both ways inside the structure, with metallic doors every twenty yards or so. Martin split them into two teams, taking opposite directions in their search. Blake joined Alex on the team headed left, and Lou went with the other team.

After a few yards, Martin's fist popped up in the air and they froze in their tracks. He then signaled with his fingers at his ear that he was hearing something, and gestured them to align along the inside wall, to take cover.

They heard footsteps approaching. Alex held her breath, getting ready to pounce. She released the safety lever on her Tavor, and she heard the others cock their weapons.

Then she saw who was approaching; two men and a woman wielding their Kalashnikovs falteringly, who froze when they saw them. One of the men lifted his Kalashnikov in a firing position, but hesitated to open fire. Her team immediately took positions on the corridor, and lifted their weapons, ready to pull the triggers. She felt her hair stand on its ends; this was wrong, very wrong.

"Hold your fire," Alex shouted. She stepped away from the wall, approaching the three people, and lowering her weapon. "Hold your fire. We're Americans; we're here to take you home."

"Really? You're not screwing with me?" one of the men asked in a choked voice, lowering his weapon.

The woman dropped her weapon to the ground and almost jumped forward, hugging Alex.

"Thank you," she said. "Thank you all."

Alex felt her eyes moisten; she hadn't expected that reaction.

"There are more of us," the same man said, "many more. And Russians too, with guns."

"Name?" Martin asked.

"Davis. Dr. Gary Davis."

"Dr. Davis, how many Russians, and where are they?"

"We don't know. We just broke free, right now. We were going to try to free the others. Five Russians are unconscious and tied up in the lab."

"All right, let's get you to safety," Martin replied, then directed them to the door, with one of his men leading. "Take them outside, behind the tree line, and wait there for my signal."

"Have you seen Adeline?" Blake asked, grabbing Dr. Davis' sleeve. "Is she all right?"

Gary Davis stopped and turned to face Blake. "I am sorry; I don't know who that is."

Blake's hand fell, releasing Dr. Davis' sleeve.

"Let's move," Martin commanded.

They advanced carefully, stopping at every door, clearing the structure room by room. Most of the rooms were empty and dark. Then they found a makeshift lab.

Martin opened the door carefully, and stiffened when he saw light. It was a large structure equipped with lab tables and equipment. His eyes met the scared glances coming from several people. Then he noticed the five inert bodies tied on the floor, dressed like the sentries he'd just taken out at the main silo entrance.

Martin entered the lab lowering his weapon and saying, "We're American; we're taking you home."

The harrowed men and women started to cheer, but Martin quickly silenced them with a quick gesture. He then directed them to leave the structure and join the others at the tree line.

"One of us was injured, and is bedridden, sedated, and unconscious," a tall, dignified man spoke with a strong German accent.

"Name?" Martin asked.

"Adenauer. Theo Adenauer."

Martin gave Alex a quick look.

"Dr. Adenauer," she said, "we will clear the structure first, make sure everyone's safe, then come back for him. Chances are if he's unconscious, he will be out of harm's way."

"You know who I am?" the man asked, emotion tingeing his voice.

"Yes, we do," Alex replied. "We've done our homework; we're not here by accident."

"Have you seen Adeline, my wife?" Blake asked Adenauer with pleading eyes. "She's five-seven, brown hair, thirty-six years old."

"No, I'm sorry. That name does not sound familiar. But there are hundreds more, somewhere in this structure."

"I know her," a woman said, stepping forward. "I'm Lila Wallace. I am—I was the flight attendant in first class. She was seated in my area."

Blake grabbed her hand with both his, holding it tight. "Where is she? Is she OK?"

"She's with the others," Lila replied. "We got separated when we got to the trucks. But she's fine, I am sure. She wasn't among the..." Lila choked a little, and then continued. "You'll find her, you'll see."

"Among the what?" Blake asked quietly, his face petrified with fear.

"Umm...the test subjects," Lila whispered, a tear rolling on her cheek. "But she wasn't, I'm sure she's OK."

"Oh, my God," Blake whispered, turning a sickly shade of pale.

Alex felt her stomach turn. She'd been right in her theories. Whoever had taken flight XA233 wanted the researchers to develop a nerve agent, and needed test subjects. Instead of feeling redeemed, all she felt was an unbearable sense of revulsion, of loathing, and a bubbling anger, driving her to want to draw blood with her own hands from the bastard who'd tortured all those people. *It will come, you'll see,* she thought. *I'll find you, you sick son of a bitch, and when I do, you'll wish you were never born.*

"Umm…excuse me?" Lila's voice got their attention.

"Yes," Martin replied. "What is it?"

"That man over there," she said, pointing at a silhouette crouched against the back wall, "is the sack of shit who brought us all here. He's the pilot."

Two of Martin's men went to get him, their faces not promising anything good.

"I want him alive," Alex called after them. "I need to find out who's behind this."

"We're moving," Martin's voice called her to attention.

They continued to inspect the structure and found no one else on the main level.

"Bravo Two, this is Bravo One," Martin said into his radio, and it crackled to life immediately.

"Bravo One, copy."

"Bravo Two, we're going underground."

"Copy that. On your six, Bravo One."

They made their way underground, descending through dark, humid, moldy-smelling stairways, and feeling the temperature drop with every step. Then they reached another curved corridor, and started following it, like they had the one above.

Within a few yards, they surprised a Russian taking a leak in a doorway. He opposed no resistance, and relinquished his weapon immediately.

"Where are they?" Martin asked.

The Russian pointed ahead.

"The first door over there, the big one. The big circle." He spoke in a raspy voice, his accent harsh.

"How many Russians?"

"I–I don't know."

One of Martin's men hit him in the stomach. "Think again, asshole."

"Three, maybe four."

"Thanks!" Martin replied, then knocked the Russian unconscious with the butt of his weapon.

They soon found what the Russian had told them about—an access way leading to a large, tall, metallic, double door, covered in rust, and guarded by an armed man who didn't even see them coming. That Russian went down silently, taken out by a lethal stab in the neck.

Team Bravo Two caught up with them, and Martin gave them the signal to stand fast and silent.

Martin cracked the door open as gently as he could, then peeked inside.

"Oh, fuck," he muttered, then closed it.

He signaled his people to approach. Alex, Lou, and Blake joined them.

"This is the ingress point to the main silo. There are hundreds of hostages in there, and the Russians are scattered among them, on elevated positions. We risk extensive loss of lives if we go direct. They'll start shooting, and scythe the hostages down in the crossfire."

"What do you want to do?" Blake asked, turning pale.

"We might try to draw them out. Or we might get one of the Russians we captured, wake him up, and force him to call them out."

"I have an idea," Alex offered. "Some of us can go in, without our gear, wearing plain clothes, and carrying knives. If the Russians are scattered in the crowds, they won't notice us. Then we take them out, one by one. In the crowd there is inherent cover."

Martin stood silent for a few seconds, weighing his options. Then he started taking his tactical vest off. The rest of the men followed.

"I need two of you to stay here, and cover our asses in case this goes bad," Martin said. "You and you," he pointed at two men. "If this goes south, remember they'll have to come out at some point. Take them out one by one; don't risk the hostages' lives." He then turned to Alex and added, "You should stay here too, ma'am."

"In your dreams," Alex replied dryly.

She'd taken off her vest, and she rubbed her back against the decrepit walls to get her tee shirt to look dirty. Some of the men did the same, even rolled on the floors covered in debris to look the part, then wiped most of the camouflage paint off their faces.

"Blake," Alex said, "You're staying behind. You have to."

"What?" he asked, surprised. "Why? No way I'm staying behind."

"If Adeline sees you, she'll react. There's no way we can control that, and we shouldn't risk it."

Blake lowered his head, accepting her argument. Then he lifted his eyes, locking them with hers. "OK. Then you bring her to me, all right?"

"I promise," she replied, touching his shoulder. "Ready," she announced.

"Roger that," Martin replied. "This is a round structure. We enter one by one, and quickly take cover in the crowd. Let's work it in concentric circles, starting from large to small. We'll take the smaller circles, where we think the most Russians will be. Lou and Alex, you take the outer circle, closest to the wall. Alex walks west, Lou walks east. Walk slowly, casually, don't draw attention. Stop, sit, observe. Find your Russian, and plan your moves. Keep chatter to a minimum. Earbuds should do it in there, and cover your mouth when you speak. The laryngophones will capture the quietest whisper. Just mark your man, and wait for my signal."

"Got it," Alex confirmed.

They snuck in, one by one. Alex was among the last, and she felt her heart in her throat when she approached the ajar door. She took a deep breath, then stepped through the tight opening.

She took a few quick steps to reach a group of hostages, then stopped, to absorb and process the information she was seeing.

The structure was vast, with a high, dome-vaulted roof that had hatched openings at the center. It was hard to tell what that space had been used for; it resembled a huge arena or a circus of sorts, in a terrible state of decay. The floor was concrete, covered in dirt and debris. The smell of human sweat and waste was pervasive, almost suffocating.

Then she looked at the people and shuddered, shocked. They were disheveled and haunted-looking, defeated, hopeless. Most of them stood, walking aimlessly, or talking quietly with one another. Some sat on the floor, or lay on the cold concrete, curled up on their sides, immobile. They were in hell.

Alex snapped out of her shock and focused on her task. She started walking slowly, checking out the people she saw, and looking for an armed Russian she could tackle. There he was, a brute, scars marring his face, arms the size of her thighs. That monster was her target.

She felt her blood chilling, turning to ice cubes. How would she do it? Would she stab him in the back? How much force did she need to apply? Why had she offered to come in here anyway? That's why they had contracted the Bravos. *Stupid, reckless, idiotic,* she called herself, almost ready to let Martin know she needed someone else to do her job.

Then she laid eyes on a thin, frail Chinese woman, sitting against the wall and holding her baby. Tears ran quietly on her checks, as she caressed and reassured the silent, immobile infant.

Alex felt a wave of rage suffocating her. "Ready," she whispered in her comm.

"Copy," Martin replied. "Go on my count. Three, two, one, go."

She made a move toward her target, her hand clutching the handle of her tactical knife, her arm lowered, hidden behind her back.

The Russian turned, startling her for a split second.

"What do we have here, huh?" he said, staring at her with obscene eyes, and grabbing her chin with his filthy fingers.

"Your worst nightmare," she growled, then stabbed the man in the chest, plunging her knife to the bolster, throwing all her weight behind the thrust.

The man buckled, his surprised eyes drilling into hers, while his mouth opened, gasping for air. She took a step back, pulling her knife from his chest, and getting ready to strike again. The man fell to the floor in a pool of blood.

"One down," she said into her comm, then signaled silence to the hostages around her, putting a finger to her lips.

One by one, she heard the team members confirm their kills. Then she heard Martin give the "all clear," and he addressed the hostages from the entrance.

"Attention, everyone, we're here to take you home," Martin said, as incredulous hostages clamored and hurried toward the door. "Please follow our instructions to stay safe. There could still be hostiles in this building."

No one paid much attention. They hurried to get out, to leave their hell, stepping over each other, screaming, running, just wanting to be free.

"Both teams, we need to contain the situation," Martin's voice came to life by radio. "Don't let them scatter in the forest. We'll never find them."

Then Alex heard Blake's voice, rising over the tumult, calling Adeline's name.

Alex followed the sound of Blake's voice, as he called his wife's name. He stood by the entrance, still on the outside corridor, unable to enter the dome against the flow of rushing people—tumultuous, desperate, frantic to get out.

That was something none of the team had given enough thought to. How would they control 423 passengers and 18 crew members, when they were running for their lives? What could they possibly say to slow them down, to get them to listen to reason? Not that they had their exfil figured out either. She had no idea how to get all those people to safety, from behind enemy lines. She needed a solution—a good one, and fast. One way or another, they were responsible for the lives of almost 450 irrationally frantic people, running, trying to escape.

Running to where, exactly?

There was no way to know what the enemy had coming. Maybe they had reinforcements nearby and some Russian had radioed a call for backup before being taken out. They had to move, get out of there while they still could, or risk a bloodbath.

She walked outside the dome with the flow of people, and soon reached Blake.

"Have you seen her?" Blake asked.

"No, but there are still a couple of hundred people inside," she replied, standing on her toes, trying to find her among the faces of the running mass.

"Adeline!" Blake called again, his strong voice covering the commotion of the crowd.

Somewhere from inside the dome, a distant voice responded.

"Blake? Blake?"

Alex smiled widely. Yes! There she was, making her way toward Blake, who tried to push against the flowing crowd to get to her sooner.

Finally, he got her in his arms, lifting her up in the air and taking her a few steps to the side, away from the stampeding crowd.

"Oh, baby," he said, burying his face in her hair.

"I can't believe you're here," Adeline said, choked with tears. "You didn't give up on me, you came for me."

"Always, baby, always."

Alex took a few steps to the side, to give them some privacy. That's when she saw him. A Russian had appeared out of nowhere, and was coming toward them fast. Anger contorted his face, and he bellowed a mix of unintelligible words in Russian. His gun was drawn and pointed at them.

"Blake!" Alex yelled to get his attention, as she pulled out her Walther.

Blake let go of Adeline and turned to see what was going on.

Then she saw the Russian pull the trigger. She fired her weapon, just as Blake stepped in front of Adeline, covering her with his own body. Alex's bullet tore through the Russian's shoulder, but didn't stop him.

She heard Adeline shriek, but kept her focus on the Russian, and fired her weapon twice more, in rapid sequence. One bullet got him in the head, the other in the throat. He fell forward, hit the concrete, and didn't budge.

Alex rushed to the fallen Russian and took his gun. Then she looked behind her, and her heart sank.

Blake was down, holding the left side of his abdomen with both his hands, while blood oozed from his wound, in small rivulets flowing between his fingers. Adeline held his head in her lap, sobbing hard.

They needed help. Their situation was turning into a disaster, fast.

She pressed the transmit button on her radio and called. "Bravo One, Bravo Two, this is Alpha, do you copy?"

"Bravo One, copy," Martin responded.

"Bravo Two, copy." That was Lou's voice.

"Bravo One, Bravo Two, follow my lead. Bravo One, I have a man down, gunshot to the abdomen. I need evac with a gurney, and get one of the doctors ready."

The radio crackled a little in her ear, then Martin's voice confirmed, "Copy. On our way."

She remained silent for a few seconds, thinking hard. What could they do?

"Alpha, you still there?" Lou's worried voice came through the radio waves.

"Copy, Lima, still here. Lima, these folks got here by trucks. Load them in the trucks; check them off the flight manifest, one by one. Make sure we don't leave anyone behind. Verify we have all the dead confirmed by at least two witnesses. Put one or two Bravos in each truck, and get ready to leave."

The radio crackled for a little while before Lou's voice kicked in, hesitantly.

"Copy, Alpha. Exfil?"

"We'll figure it out. I'll hang back until evac takes over here, then we have some cleanup left in the lab. Five terrorists are in there, waiting to get our attention."

"Alpha, Bravo One," Martin's voice crackled to life. "Lab cleanup executed."

"Copy, Bravo One. Any intel extracted before cleanup complete?"

"Negative, Alpha," Martin's voice replied after a short hesitation.

Damn it!

"Copy, Bravo One, Alpha out," she replied, feeling a sense of weariness. How was she ever going to find V, if no one got any intel from the enemy? Yet she understood Martin's call. With nearly 450 desperate civilians in tow, they couldn't deal with prisoner transport and interrogation. By all laws, the Russians were terrorists, caught in an act of terror. They deserved to die. She looked at Blake, shivering, lying in a pool of blood, and felt a lump in her throat, a wave of suffocating anger. Yes, they did deserve to die. Screw the intel; she'd find another way.

She kneeled next to Blake and Adeline, feeling tears coming to her eyes, not knowing what to say.

"You'll be all right, you'll see," she whispered. "You're tough. You drive people crazy with how tough you are. You'll be fine." She touched Adeline's arm and added, reassuringly, "He'll be fine. We have doctors here, good ones, the best."

Dr. Gary Davis followed behind two men carrying a gurney, running toward them.

"See? Help is here," Alex said, then stood up to make room for the doctor and the gurney.

Dr. Davis kneeled and checked the wound briefly, then instructed the men.

"Let's load him up, gently. We need to stop by the lab. I have what I need to stabilize him in there. I'll pack us some first-aid kits too."

She walked briskly behind them, but then headed out of the dome, while they went to the lab. Outside, the trucks were pulled in front of the silo's entrance, and pure chaos ruled. Bravo teams tried to mark people off the manifests as they loaded them in the trucks, but it wasn't working all that well. People were desperate to secure a place on the trucks, and were boarding the trucks as fast as they could, paying little or no attention to the Bravo teams giving instructions.

Then it suddenly got worse.

Two trucks filled with armed Russians approached fast on the road coming from the mountain, not giving them much time to react.

She yelled into her comm, "Take cover!"

Then she fired her Tavor, sending a few shots in the air, to get everyone's attention. People ran shrieking, some toward the field, most of them toward the forest. Those who had already climbed inside the trucks didn't dare get off and run for cover, but the trucks were not going to shield them against bullets. It was going to turn into a massacre.

"All Bravo teams," she yelled into her radio, pressing the laryngophone against her throat, "Russians cannot get to the trucks, no matter what. Copy?"

"This is Bravo One, copy," Martin's voice responded.

"Copy," Lou's reply came in next.

They had already started shooting. Most Bravos took positions around the front of the building, taking cover behind tree trunks or big rocks. Alex crouched behind a large tree trunk, her Tavor in position to fire, waiting for the Russians to come close enough. She saw Lou running toward the incoming Russian trucks, behind the tree line, holding a grenade in his hand. As soon as the first truck drove by, he threw it in the back of the truck. Seconds later, it blew up, sending smoldering pieces everywhere.

The second truck stopped and dozens of Russians climbed down, scattering toward the building and shooting their AK47s on automatic fire. Despite the total chaos, Alex remembered Lou's training in the firing range. "Slow is fast when you fire your weapon," he had said. "Pick your man and take him out. One bullet is all it takes."

She aimed her Tavor at one of the first Russians, and squeezed the trigger. The man fell on his back, firing his Kalashnikov as he fell, sending a stream of bullets in the air. She aimed toward a second Russian, and her bullet hit him in the leg. She fired again, and took him out. A third one started shooting in her direction, providing cover for the rest of the Russians, but one of the Bravos killed him within a second.

She saw another Russian approach, and aimed carefully, then squeezed the trigger. She missed. Cussing under her breath, she fired again and the second time she didn't miss. Focused on the targets in front of her, she completely missed the Russian who approached from her left side, hiding behind trees as he drew near.

She heard footsteps really close and froze, adrenaline shooting up her spine, her heart pumping hard and fast. She turned and saw a Russian holding his weapon trained on her chest, only a few feet away. She didn't get the chance to decide what to do. Lou crept up on the Russian and stabbed him in the ear with one swift blow.

"Thanks," she whispered.

"Anytime," Lou replied and disappeared behind the trees, looking for another target.

She resumed her position, searching for another Russian to kill. She didn't see any; slowly, carefully, she headed closer to the silo, using every tree as cover.

Then she heard the "all clear" message come in by comm.

She looked up at the sky and frowned. Still cloudy, but toward the west she could see a few stars. The sky was clearing, which meant the enemy could have satellite eyes on them soon.

She found Lou.

"Where's Sam?" she shouted, trying to cover the commotion.

"In the first truck. A doctor is with him."

"Let's go," she said, and climbed in the back of the truck.

The truck's canopy, moist and smelly, didn't do much for comfort. The earlier rain had soaked it and water was dripping here and there. Sam lay on a gurney toward the front of the truck, near the cabin, and a tall, distinguished-looking man she vaguely remembered from before sat by his side.

"How is he?"

"He needs a hospital," the man replied with a thick German accent. "He's bleeding internally. I've done all I could here, but that's not enough. He needs surgery." The man averted his eyes and lowered his voice. "It's urgent; he won't last much longer."

Oh, no! Where? Where could they go? Sam would know.

"Sam?" she called gently, reaching out and holding his hand. "You in there, somewhere?" she tried to joke, but felt her eyes well up with tears.

"Yes, I'm here," he whispered faintly.

"Sam, I need your help. We're going to head out to the coast in these trucks. We have the maps and everything. Where would I take you to a hospital?"

He gave a long sigh, then closed his eyes.

"You wouldn't, kiddo. The Russians would kill all these people. Not worth it. This is the end of the line for me."

"Sam!" she protested. "Not an option, you hear me? Think of something, please!"

She couldn't bear the thought of losing Sam. No...there had to be a way.

"If we make it to the coast," Lou intervened, "we might have a chance. There's an American base on Hokkaido, near Wakkanai. There's a Wasp-class ship there we could call in for help. It could come and get us."

"Confirmed, I've seen the Wasp," Martin added. "The USS *Okinawa*."

"What's a Wasp?" Alex whispered, trying to contain her sobs.

"It's an amphibious assault ship," Lou said, "Wasp class. It's big, and it has helos, six or eight Super Stallions at least. It's almost like an aircraft carrier for helos and a lot of Marine Corps Expeditionary forces. They could evac all these people in one move. They'd also have surgeons on board."

She felt a surge of hope swell her chest.

"What does it take to call them? How do you get a military warship rerouted here, near the Russian shore?"

Martin and Lou looked at each other, and Lou pursed his lips before speaking.

"You mean, in Russian territorial waters? We'd need—"

"A presidential order," Sam whispered. "It's technically an act of war against Russia."

"Shit…" she muttered, thinking hard. "Well, what the hell, I'll give it a shot," she decided. "Got nothing more to lose at this point. Time to pray is now, people."

She grabbed her sat phone and retrieved a number from the phone's memory. She almost smiled seeing how puzzled Lou and Martin glanced at her. Even Sam had opened his eyes, watching her press the buttons to make her call. She winked in his direction, then put the phone on speaker.

Someone picked up at the other end of the line immediately.

"Central Intelligence Agency Headquarters, how may I direct your call?"

"Yeah, hi, I need to speak with Henrietta Marino. This is an emergency."

A few seconds later, a woman's harsh voice answered, "Marino."

"Ms. Marino, not sure if you remember me, it's Alex Hoffmann."

"Oh…I don't have time for this. I'm hanging up."

"No, no, please don't hang up!" Alex pleaded. "Listen, I found flight XA233. In Russia."

"If this is another one of your crazy theories, I promise you this time you'll go to prison and do some serious time," Marino replied dryly.

"No, listen, I am here, right now, in Russia, with the passengers of XA233, about 450 people. We need exfil, now. We're desperate."

The line went silent for a few long seconds.

"Hello?" Alex said, afraid Marino had hung up after all.

"You better be for real," Marino replied. "What do you need?"

"We need a warship rerouted, the *Okinawa*, so we can all go home."

"Send me details, some proof—a picture or something, and hang tight," Marino replied, her voice sounding a tad warmer. "I'll text you my number," she added and then hung up.

"Whew," Alex exhaled. "Now let's hope this works." She checked the clearing sky again, then added, "We need to hit the road, and we need some backup."

"I think I have that covered," Lou replied. "Remember the recon drones we used to get pictures of the silo? Their operators are willing to fly them in here, armed with Hellfire missiles, as air support. They've cleared it through channels using NanoLance connections. The drones are inbound as we speak, but it will take them a while. They're flying in from Hokkaido."

The cabinet of the United States was in session. The members were assembled in the west wing of the White House, in the Cabinet Room, and running behind schedule. President Krassner liked his meetings to start on time and end on time, yet the cabinet members were constantly veering off the agenda.

Twelve people sat around the grand mahogany table, with President Krassner sitting at the center of the table, his back toward the large, arched windows that faced the Rose Garden, flooded in the sweet light of a clear-sky spring morning. The cabinet members had been served coffee in small, delicate china cups, and the staffers had since left the room.

The secretary of commerce frowned, looking disapprovingly around the table, where several sidebar conversations were in full flight, while the president finished flipping through the pages of a brief. As soon as he put down the brief, she cleared her throat.

"We're ready to proceed, Mr. President."

The room, brought to order, fell silent. The only sounds heard were the occasional paper shuffle and the clinking of china, as coffee cups were set back on their delicate saucers.

"Good morning, everyone," Krassner greeted them in his usual manner. "I have one agenda item for today, and that is unemployment reporting."

Krassner, famous for his direct, engaging, blunt style, looked straight at the secretary of labor before proceeding. The man shifted uncomfortably in his seat.

"So, what is it, really?" Krassner continued. "Is 5 percent the real unemployment number in this country? Or is it that only 5 percent of the eligible population is drawing unemployment benefits? If we're going to revisit our immigration policy, I want to know first, how many Americans are truly unable to find work. How many have given up searching, but would gladly rejoin the work force if given the opportunity. Is it five million, or fifty million? I'm definitely not supporting this ridiculous race to undercut the American worker in favor of cheaper workers brought on temporary visas, only to benefit corporate greed. Bring me data, data that makes sense."

Krassner stopped talking, waiting for the secretary of labor to answer.

"Ahem...Mr. President," the secretary of labor replied, "our numbers indicate—"

The Cabinet Room door opened, and an apologetic staffer made his way quickly to the secretary of defense, then whispered something in his ear.

Everyone held their breaths when an urgent message was delivered to the secretary of defense, interrupting a cabinet session no less. Only bad news could be that urgent.

The secretary of defense turned toward the staffer and whispered, "Are you sure?"

The staffer put several photographs printed on glossy paper in front of him, and he reviewed them in less than two seconds. Then he stood abruptly, and approached Krassner.

"Mr. President, if I may..."

"Go ahead," Krassner invited him, intrigued.

"Flight XA233 has been found. In Russia. CIA Director Seiden is on the phone for you. He needs to speak with you immediately."

Murmurs, whispers, and gasps took over the Cabinet Room as the president stepped out, followed by the secretary of defense.

Within seconds, Krassner entered the Oval Office, sat down, and picked up his phone. The secretary of defense continued to stand.

"Director Seiden," Krassner said.

"Mr. President," Seiden greeted him with deference. "We've found Flight XA233, somewhere in eastern Russia. We have a battle group in the area, the USS *Okinawa*, engaged in training exercises with the Japanese Navy. We need your approval to reroute the *Okinawa* to extract the passengers and crew, and the team who found them. We need the *Okinawa* to enter Russian territorial waters and airspace for a couple of hours. We also need permission to open fire if fired upon."

"What's your theory?"

"Terrorist attack, Mr. President. We have proof."

"Congratulations to your team, well done!"

"Umm...sir, it wasn't my team. They are a private investigations team hired by Blake Bernard, whose wife was aboard that flight."

Krassner remained silent for a brief moment.

"I see. All right, I'll give the order. Tell them to hang tight, we're sending in full support. Thank you, Director Seiden."

He hung up the phone and pursed his lips, the short-lived look of disappointment on his face quickly replaced by anger.

"Get me the *Okinawa*, let's bring these people home, right now. I'll deal with the Russians later."

"Yes, sir," the secretary of defense replied.

"Who's the commander?"

"It's Captain Kevin Callahan, sir," he replied, after briefly checking the notes brought by his assistant.

Krassner's frown deepened. He loosened his tie and took off his jacket, then rolled up his sleeves. He shook his head in disbelief, and then continued, swallowing a sigh of frustration.

"After we reroute the *Okinawa*, can you please find out how the hell the entire world is looking for XA233's wreckage in the middle of the Pacific, and a bunch of civilians find it on mainland Russia? Open everything for this mission, all available support. Reroute satellites."

"Umm...yes, sir. They already have satellite support," the secretary of defense replied, after checking his notes again. "We're tapped into their feed."

"Who the hell are these people?"

Every few minutes, Alex looked up at the sky, more and more worried. One after another, myriad stars became visible, as the heavy clouds moved away. A moonless night, pitch-dark, and, within minutes, direct satellite line of sight would be opening up right above them, as the last of the clouds disappeared fast.

The Russians had to have a satellite or two monitoring the operation; one doesn't pull off that kind of endeavor, and then decide to ignore it. It made sense. V would definitely keep his eye on the silo and the status of his op; he was a logical, thorough, resourceful strategist. They were about to have company, she could bet on that. V wasn't going to give up his operation without a fight.

Her radio crackled to life.

"Alpha, Tango One ready for departure."

"Copy that, Tango One, on my way."

That was the code name for the first truck in their escape convoy. Numbered one through nine, the trucks were loaded with people and ready to leave, hotwired by the Bravo teams and driven by passenger volunteers. Each truck had at least one Bravo team member riding in the back, ready to open fire on any attacker. Tango Nine, the last of the convoy, had three Bravos at the back of the truck, and Lou rode with them.

Alex had the passenger seat in Tango One, from where she could help Tango One's driver navigate. She headed there fast, satisfied that all trucks were loaded and ready to leave.

They had found an escape route toward the coast, a curvy, narrow, mountain road meandering forty kilometers or so toward the coastal town of Vanino. Of course, they would never get to Vanino; they couldn't risk it. Vanino, being a coastal town, had to have Russian Coast Guard forces. They couldn't risk being seen and captured. A convoy of nine military trucks loaded with people was not that inconspicuous.

No, they would cross the mountains on the road to Vanino, then veer off that road heading south, taking a road hardly worth being called a road, just to get out of swamp territory and onto hard terrain, where rescue helos could land. The so-called road was more like an unpaved trail, not even visible on maps. But the satellite feeds from DigiWorld confirmed it was there, barely wide enough for the trucks.

Then the trucks would take them to the clearing they had identified via satellite, just about ten kilometers after leaving the paved road to Vanino. She had given those coordinates to Henri Marino as a landing zone for their extraction. It was wide enough, and the terrain was flat and firm. No one had confirmed those coordinates yet, but she couldn't wait any longer. No one had confirmed the exfil mission had been cleared either, but she couldn't afford any doubt. She had to believe they'd be there.

She knew she was asking for a lot...rerouting a US Navy vessel into the territorial waters of Russia was crossing the point of no return to what could potentially read in tomorrow's papers as the start of WW III. Nevertheless, the USS *Okinawa* and its fleet of Super Stallion helicopters were their only chance of survival. *Go, Marino go! Make it happen, girl!*

It wasn't going to be easy. They'd found 434 survivors; 7 people had been killed since XA233 had been hijacked, including the flight's captain. Those trucks held 434 men, women, and children in very poor shape, some wounded badly. There were 434 people who counted on her and the team to take them home safely.

They needed to get going. The sky was almost completely clear.

Satisfied they had everyone loaded on the trucks, Alex hopped into the passenger seat in Tango One and radioed, "This is Alpha in Tango One, ready to go."

One by one, all Tangos confirmed.

The trucks set in motion, going east, their lights on low beam. Their convoy, moving slowly on the curvy road, seemed eerie to her, like moving though an alternate reality. She felt a pang of fear, thinking just how vulnerable they'd be once they entered the stretch of curvy, narrow, mountain road, with no place to turn or take cover if things got ugly. It was the perfect place for an ambush.

She pushed her dark thoughts away, and turned toward the back. Through the opening between the truck's cabin and the cargo hold, she reached out and touched Sam's hand. He lay on the gurney covered in dirty blankets, in and out of consciousness, barely alive. His skin felt ice cold and damp. He was going into shock.

She squeezed his hand.

"Sam? You holding on? We're moving, see? Just a little while longer. Just hold on. Promise me you'll hold on."

Sam didn't reply, didn't even open his eyes. Dr. Adenauer, still by his side, shot her a worried glance as he placed two fingers on Sam's right carotid, feeling for a pulse.

"Please hang on, Sam, please," she whispered. "We're almost there."

Next to him, lying on another gurney, Blake was conscious, although pale and wincing at every bump in the road. Adeline sat crouched next to him, holding his hand with both of hers, while her big, round eyes searched Alex's with unspoken fear glinting in them. The doctors had patched Blake's wound enough to help him survive the journey, but not much more. She locked eyes with Blake, trying to encourage him. He nodded slightly. He was holding on.

A third gurney held an unconscious man; Alex had learned he was a doctor, and the Russians had smashed his ribs to make a point. He was heavily sedated, his vitals monitored closely by an American doctor, Gary Davis.

A short vibration coming from her phone caught her attention. A text message from Tom. It read, "We have you on satellite, from DigiWorld. Godspeed and be safe!"

Her heart swelled. They were not alone. She opened a comm on her radio.

"Lima, this is Alpha."

"Go for Lima," Lou's voice replied, with a little static in the background.

"Lima, Father has visual, says hi."

"Copy, Alpha. Tell him to look wide."

That was a good idea. If the DigiWorld satellite would zoom out a little, they would be able to see if anyone approached their convoy, by air or by ground, and give them the heads up.

She texted Tom. "Will try. Go wide with visual, keep us posted."

The truck was slow, going sixteen, maybe twenty kilometers per hour. The road was bumpy, making the wounded in the back groan in pain.

She craned her head out of the window and looked back at their convoy snaking through the wooded mountain road. The other trucks were holding close, none had straggled. She checked the sky again; it was all clear. If Tom had eyes on them, so could anyone else. So could V. Their headlights in the perfectly dark forest made them easy to spot from above, even with the dense tree foliage cover.

She felt adrenaline hit her gut. Something was wrong. Behind them, the sky was slightly less dark. At times flashes of light ripped through the hazy darkness, sending long shadows everywhere. Something, someone was coming.

Her phone chimed again, at the same time Lou's voice came alive on her radio.

"Alpha, this is Lima. We have company."

She checked the new text message from Tom.

"Multiple armored vehicles approaching fast from behind. Five Ansyr, two BTR-80 armored personnel carriers, two trucks carrying troops."

She pressed the radio button fitted on her wrist and replied, "Copy, Lima. Get ready. We have nine miles left to go until we turn south. Multiple armored vehicles inbound, Ansyrs, BTR-80s, troops. We can't outrun them."

Ansyr was the latest Russian assault vehicle. It was bad news. The Ansyr was an armored vehicle that could go a maximum speed of 120 kilometers per hour for 800 kilometers without refueling, and could carry three troops and a heavy-machine gun. The vehicles would have no difficulty catching up with the trucks. There was nothing on those trucks that could stop an Ansyr.

"Copy, Alpha. Ready to engage," Lou replied, not a trace of hesitation in his voice.

"Bravo teams, we have company," she added, although all teams had heard her exchange with Lou.

"Tango Two ready," she heard Martin's voice confirm, followed by the rest of the trucks.

Yeah, ready, she thought, clenching her jaws. *As we'll ever be.* A bunch of people armed with MP5s, Tavors, and handguns, maybe a couple grenades, against Russian armored assault vehicles, and who knows how many soldiers. Not a fair fight, but she wasn't going to shy away from it. They'd come here to do a job, damn it, and they were going to do it. They were going to take these people home, no matter what.

Their only strategic advantage was the narrow, mountain road. The assault vehicles could only approach them one by one if they kept on moving. With a little bit of luck and some decent gunmanship from the Bravos in Tango Nine, they could take them out one by one. Or at least she hoped so, considering the Ansyrs were fully armored.

"Step on it a little," she asked the driver. The man nodded and increased the speed.

Alex looked behind her, at the people riding in the truck. They were scared, packed closely together, the way gazelles gather when lions are circling the herd. Most of them had their eyes on her, looking for hope, for safety, for a way home out of that dark, endlessly miserable hell. She had to say something to them.

She took a deep breath, and then spoke into her radio, while maintaining eye contact with the people on her truck.

"All Tangos, this is Alpha."

"Go for Tangos," Lou replied.

"All Tangos, please repeat my message to your passengers."

She cleared her voice, then continued.

"Things are going to get a bit ugly," she started saying, cringing at the way it sounded. "The Russians are catching up with us. Please know we'll do everything it takes to get you back home to safety. We have air support on the way, and we *will* make it. This is my promise to you, to all of you."

She checked the back of the convoy, and noticed the sky was lighting up closer behind them. The Russians were getting near.

She spoke into her radio again, while her right hand clutched the Tavor's handle tighter.

"Lima, this is Alpha. ETA on air support?"

The radio went silent for a little while, and then static picked up before an unfamiliar voice chimed in.

"Alpha, this is Firefly Nest. ETA is sixteen minutes. We have you on remote visual. Hang tight."

Captain Kevin Callahan woke up with a start. His XO knocked twice on his stateroom door, then walked right in, not waiting for permission. What the hell was going on?

His current assignment was a tricky one. He was leading battle group *Okinawa* into a series of tactical naval exercises off the coast of Japan, in collaboration with the Japanese Navy. As captain of USS *Okinawa*, a Wasp-class amphibious assault ship, he was the commander of the entire battle group: one Arleigh-Burke class destroyer, two Freedom-class and one Independence-class littoral combat ships (LCS), two GHOST super-cavitating stealth ships, and several support vessels.

But that wasn't the tricky part of his current assignment. The tactical exercises were going well, and the Japanese Navy was a worthy partner with naval strategy valor. However, they rarely operated more than fifty miles away from Russia's territorial waters. Most days they'd come as close as ten miles, irritating the crap out of the Russian Coast Guard, their vessel commanders, and everyone else for that matter.

Naturally, the Russians were worried, knowing the *Okinawa*, a Wasp-class, landing helicopter dock (LHD), amphibious, assault ship, essentially an aircraft carrier for helicopters, deployed and maneuvered so close to their coast. The *Okinawa* carried almost two thousand Marines aboard, in addition to the ship's complement of almost twelve hundred. Her own fleet of seven Super Stallion helicopters, four MV-22 Osprey aircraft, four Super Cobra attack helos, and six Harrier II attack aircraft packed a serious, worrisome punch. Her stern gate could drop and launch additional armed landing hovercraft, challenging the enemy with its versatility. Hence, it was not surprising that the *Okinawa* and its battle group made the Russians wary, anxious, and irritable. Yet, while she was executing joint tactical exercises with the Japanese, staying just barely outside of Russian territorial waters, there was little, if anything, the Russians could do.

The Russians had two powerful radar stations, tracking every move the ship made. One station stood high on a cliff near a lighthouse called Red Partisan, and the other was farther south, right on the coast, near Terney. Those two radar installations could track everything, from surface vessels to air traffic. The facilities were heavily guarded, and most likely were humming with intense activity every time one of the battle group ships started her engines, or lifted her anchors.

They had received significant diplomatic pressures to take their joint exercises farther out into the Pacific as a sign of goodwill, but Washington and Tokyo had held equally strong. As long as battle group *Okinawa* was not entering Russian territorial waters, there was nothing Russia could do about it other than foam at the mouth.

Before Captain Callahan had finally gone to bed for the night, sometime after midnight, his battle group was sailing around Wakkanai heading east, just five miles off the coast of Japan, but only a few miles away from the territorial waters of Sakhalin. He hoped his XO didn't bring the news that someone had made a mistake and had veered into Russia's waters by accident; there'd be hell to pay.

He sat on the side of his bed, rubbing his eyes.

"What is it, XO?"

"I have the president for you, sir."

Sleep still fogging his brain, Callahan asked, "You have who?"

"The president of the United States, sir, on encrypted voice comm."

All his remaining brain fog instantly dissipated under the wave of adrenaline that hit every nerve in his body. The president? Calling him? That had never happened before, in his entire career. It had to be serious.

He hopped to his feet and threw his working blues on within seconds. Then he ran to the bridge, followed closely by his XO.

"Captain on the bridge," one of the lieutenants announced, standing at attention.

Callahan went straight for the communications desk. He put on the headset handed him by his communications officer, cleared his throat a little, then signaled to the young man to open the line.

"Mr. President, sir," he greeted. "This is Captain Kevin Callahan, Battle Group *Okinawa*, off the coast of Japan."

"Captain, we have a situation on our hands, and you're the only one who can help," President Krassner said, skipping the pleasantries and going straight to the core of the issue.

"Sir?"

"Flight XA233, the flight that was presumed crashed in the Pacific, was in fact hijacked by Russian terrorists. A small American team found the plane and was able to free the passengers and crew being held as hostages. They're heading toward the coast, taking heavy fire, right in the area where you are now. There are nearly 450 people, most of them American. They need your help, captain.

We have to bring them home."

Captain Callahan felt sweat beads forming at the roots of his hair. He was being asked to commit an act of war against Russia.

"Mr. President, sir, are you authorizing me to enter Russian sovereign air space with armed military aircraft, engage the enemy, and exfiltrate the rescued people?"

"Precisely. If it can be avoided, I would prefer not to start World War III with Russia over this, but do whatever is necessary to bring those people home. I am 100 percent behind whatever you decide to do, captain. Just get them home."

"Yes, sir," Captain Callahan acknowledged the orders.

"We're sending maps, satellite imagery, and coordinates as we speak. What else do you need?"

"Nothing else, sir. It's an honor to be chosen for such a mission, sir. We'll get the job done; we won't let you down. You can count on us to bring our people home."

"I know that, captain. Good luck!"

The connection ended, leaving Callahan with two parallel ridges of deep worry on his forehead. An incursion like this typically took months of preparation, of careful planning. He had a few minutes, not more.

"XO," he called.

"Sir?"

"Get all Stallion crews ready, two Harriers, four Cobras. Arm and fuel them, have them ready on deck. Let's look at the map."

He walked toward the navigation desk, followed closely by the XO, the weapons officer, and the flight operations officer.

"Get me a satellite feed for the rescue location. How do we communicate with them?"

The XO checked the recently decrypted communication.

"We have their comm frequencies and their sat phones. We have codes to tap into their satellite support, sir. They've suggested LZ coordinates for extraction."

"Put it on the screen," Callahan said.

The XO typed quickly some numbers, and a red dot appeared on the regional map. Green dots marked the locations of the USS *Okinawa* and its battle group. A dotted line marked the limit of Russia's territorial waters, and two red triangles marked the locations of the Russian radar stations.

On a separate screen, an officer brought up a live satellite feed, showing a slow-moving convoy of trucks taking fire from Russian assault vehicles. It was still dark; the feed barely showed anything other than flashes of light accompanying whatever projectiles were fired and briefly illuminating the convoy and its attackers. A vehicle had been left behind, burning on the side of the road. Some projectiles were fired at the enemy, hitting the targets, and causing explosive damage, but Callahan couldn't tell who was firing what at whom. There wasn't any time to figure out what was going on with the convoy; he needed to act.

"Switch to infrared and get me a sitrep," he ordered one of the lieutenants.

Then he went back to the comm desk and grabbed the microphone that opened channels to every station on the vessel.

"All hands, this is the captain speaking. We are now at condition Delta. This is not a drill. We have been tasked with the rescue of about 450 civilians from behind the Russian border. We will engage in immediate combat action."

He hung up the microphone, and a second later an officer grabbed it and called, "Battle stations. Battle stations. This is not a drill." Then he hit a button, and a familiar alarm went on for a few seconds.

Callahan went back to the digital map and studied it intently for a little while.

"This is what we're going to do," he said. "We need a diversion, and we have to take out these two radar stations."

"Diversion, sir?" the XO asked.

"There are just too many Russian vessels and helicopters patrolling the area. If they see us too early and they send in their MiGs, we won't be able to pull the civilians out; we're finished. There's an air base on Sakhalin holding at least four MiGs, only minutes away in flight time; we have to move lightning fast." He stopped for a second, frowning deeper at the digital map. "I'll ask Admiral Tochigi for a favor. If one of his battleships here, off the coast of... umm... Mashike, should send an SOS, and we deploy our group for search-and-rescue operations, all the Russians will gather there to keep an eye on us. We'll head out there with the entire battle group, but right before we'd have to turn south, here," he added, pointing at the northern tip of the Japanese island of Hokkaido, where Wakkanai was, "the *Okinawa* will claim engine trouble, and stay behind with only the GHOST vessels and some armed RHIBs."

"Sir, if I may?" the XO asked.

"Yes, what is it? the captain answered.

"We'd be vulnerable with only two GHOSTS; we'd be sitting ducks. Our helos would be gone, our escort too. The Russians could take advantage of the situation we created."

"We'll keep two Harriers and a Cobra. But that's why we'll start by sending a couple of SEALs to take out those radar stations. Send out a Cobra with two SEAL teams armed with RPGs. Let's take those radars out first. This will give us a small window of darkness to get to the coast and out again with the civilians."

His XO's face lit up, as he understood the captain's strategy. A faint smile fluttered on his lips.

"Sending SEALs now, sir."

"Good. As soon as they confirm the radar stations are out, send in all seven Super Stallions to the LZ, with two Cobras and two Harriers as escorts. Confirm extraction with the ground team, confirm LZ coordinates. Get their ETA for the LZ."

"We're 250 klicks from the LZ. Stallions will take almost one hour to get there."

Callahan frowned again.

"Let's synchronize with the rescue team on the ground. We shouldn't remain in Russian airspace one second longer than strictly necessary."

One of the lieutenants approached them.

"I have the satellite sitrep, sir. The convoy has drone support."

"Drones? Who's flying them?"

"Unknown, sir. But the Russians are sending in helos. Several Russian armored vehicles are still engaged in battle with the convoy, and three helos are approaching from the north. They should reach the convoy within thirty minutes or so."

Callahan clenched his fists in a rare display of anger.

"Damn it," he muttered under his breath.

Their exfil plan needed more than an hour to execute; more likely two.

It was hell. Weapons fire and explosions lighting up the sky, blinding her night vision, and deafening her. She was still riding in the first truck, leading the convoy. Alex put her head out of the window and looked behind her, at the rear truck, Tango Nine, engaged in fierce battle with the Russian assault vehicle, and losing.

She heard bullets flying through the air, smelled the heavy scent of burnt gunpowder, and heard the bullets hit trees and rocks, just a couple of feet away. Her heart pounded in her chest, and she breathed heavily, almost panting, not even aware of the sharp pain felt in her sternum with every breath.

Oh, my God, what the hell are we going to do? Alex thought, watching in disbelief just how ineffective the fire laid down by the Bravos and Lou was. The armored vehicle behind Tango Nine kept on coming, catching up with every second. All their bullets ricocheted off the Ansyr's armor, not even slowing it down.

Then, suddenly, the Ansyr blew up, engulfed in a ball of fire.

"Yeah, baby," she couldn't help but cheer. She pressed the button for her radio, yelling to cover the battle noise.

"Lima, this is Alpha, do you copy?"

"Go for Lima," Lou replied, barely intelligible over the heavy firing.

"What did it?" Alex asked.

"Grenade," he replied, "under its belly."

She craned her head out of the window some more, swallowing hard, forcing herself to ignore the sound of bullets flying through the air. One Ansyr blown to hell, but four more were coming, and behind them, even more trouble. The next Ansyr in line on the narrow road, closest to Tango Nine, was firing continuously, getting awfully close to the limit where their large caliber rounds would start tearing into Tango Nine, killing everyone in it.

Then she had an idea. She pressed her comm link button. "Lima, sever a tree, a big one, copy?"

"Alpha, did you say tree?"

"Block the road, Lima, block the damn road!"

"Copy," Lou confirmed, then, before releasing the comm button, Alex heard him give instructions to the Bravos with him. She saw Tango Nine slow, almost to a stop.

A few seconds later, a huge, majestic oak fell sideways, barely missing Tango Nine, and blocked the road.

"Great job, Lima, now catch up," she radioed.

"Copy," Lou replied, more intelligible now that the heavy firing had ceased and the Russian armored vehicles had stopped their pursuit.

"How much time did it buy us?" Alex asked, smiling involuntarily as she noticed the expression on the Tango One driver's face. The man was grinning widely, despite the tension in the air.

The radio crackled static for a short while, then Lou's voice came through.

"Not that much. Maybe five, ten minutes at the most."

The driver's grin vanished.

"What?"

"They can cut through it, Alpha, just like we did, only they have bigger caliber bullets."

"Copy," she replied, unable to hide her disappointment.

They needed a break...a bigger break, not five minutes. This wasn't going to cut it.

She spoke into the radio again.

"Firefly Nest, do you copy?"

"Copy, Alpha. ETA is two minutes."

"Copy, Nest. Step on it." Then she turned to the driver at her left and added, "You too."

The truck accelerated, bouncing heavily on the poorly maintained road as it hit potholes, scattered rocks, and fallen tree branches.

Alex allowed herself a moment to breathe, and leaned against her backrest with her eyes closed. Maybe they had a chance after all with help from the drones. She'd seen them in action before. Each UCAV could carry up to 16 Hellfire missiles, and their targeting was deadly accurate; they were incredible weapons, a thing of beauty when they were on your side in battle.

She turned toward the back, to check on Sam and Blake. Blake locked eyes with her, encouraging her with a quick nod. Sam lay unconscious, the German doctor checking his vitals every few minutes. The doctor's pursed lips and deep frown made her stomach churn in fear for her friend's life. She reached and grabbed Sam's hand, holding it tight. It was still cold to the touch and damp. *Hang in there, Sam, please! We're gonna make it, you'll see. Just hang in there!*

Her phone's vibration caught her attention. She had a new text message, from Henri Marino. It read, "Eagle Base is your ride home. Good luck!"

Yes! They were coming! Way to go, Marino! And thank you, Mr. President!

Now all they had to do was get to the extraction point, and stay alive until they came.

She spoke into the radio to share the news.

"All call signs, this is Alpha. We have a ride home. Do you copy?"

She knew they copied, because instant cheering erupted from all trucks. Some honked their horns and flashed their lights, forgetting for a second they were in the middle of a battle. Knowing they were not alone, knowing that someone was going to come for them gave them hope, a much-needed shot in the arm for everyone.

They weren't out of the woods yet, literally and figuratively speaking. She saw the lights from the Russian armored vehicles starting to approach again; they'd only delayed them by four minutes or so.

Her radio crackled, then a new, unfamiliar voice spoke, patched in via her sat phone.

"All call signs, this is Eagle Base. Do you copy?"

She replied cheerfully. "Eagle Base, Alpha. Copy loud and clear."

"Alpha, coordinates for pickup confirmed. ETA sixty minutes. What's your status?"

She hesitated before responding. How could she summarize in a couple of words the desperate situation they were in?

"Eagle Nest, this is Alpha. We're precarious and low on resources, taking fire. More bogeys inbound, both air and ground. Not sure we'll last sixty minutes, but we'll try."

She released the comm button, waiting for Eagle's response. A few seconds of radio silence ensued, then the voice replied, "Copy, Alpha, good luck."

She couldn't help a bitter chuckle hearing Eagle's encouragement. Too many people wished them good luck; that meant their situation actually needed it. Every bit of luck possible.

Alex looked out the window toward the end of the convoy; the headlights were approaching fast, and the Russian armored Ansyrs were resuming their fire.

Then, from somewhere above her head, she heard a whoosh, followed by an explosion. A drone had fired a missile, blowing up the Ansyr closest to them.

"About bloody time, Firefly," she radioed.

"Roger that, Alpha," the drone operator replied, barely intelligible. "Alpha, we have an issue. It's dark, and you're under forest cover. We can't distinguish between you and them enough to fire safely. We can only target them if they're firing at you."

Oh, crap... "Copy that, working on a fix," she replied.

She thought for a few second, then pressed the radio button again. "Lima, can you paint a target?"

"Affirmative," Lou's voice confirmed.

"All Tangos except Tango One, kill your beams. Lima, paint the fuckers."

A few seconds later, the only lights still flickering in the darkness of the forest were the Russian Ansyrs, marked red by several laser spots.

The drones didn't waste any time. Two missiles were fired and both reached their targets, blowing to bits two Russian armored vehicles. Only one Ansyr was left, followed by the BTR-80s and the trucks carrying troops.

Before a drone could take that last Ansyr out, it fired a large caliber projectile, but missed Tango Nine. The road was curved, so the projectile hit the rear right wheels of one of the other trucks, sending it in the air, sliding on its side, and screeching to a stop. The trucks braked hard, barely avoiding it, and the rest of the convoy stopped.

The radio crackled and then the voice of one of the backup team members screamed.

"Alpha, this it Tango Five. We're hit! We're hit!"

"Stop the truck and kill your lights," she instructed her driver.

She jumped off the truck and ran to Tango Five, just as people were starting to come out of it. Some were just dazed, shocked, while others were wounded and needed help.

One of the Bravos approached her.

"The road is blocked," he said. We can only use the first four trucks, and we can't fit everyone in them.

She frowned, thinking hard. The truck was huge, effectively blocking the narrow road. But they had manpower, the power of many.

"All Tangos, instruct your able passengers to climb down and help us push Tango Five out of the way, and then they are to go back to their trucks. All passengers in Tango Five and Tango Nine will have to travel in other trucks. The civilians are too exposed in Tango Nine. Only Bravos in Tango Nine. Copy?"

Another drone, flying low above them, shot a missile, and took out the last Russian Ansyr that had just opened fire.

Within a minute, Tango Five was pushed to the side of the road, where it fell into a ravine and exploded on impact on the rocks below.

Everyone rushed to the trucks, and, one by one, the Tangos confirmed by radio they were ready to continue on their escape route.

Alex took her seat in Tango One, and checked the GPS. Only a few more minutes until they turned south, heading for the LZ. She noticed a message from Tom, arrived just seconds earlier. It read, "Russian helos closing in, ETA two minutes."

Really? That was not happening...It was about time they caught a goddamn break. She felt tears of frustration burn her eyes. There was no way they could take on three armed helicopters attacking them, drones or no drones. They were low on ammo, the drones were busy with the rest of the Russians catching up from behind; it was just hopeless.

She directed the driver to turn right, and leave the main road. Maybe their chances would be better if they dumped the trucks and scattered everyone in the forest, to continue to the LZ on foot. But they had a lot of wounded, and some of the people couldn't walk. Some of the people had been shot; no, that wasn't going to work.

As they turned, she saw an explosion toward the coast; a large ball of fire erupted, illuminating everything around it for a short while, then continuing to burn. She texted Tom, who watched them via satellite, "What was the explosion ENE of us?"

His reply came in immediately. It read, "Your friends took out a radar station called Red Partisan. All good."

That was logical. Probably Eagle Nest preferred radar darkness to having to fight the entire Russian Army over their rescue.

Then her radio came to life again.

"All call signs, this is Eagle Nest. We see three enemy helos approaching fast. Moving to intercept."

"Copy that, Eagle, you saved the day."

Maybe they'd caught that break after all.

They drove south on an unpaved, bumpy road that followed the edge of the forest. Behind them, the drones still engaged the remaining Russian vehicles, and Alex had counted two more explosions since they had taken the turn onto the unpaved road. Probably they were finishing off the remaining trucks filled with Russian soldiers.

She swallowed uncomfortably, thinking for a minute of all the Russians who were losing their lives that night. Then she thought of what might have happened to all the passengers and crew if they'd been recaptured by the Russians. That was what war was all about...One had to kill to survive. They hadn't started that war; the people who took XA233 had started it. V had started it. She and her team were there to end it.

She checked her GPS again, seeing they were approaching on the left, the flat, rocky clearing she had chosen for the landing zone. They were there...they had made it.

Now all they had to do was survive for another forty minutes or so.

She spoke into her radio.

"All Tangos, we're here. Instruct your passengers to disembark, walk south for a few hundred yards, not more, and take cover behind the tree line."

"Copy that, Alpha," Lou's voice responded, almost cheerfully. Hope was a wonderful thing.

She hopped off the truck and stretched her legs, feeling the tension ease a little. She looked toward the rest of the trucks, and nodded, satisfied, seeing how they arrived, one by one, killing their lights and cutting their engines.

The distant roar of jet engines caught her attention, and she looked toward the northern sky. In the distance, she could see the sky light up occasionally, as Eagle Nest's forces engaged the enemy.

She climbed in the back of Tango One and handed Blake her phone.

"We're here, we've made it. We have a ride home. Tell your pilot to get out."

Dylan Bishop ended the brief conversation with his boss with a long sigh of relief. He wasn't very brave; he had to admit. He was just a guy who liked to fly planes, nothing more. His charismatic nature, combined with his excellent record of achievement as a pilot had gained him the cushy, generously compensated job of personal pilot for the banking magnate, Blake Bernard.

Cushy until now, that was. Mr. Bernard's typical outings were mostly business trips to a variety of American cities, or, in some cases, leisure outings to destinations like Ibiza or Paris. But Russia? With 500 pounds of guns and ammo onboard? That was scary.

Dylan shuddered. He was glad it was over; he wasn't cut for that kind of stuff. His boss had told him to get out of there, and he wasn't going to waste another minute. Deciding on the quickest, most superficial preflight check of his career, he hopped out of the plane and quickly circled it, removing the wheel blocks and the air intake covers. He moved fast, feeling the tingle of fear chilling his blood and creeping up his spine. He ran his hands quickly on the wings' edge of attack, making sure no dents had appeared. Nothing could be wrong with the plane anyway; he hadn't left it for a minute since they had arrived, too terrified to set foot outside the eerily quiet hangar. No one had even come close to it since they had landed.

The Phenom had enough fuel to make it to Japan, and was ready for takeoff. He closed and locked the aircraft's door, securing it for departure. Then he took his seat, buckled his harness, and did a quick instruments check before starting the engines. He smiled with relief as the engines revved to life. Everything was going to be fine; he was way past ready to leave that godforsaken, creepy place.

Unseen, engulfed in the darkness shrouding the hangar, a man sneaked quietly toward the landing gear with a block of plastic explosive in his hand. He almost swore aloud when the plane's engines came to life, startling him. He crouched lower, and nearly fell when the plane started rolling. He was running out of time.

The plane started moving faster. He attached the PVV-5A explosive to the wheel strut while walking next to it. Then running next to it. He barely managed to roll the tape around the block of explosive a couple of times, and inserted the detonating pin while wholeheartedly running right behind the Phenom's wheel, panting hard, barely able to keep up with the accelerating plane.

Then he stopped running, breathing hard; the job was done. In a few minutes, the PVV would detonate, taking the Phenom out of the sky in a raging blaze of fire. That was his plan, and he never failed.

Just as the Phenom took off, the poorly attached PVV block fell off the plane's landing gear and hit the ground a few yards from where the man stood, short of breath, watching the plane soar. Upon impact, the explosive detonated, sending pieces of burning concrete high in the air, and leaving a smoldering crater behind. Khabarovsk Airport was gone.

The Phenom surged and retracted its landing gear, already too far from the explosion to be impacted in any way. Immediately after that, Dylan changed the heading, eager to leave Russian airspace as soon as possible. As the plane turned, he noticed the blaze on the ground, where the airport had been.

"Holy shit," he said, wiping the sweat off his forehead with a trembling hand, "that's what I'd call a timely departure."

Alex walked along the tree line, heading back toward Tango One. That's where the wounded were, and that's where she wanted to go, to check on Sam and Blake. She started to feel how tired she was. She had difficulties breathing; a strong, sharp pain in her sternum keeping her from filling her lungs with air.

Probably most of the excess adrenaline and cortisol in her blood were gone by now. The wonderful chemicals that kept her body focused on survival and blocked her pain receptors were dropping to more normal levels, allowing her to feel the hurt from her injuries. Her head pounded, the dull throbbing centered around the cut on her forehead. Her chest hurt with every breath, probably a couple of cracked ribs were to blame for that. She vaguely remembered the explosion at the hangar where they'd found the missing plane; it felt like centuries had passed since then.

Lou startled her, appearing out of nowhere and hugging her hard, lifting her off the ground.

"Hey, boss, told ya you're gonna be great at this, didn't I?"

Martin, the Bravo team lead, watched with amusement.

"He's right, you know," Martin acknowledged with a quick grin.

"Put me down," she said, fighting to break free. Unknowingly, Lou's hug was hurting her badly, putting pressure on her ribs and sternum.

He let her go immediately, alerted by the urgency in her voice, scrutinizing her.

"You're hurt," he said, his half-question turning into a statement. "Damn...I didn't know."

"It's OK, Lou, I'll live. We've got some stuff we need to do, all right? I need your help."

"Shoot," he replied.

"We need to make sure we're not leaving anyone behind. The wounded have to leave in the first helo out of here. We'll be in the last." She thought for a second, feeling more and more pressure in the chest as she struggled with breathing and talking at the same time. "Martin, can your men count everyone who gets aboard the evac helos?"

"Yes, ma'am. What's the total headcount we need to account for?"

A long sigh escaped from her lips, interrupted by another sharp pang of pain in her chest. Seven had died before they could be rescued...Five more, shot by the Russians on their way here. She did the math in her head, then replied, a wave of sadness overwhelming her.

"We're down to 429, that's all that's left—429 civilians, plus 14 Bravos, and the 4 of us. That would be 447."

Martin looked down for a second, then replied, "Twelve Bravos, ma'am. Only twelve left."

She looked at him, feeling a renewed sensation of overwhelming sadness and frustration. She reached out and touched his arm.

"I am so sorry, Martin, so sorry..."

"Thank you, ma'am. This is what happens in our line of work. At least it was for a good cause. I am proud to have served with you and your team, and so were they."

She nodded her silent appreciation, confirmed the final headcount of 445 with Martin, and then she resumed walking toward Tango One, looking for Sam.

There he was, lying on his back on the gurney, probably unconscious. The tall German doctor was by his side, keeping a close eye on his vitals. She crouched on the ground next to Sam's gurney, shooting the doctor a glance of gratitude for the care and attention he had provided to Sam. Then she reached out and grabbed Sam's frozen hand, holding it tight with hers, and whispering gently words of encouragement.

"We're here, Sam, just hold on, we're here. You're taking the first flight out, going straight into one of the best trauma centers on this side of the world."

"Hey, kiddo..." he whispered with difficulty.

"Sam!" She sprung to her knees, her heart soaring. She kissed him on the forehead with a loud smooch. He was going to be all right.

"Yeah, kiddo, it's me," he replied, faintly. "Did you find your man, V?"

She let out a groan of frustration. "No, Sam, no trace of the bastard."

"Any proof, anything?"

"None, Sam, not a trace," she admitted after a second of hesitation. "Nothing. But I *know* it was him, I just know it."

"You'll find him, I'm sure..." he added, then closed his eyes again, exhausted. "Look what you've done here today. You can do anything, kiddo, anything you set your mind to do."

"Shh..." Alex whispered, not letting go of his hand. "Don't talk. Just rest. I'm right here."

They remained quiet for a few minutes, one almost unconscious, and the other deep in her thoughts. Yes, not a single shred of evidence tying V to yet another terrorist attack of unprecedented boldness. None of the captured

Russians had any idea about anyone leading operations other than Bogdanov. As for Bogdanov, the Bravos had taken him out before she'd had a chance to interrogate him. But the Bravos weren't to blame. They had operated by the rules of antiterrorism engagement in a hostage situation. People's lives come first, safety second, intel third. This time, they never made it to third.

The pilot, roughed up by the Bravos and tied up with plastic cuffs, awaited his fate almost indifferently, a few yards away. She didn't hold high hopes to extract any intel from him. V was too smart for that; he wouldn't have engaged the pilot personally. To make things worse, the moment they'd set foot on the *Okinawa*, he would be placed under arrest, and she would lose all access to him. After all, she was just a civilian, operating without any official sanction.

That's why she had no intel whatsoever. She had nothing on V. *Damn it to hell...and back...*The slippery bastard managed to stay hidden again. She had nothing, no evidence, but she believed more than ever that it had been him all along.

"Sam?" she called quietly.

"Uh-huh," he mumbled.

"What do you think is going to happen? Did we just start World War III?"

"Nah...The Russians will issue a statement," he replied, speaking slowly, with difficulty, making her regret she asked. "They'll say it wasn't sanctioned and apologize. Then we, the Americans, will issue a statement and apologize for entering their airspace. It's all politics, kiddo...no one really wants to go to war."

"How about us? Will we go to jail? We did so many illegal things today I can't even count."

"Nah...the public wouldn't go for it, and we have more than four hundred witnesses on our side. No jail for us."

"Good. Good to know," she replied, feeling a little relief. "Now hush...don't talk anymore."

The sound of multiple helicopters approaching was the first sign that help had finally arrived. Then she saw their dark silhouettes, barely visible against the very early dawn on the eastern horizon, as numerous helicopters approached. Their evac transport was finally there.

The radio came on.

"All call signs, this is Eagle Nest. We have visual on you."

"Eagle Nest, this is Alpha, copy. You're a sight for sore eyes, Eagle Nest."

Alex caught a different sound, coming from the north. Nothing was supposed to come from there.

"All call signs, maintain cover. We have inbound bogeys." Eagle Nest's voice sounded worried, almost surprised.

Several Russian helicopters appeared out of nowhere, firing at the trucks, and blowing a few of them up. *They must have flown low on the river, escaping detection, and sneaking up on them from behind,* Alex thought. *But if they are here, why isn't the entire Russian army? Sakhalin has a huge contingent of air, ground, and naval forces. We should be already dead by now.*

Then she remembered Sam's weak voice, whispering, "They'll say it wasn't sanctioned." What if it wasn't? What if V was not acting officially, under Russia's authority? What if he's a rogue player?

A few of Eagle's approaching fleet of helos engaged the Russians, but a drone was the first one to score, sending a Hellfire missile whooshing through the dim dawn light. It ripped through one of the targets, blowing it up in mid-air. An Osprey approached from the left, surprising another one of the Russian bogeys, and took it out with a long round of shots fired at the bogey's tail rotor from its belly gun. The remaining Russian helicopter turned around and tried to bug out, but exploded when a missile fired from a Cobra hit it center mass. The explosion sent flying pieces of debris toward their location, making the people scream and crouch close to the ground. Alex covered Sam with her own body, shielding him from the flying, smoldering debris.

As soon as the sound of the last explosion died down, the approaching heavy transport helicopters became more noticeable. Their rotors spun with a low-pitched sound, and their light-gray, elegant silhouettes contoured in formation against the early dawn.

"All call signs, this is Eagle Nest. Get ready. Move fast. The area is heating up, we have to go."

She let go of Sam's hand, and two men carried the gurney to the nearest Super Stallion with the rest of the wounded.

The individuals ran toward the approaching helos, and as soon as the Stallions landed, they climbed aboard, assisted and counted by the Bravos, not wasting a single minute.

"Let's go, boss," Lou said, grabbing her arm and taking her toward the last Stallion. "Time to go home."

Alex looked around, taking in the details of the early dawn battlefield, still smoldering here and there. Some Stallions had taken off already; others were almost full, getting ready to go. She had nothing...not a trace that could lead to V, nothing whatsoever.

Lou didn't let go of her arm, leading her to the remaining Super Stallion at a running pace. The few remaining people were already aboard; the two of them were the last ones left on the ground.

As she approached the helicopter, she looked up and saw the clear sky, the sky from where DigiWorld's satellites had watched over them and their mission, sending them valuable tactical information. The sky from where V would have kept a satellite eye on his operations.

She couldn't leave, not yet.

She hopped aboard the helo, then asked the pilot, yelling to make herself heard, "You got any flares?"

"Huh?"

"Flares, got any?"

"Yeah, over there," the pilot replied, pointing at a large flare bag secured against a wall mount.

Without hesitating, she grabbed the bag of flares and jumped off the helo, yelling over the sound of the rotors, "Give me a minute, OK?"

With the corner of her eye she caught a glimpse of consternated Lou, his jaw dropped, signaling to Martin and the pilot to wait.

She ran a hundred feet or so away from the helicopter, then lit the first flare and put it on the ground. One by one, she lit nine flares, spacing them several feet apart from one another, and placing them in a V pattern. The V, marked by brightly burning red flares, was clearly visible and distinguishable by anyone watching her via satellite.

She looked up toward the sky, where the satellites would be watching intently. She couldn't see anything, but she didn't really expect to. She tilted her head a little, smiled, and made a wide, inviting gesture toward the sky. *Come on, you son of a bitch*, she thought, *take the bait!*

Then she ran toward the helo as fast as she could, hearing its rotors revving faster and faster as she approached it. She hopped aboard, taking Lou's hand and sat down next to him, catching her breath.

The Stallion took off and immediately increased speed. She relaxed a little; they were finally going home.

Lou leaned into her side, screaming in her ear to cover the rotor's noise.

"What the hell were you doing down there?"

She looked out the window. From their increasing altitude, the red V stood out clearly against the dark landscape.

"Calling him out," she replied.

"For Christ's sake, Alex, this is not a game!"

"Ahh, spare me, Lou. You guys don't even believe he's behind this anyway. I'm not even sure you believe he exists. So, tell me, what's the harm, really?"

Vitaliy Myatlev hadn't moved from his chair the entire night, or day by Moscow's time zone. His bloodshot eyes, transfixed, glued to the monitors, watched in disbelief how his entire operation was falling apart.

For hours, he watched powerlessly how these strangers, a handful of people, thoroughly destroyed everything he had carefully built. The most secret of his operations, buried deep in the Russian far east, exposed, blown away in just a few hours. How the hell did that happen?

He barked orders every now and then, sending reinforcements, and Ivan rushed to execute them with increasing reluctance. Ivan wasn't an idiot; he knew very well that all people exposed to his boss's top-secret operation would have to be eliminated. His Spetsnaz background still fueled loyalties to Russian armed forces, loyalties that sometimes stood in the way.

And yet, no matter how many reinforcements they had sent, how many armored vehicles and how many aircraft, these strangers took them out one by one. Drones, appeared out of nowhere, fired countless missiles, annihilating them.

He had lost...again. This time, there'd be hell to pay.

On the screens, in the early light of dawn, he watched a fleet of American helicopters land. His face a sickly shade of pale, his jaw clenched so hard it hurt, and his fists white-knuckled in anger, he could do nothing but watch powerlessly as every single person was airlifted away.

Then something caught his attention. Someone was lighting flares in a pattern, laying them on the ground. He watched petrified, through dilated pupils, as the flares lined up one after another to form the letter V.

His blood instantly turned to ice, and adrenaline kicked him in the gut, setting off familiar alarm bells. He zoomed in the satellite feed just in time to see clearly the woman who just finished lighting the flares. He saw her turn her face toward him, staring him directly in the eye through the monitor, as if she were in the room with him. He felt her eyes drill into the depths of his heart, making him shudder. Then she waved at him, smiling, as if she knew he was there, observing.

Shocked, he pushed his chair away from the desk and sprang to his feet, pacing nervously.

"Motherfucker," Myatlev swore loudly, his voice raspy and strangulated with fear and anxiety. How could they know he'd be there, watching? How could *she* know? Who betrayed him?

Then he approached the desk where the satellite monitors were installed, and slammed both his fists against the shiny, cherry-wood surface, making the video equipment rattle.

"So, it's personal, huh? Alex Hoffmann, you fucking bitch...You want to play? You're on!"

~~~ *The End* ~~~

Did *The Ghost Pattern* keep you riveted to the pages as you raced through the story, gasping at every twist? Find out what happens next for Alex Hoffmann and her team, in the next unmissable Leslie Wolfe thriller.

Read on for an excerpt from

OPERATION SUNSET

Alex Hoffmann Series Book Five

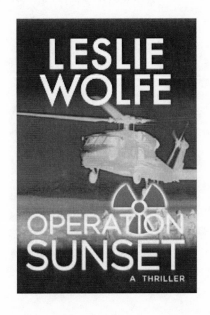

THANK YOU!

A big, heartfelt thank you for choosing to read my book. If you enjoyed it, please take a moment to leave me a five-star review; I would be very grateful. It doesn't need to be more than a few words, and it makes a huge difference. This is your shortcut: http://bit.ly/GhostPatternReview

Did you enjoy Alex Hoffmann and her team? Your thoughts and feedback are very valuable to me. Please contact me directly through one of the channels listed below. Email works best: LW@WolfeNovels.com.

CONNECT WITH ME

Email: LW@WolfeNovels.com

Facebook: https://www.facebook.com/wolfenovels

Follow Leslie on Amazon: http://bit.ly/WolfeAuthor

Follow Leslie on BookBub: http://bit.ly/wolfebb

Website: www.LeslieWolfe.com

Visit Leslie's Amazon store: http://bit.ly/WolfeAll

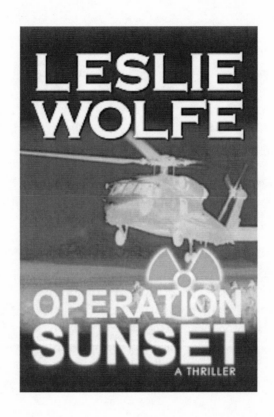

...Chapter 1: Welcome Home
...Wednesday, May 24, 5:45PM Local Time (UTC-8:00 hours)
...John Wayne Airport
...Santa Ana, California

Alex shifted in her seat as the Phenom turned gracefully, on final approach to Santa Ana's John Wayne Airport. She stretched her neck, her eyes glued to the plane's small window, to see the sunny coast she called home. The heart-piercing deep blue of the Pacific, as is glittered when sunrays hit its restless surface and reflected back in a million shards of diamond, the golden sands of shore, safety, warmth, and familiar places. That was home. She'd missed it. She'd feared she'd never see it again. Her heart swelled and her eyes welled up.

She cleared her throat, embarrassed by her own weakness. *Look at me, the sentimental soldier. Argh...*

She turned toward Lou, but shifted too abruptly in her seat. A pang of sharp pain in her sternum caught her breath and reminded her she was still convalescing. The pain was nothing like it had been a few weeks before; it was just a reminder to take it easy still. Three cracked ribs and a hairline on her sternum, they had said. A couple torn ligaments in her left shoulder, and a pretty bad cut on her forehead. That, unfortunately, had left a scar. Her first battle scar, hopefully her last. Scars aren't sexy in women... only in some men. Damn. Alex hated long bangs, but probably she'd have to consider them now. A curtain of hairstyle camouflage to hide the wounds of battle. Huh. Like that was going to work.

"Hey Lou," she said, then cleared her throat again, still choked up a little.

His eyes were glued to the window. From his side of the plane, he could see the city, and farther out, the hazy Los Angeles skyline, almost lost in the smog.

"What's up," he replied, then cleared his throat a little, quietly.

"Are you getting emotional, seeing that we're finally coming home?"

He turned and looked at her, a little surprised.

"Come on, you can admit it," she pushed him, smiling widely, making him frown and purse his lips. "It's just the two of us here."

"Yeah... a little," he eventually confessed, shifting uncomfortably in his seat.

"It's okay to be happy to be home, you know," she pressed on. "What are you planning to do in the next few days?"

"As little as possible," Lou quipped, then chuckled lightly.

"Yeah, we got time. I'm planning to work on my tan more seriously. The Japanese doctors told me to spend as much time as possible lying on my back, resting. On the beach sounds like the perfect place for me."

"Then, in about a week's time, we'll resume your training routine, right? They said in five, six weeks you should be back to normal. That's coming up."

"Lou, I hate you right now. Words cannot express." She made a strangling gesture with her right hand, grunting a little.

"Yeah, yeah, right. Heard that one before."

"The doctors said at least two more weeks of R&R," she said. "I won't let you ruin that. Plus, we got some time, until Sam and Blake return."

"We shouldn't have left Japan without them, you know. No man left behind, that's the right way to do it."

"They are fine, well taken care of, and out of harm's way. They're not exactly left behind on the battlefield."

"Yeah, but still."

"Lou, they have protection round the clock. The Bravo Team is with them. They are surrounded by top-notch medical professionals, caring for them in one of the most exclusive, most expensive health clinics this world has to offer. They rest, they relax, they do physio; that's all they do. They're probably going to make a full recovery before we do. And they're coming home in a week or so."

"Yeah, I guess…"

A chime interrupted them.

"That's it, folks. Buckle up for final descent." The pilot's voice was loaded with the same kind of excitement they were feeling.

"I'm actually impressed with this guy," Alex said.

"Who?"

"Dylan, the pilot," she clarified, lowering her voice a little. The door to the cockpit was wide open.

"Why?"

"I didn't think he'd make it out there without losing his shit. He's not military, you know. He's just a civilian, who landed a cushy job flying a big shot banker, *the* Blake Bernard, around the world."

"Yeah, he's okay, I guess."

The landing gear made a squealing sound as they touched down, followed by the roar of the engines thrown in reverse. The Phenom slowed down, then taxied to the VIP terminal at John Wayne Airport.

Alex unbuckled her seatbelt and jumped to her feet, holding on to the seat for balance. She winced when her ribs reminded her again to take it easy, but that reminder quickly faded away under the excitement of being home.

"There they are!"

On the tarmac, lined up to meet them, stood Tom and Claire, and, a little to the side, Steve. Steve looked a little grim; there was tension around his mouth, and a frown line crossed his entire forehead. Alex's smile froze on her lips.

"There's going to be hell to pay, I guess," she said, softly.

"What did you expect? I'm not sure I forgave you either, you know." Lou's words were harsh, but the warmth in his voice softened them a little.

She was the first one to get off the plane, landing in Tom's bear hug.

"Welcome home," he said. "We need to talk."

Ugh.

Then Claire was next to hug her.

"Good to have you back, my dear," she whispered warmly.

She moved to greet Steve next, and she managed to do that awkwardly, averting her eyes, and feeling like she wanted the earth to open up and swallow her right where she stood. Not a word was spoken between the two of them. Just a hasty, hesitant handshake, and she pulled away.

She took a deep breath, bracing herself, and opened the conversation as if nothing ever happened. She turned to Tom and smiled.

"So, what's for dinner?"

"Ah, all kinds of good stuff," he replied. "Portabellas on the grill, skirt steak, and a side of... What the hell were you thinking?"

She took a small step back.

"What do you mean?" she managed.

"The flares stunt you pulled." Tom's eyes were dead serious, glaring at her mercilessly.

"I thought I'd bring him out, that's all. I'm tired of chasing a ghost. All this time, and all I have is one letter. One initial, the damn letter V. A letter I've grown to hate."

"He's a terrorist, for chrissake, Alex, a terrorist! You don't bring out terrorists like that."

"Oh, no? Then how? How exactly am I supposed to bring him out?"

"Why is it your job, to begin with? I'm your boss, Alex, and I'm telling you this is not your job."

"Ah, so now you pull rank on me, Tom, is that it?"

"Well..." Tom hesitated, taking it down a notch. His wife reached out and gently squeezed his hand. "You leave me little choice, Alex. This is not what we do. We're not equipped to chase down terrorists. We're a corporate investigations agency, and a small one. That's all we are, all we do."

"I—I know," Alex said with a sigh. "But these cases, I didn't choose them, you know. They chose me, *you* chose me to work them. Because this bastard's still out there, I can't call these cases closed, and it's killing me. I thought I'd draw him out, that's all. Play on his ego, tease him a little."

Steve approached the two of them.

"Did you stop and think you're endangering all of us by doing that?" Steve asked. His frown grew deeper.

She felt her heart break a little, seeing Steve turned against her. What could she expect? Her disappointment quickly became anger, and she spun on her heels to face him.

"Wait a minute there, Steve. Weren't you the one who lectured me on how I'm becoming obsessed with someone who doesn't even exist? Well? Make up your mind, then. Does he exist? Or doesn't he?"

"*Someone* does exist. Someone who might have been watching that satellite feed when you lit up the flares and looked straight up, so they can see you grin at them as you destroyed their operation. In my line of work, that's called adding insult to the injury. You just motivated your enemy, that's all. Whoever that is, V or not." His voice was firm, but sad at the same time.

She still resonated to the undertones in Steve's voice, more than she cared to admit. Damn it to hell... the heart doesn't belong in the office... or on the battlefield. Lesson learned.

"Yes I did. That's exactly what I wanted to do. A motivated enemy will come out and attack."

"Sure he will," Steve continued. "He can kill you in your sleep, or rig your car to explode. How are you calling that a good outcome? What if you can't see him coming, to do anything about it?"

She pursed her lips, a wave of deep irritation scrunching her features. She shook her head gently, almost imperceptibly, as she kept her eyes glued to the tarmac.

"I'm still struggling to hear you talk about this, when you were the most adamant non-believer in this man's existence. You were the one who reassured me that there's no Russian terrorist leader behind everything. You said it was all in my imagination. You made me doubt my sanity. So, why the change in spirit? Because if you did in fact reconsider, and now you do believe that V is really out there, then you owe me an apology." She ended her ranting in a defiant tone, and lifted her gaze to meet his. She drilled her eyes mercilessly into his, until he looked away.

"Truth is, I don't know," Steve conceded. "I don't know if you were right, or if I was right. I don't know if there's a Russian terrorist out there or not. One thing's for sure though. What you did was reckless, because you endangered your life and everyone else's for no good reason. For no clear outcome whatsoever. You've now set a trail, a trail that someone can follow with ease, all the way here, to all of us."

Her jaw dropped. She was stunned, and angry with herself for not seeing it, in her egotistical excitement with the possibility of catching V. Steve was right; she hadn't thought of them for a second. High on the moment's adrenaline and only caring about exposing and hunting down her elusive Russian terrorist, she had jeopardized the lives of the people she cared about the most. They weren't just coworkers. They were her family, her friends. *Oh, my god…* Her hand went to her mouth, shaking, and cold as ice.

"You're no longer the stealth hunter, Alex," Steve added in a low, conclusive pitch. "You've become the hunted, and so have we. This is the mistake you've made."

She stood there, speechless for a while. Pallor descended on her face, turning her features spectral. As realization hit, she felt a million pinpricks on her skin, as wave after wave of adrenaline hit her insides.

"I'll—I'll just disappear," she whispered. "I'll go away, fall off the face of the earth. That way, you'll be safe."

"You'll do no such thing," Tom intervened forcefully. "We're in this together, no matter what."

She felt her eyes well up, and a tiny smile of heartfelt gratitude appeared on her lips. Then she turned to Steve.

"How about you? You feel the same way?"

"Absolutely," he replied, not a trace of hesitation.

"Lou?"

He'd been leaning against the car for a while, his leg injury causing him some grief. However, he bounced up on both his feet and approached her.

"Hundred percent. Never leave a man behind, remember?" He smiled, then added, "I also happen to trust your judgment, you know. So far, I've seen some pretty awesome results. Maybe, who knows? You'll draw this bastard out, so we can rid the world of him. Whatever his name is."

She nodded toward Lou, then turned to Claire.

"How about you, Claire?"

"I will repeat what I said earlier. It's good to have you home, my dear. That's all that matters to me. The rest, you will fix, together. I have no doubt."

Tom opened the door to his car, inviting everyone to join him with a jovial, wide gesture, and a slight bow. She felt a wave of emotion swell up her chest. They were her family, and they had forgiven her. She swallowed hard, trying to refrain from crying. She tried to hide it with a quick joke, as she boarded Tom's car, sliding with difficulty on the back seat.

"So, I take it I'm not fired, huh?"

Tom made eye contact with her in the rearview, for a split second, but enough for her to register the smile in his glance.

"Don't tempt me."

The heavy velvet draperies were half-closed, a little unusual for that time of the morning. It could only mean two things. Either President Abramovich had a fierce migraine, or he was mad as hell. Neither scenario showing any promise of a good meeting, Dimitrov repressed a sigh, and continued pacing the carpet slowly, waiting for the man to show his face.

He focused on his steps for a while, taking one step at a time, studying the intricate design of the rich Oriental rug, aligning his fine leather shoe to the delicate curves drawn in wool. No matter how heavily he stomped his foot, the rug swallowed all the noise. The lavish design, a million gold arabesques dancing on a dark, deep red with hues of burgundy, matched the wallpaper, the famous Kremlin gold-encrusted ceilings, and the massive, sculpted hardwood doors, also covered in gold foil.

So much detail for the mind's eye to perceive, register, and analyze. So much gold, infatuation, and pretense. After having spent the past fifteen years of his life serving as Russia's controversial, yet balanced defense minister, Dimitrov craved some simple, white walls, maybe with a wall rug or two, just for the sake of tradition.

"Ah, you're here," Abramovich said, surprising Dimitrov.

He snapped out of his reverie and turned to greet his boss.

"Good morning, *Gospodin Prezident*."

"Drop the formalities, Mishka, it's just us here, in my private quarters."

He took the invitation, and relaxed his demeanor a little. After all, they'd been friends since their earlier days as junior officers in the KGB. That seemed like centuries ago.

"Morning, Petya."

"That's better," Abramovich acknowledged. "Do you know why I wanted to see you?"

"I—no, I don't think I do," Dimitrov replied cautiously. Abramovich was world-famous for his short fuse, irrational thinking, and ultra-sensitive ego. Not someone you'd want to assume things about.

"I have the press conference in under an hour."

"Ah…" Dimitrov said, before he could stop himself. So that's why the semi-darkness in the presidential quarters. Deeply hurt, Abramovich was hiding from the world. The damn press conference was going to cost a lot of people, dearly.

"Yes, yes, Petya. Yes, you understand. I have to apologize to the entire world on live television. Can you believe that?"

Dimitrov didn't answer. He let his eyes speak, encouraging the volatile Abramovich, while offering him a cigar. Maybe smoking would soothe him a little.

"I have to explain to the whole world that I had no idea what was happening in my own country, goddamn it. I will be the laugh of this entire globe. They'll think me impotent, clueless, a puppet! A trinket, bounced around by someone else, more powerful than I am!"

Abramovich paused his lament to light up the cigar. Dimitrov held the match with steady hands, steadier than he'd expected.

Then Abramovich resumed his deploration, his pitch higher a notch or two.

"How am I going to explain that such a massive undergoing had happened without my knowledge? Tell me, Mishka, how?"

Abramovich stopped, this time waiting for an answer.

Dimitrov let a second or two pass by before speaking. When he spoke, his voice was calm, reassuring yet not dismissive, supporting, and firm.

"Petya, this has happened many times before in history. Today it's harsh, I agree… it's humiliating for you, and demeaning for our country. But you can say that the terrorist attack was a complete surprise to the Russian people, as it was to the rest of the world. You can say no one knew that, hidden in the forested depths of the Far East, evil had found a place to nest and weave its plans. And you will say that you will not rest until you uncover the roots of this evil. You will say all that, while looking straight into the main camera, and believing it with all your heart."

Abramovich stood immobile, following keenly every word that came out of Dimitrov's mouth. Then he turned and took a couple quick steps to his desk, to jot notes on gold letterhead stationery. He held his cigar between the index and middle finger of his left hand; tiny specs of ash found their way onto the shiny, inlaid hardwood desk top.

"What else?" he asked, still leaning on his desk, ready to take more notes.

"Nothing else, Petya, nothing else. If you wish, you can blame it on the Chechens; we always do that. Whatever you decide, keep it very short. All you need is to make a statement. Once you've made it, you don't need to say anything else. Take a couple of questions though; it makes you appear open, honest, and human."

"Ahh… the press and their damn questions."

"Regardless what they ask, all you have to say is how committed you are to finding and punishing the source of this evil. That's all."

"I am, you know," Abramovich stated, with a hateful glint in his eye.

"You're what?" Dimitrov's eyebrows shot up, aiming to get closer to his receding hairline, and adding a few more transversal ridges on his forehead.

"Committed to punishing this evil. I'll give it to Myatlev; I'll give it to him so badly that he'll never forget who he failed."

"I see what you mean," Dimitrov said quietly. "You must be mad."

"I am more than mad. I am more humiliated and angrier than I've ever been in my entire life. Do you know why Myatlev's still alive, at this very moment?"

Following along like a good sport, Dimitrov replied, careful to quickly repress an eye roll.

"No, Petya, why?"

"Because he's got some balls, this guy. Balls the size of Barents Sea icebergs, that's how big they are. Too bad he failed, and he got caught. By the Americans, no less. For that, yeah, I want to kill him myself, with these two hands," he continued, illustrating by holding both his hands firmly outward. "Nevertheless, can you imagine what the world would have been like if he'd succeeded? Can you imagine? Having the power to dictate what everyone of any importance will do, will think?"

Dimitrov remained silent, a crooked smile twisting his lips somewhat. Then he decided to push the issue a little, just to take a temperature read.

"So, it's not because the two of you go way back, even further back than the two of us?"

"Nah... No. He screwed up really badly, but he meant well. He's loyal, dedicated, and trustworthy."

"Then he's forgiven?"

"No, not at all. He still didn't deliver, and neither did you. The two of you work together every day, share the same floor, and have promised me one thing. Yet I get nothing, after so much time. Only promises and failures."

"Petya, we are both trying to avoid the nuclear option. We don't want to bring radioactive air on top of Russia, for our children to breathe. That's why he's been thinking up all these ballsy plans, to give you what you want without destroying the entire planet."

"While in the mean time the Americans grow more arrogant, more defiant, and their superiority is pissing me off!" Abramovich bellowed, the sound of his voice reverberating in the huge room. "Is it too much to ask? For a power like Russia is today?"

Dimitrov swallowed hard. "No, sir."

"Don't sir me, Mishka, don't be an idiot. You've done well rebuilding the army, the arsenal, everything. The *Armata* tank is a thing of beauty. But I want the Americans on their knees, defeated, begging for my mercy! *My* mercy! How do you plan to deliver on that, you and your dear friend Myatlev?"

Abramovich's anger was ramping up again... Dimitrov suddenly realized he was too old for this job, too old for Kremlin, too old for Abramovich's tantrums. He considered it for a split second, but then decided it was the absolute wrong moment to hand in his resignation right then and there. Abramovich still took pride in throwing the insubordinate few in Siberia, where remnants of the Gulag still existed, under new, reformed names, but the same leadership, and employing the same methods.

Dimitrov's eyes darted at Abramovich, then looked away. He was afraid the sociopath standing combatively in front of him would see right through him, and hear his thoughts. *God help us all, and forgive us the cowardice we are showing by letting this man live.*

"He surprised me a little a few weeks ago when he ordered a few backpack nukes," Dimitrov eventually said, hating himself. "We delivered the order. I don't think he's planning to hold on to them for too long."

"He did? Really?" Abramovich's voice bubbled with excitement.

"Yes... I was surprised to see he finally adopted the nuclear path. You've been trying to convince him for a long time, and he held strong. He was afraid we would ruin this world for all of us, for generations to come, not just teach the Americans a lesson. But he came around; he changed his mind, recently. He must have thought of something. He must have a plan."

"It was about time," Abramovich replied serenely.

"You should speak with him, see if you agree with his new plan. No more surprises for you this time, right?"

Vitaliy Myatlev's office was abuzz with activity. Myatlev himself directed traffic like an effective street cop, while his aide and personal bodyguard, Ivan, took notes impassibly on his plastic clipboard.

"Alright, boss, what else?"

"Um, let's make sure the safe at the house is emptied out. I think it is, but check to make sure," Myatlev asked, a little impatient.

"I cleaned it out myself just a few months back, but I'll drop by tonight and take another look."

"Good. Have the jet fueled and the pilot in it, on standby, day and night."

"Done."

"Who's taking care of the stuff at the house?"

"I am, after dark, just like you said."

"Good. Leave the bulky stuff behind. Leave the furniture; just take my clothes, documents, that kind of stuff. How about Kiev? Is the villa prepared?"

"Yes, it is. Everything is ready for your arrival."

"Good." Myatlev sighed, and allowed himself to calm the frenzy of his just-in-case departure preparations. They were good on time. He was prepared to leave on a moment's notice, should the case present itself. It was better to be safe than sorry.

He also needed to be very discreet in his preparations. Abramovich wouldn't take too nicely to him getting ready to run, albeit only to Kiev, at his favorite residence. However, Kiev was now in a foreign country, Ukraine. Abramovich would consider his departure to a foreign country as desertion, and everyone knew what Abramovich did to deserters, lifelong friends or not.

His thorough preparations were more of a precaution than anything was. He wasn't planning to run, just for the sake of becoming Abramovich's next hunting target. No matter how rich and powerful Myatlev was, once Abramovich had decided he wanted him dead, he couldn't survive for long. Division Seven had the best cleanup crew a secret service had ever had. Myatlev knew just how good they were, because he'd trained some of them himself, and seen most of them in action.

Nevertheless, he intended to carry out the president's vengeful plans, without hesitation, even if that meant the detonation of numerous nuclear devices within the continental United States. Now more than ever, Myatlev shared Abramovich lust for vengeance, after having been bitterly humiliated by that Hoffmann bitch. Fuck her. Fuck that bitch from hell.

He felt alive again, and thrived in the feeling, rejoiced in it. For almost two years, he had believed he was losing his mind. Crippled for months by rampant anxiety and bouts of paranoia, at times he'd believed he had an imaginary enemy, who saw through all his strategies and ruined all his plans. Other times, he'd feared it was the hand of God himself. Senseless fears had crept up on him, augmented by the very alcohol he had used to try to silence them. Thus, he'd forgotten who he was: a powerful energy and weapons magnate, who never failed, and never took no for an answer. Who had no enemies, because the moment an enemy would surface, that enemy would soon find an early demise. Now he finally remembered, with every bone in his body and every breath he took; he was back in the power seat.

Once the source of his irrational anxieties had gained a name and a face to go along with it, he transformed overnight, returning to his old self. His drinking habit almost entirely gone, the dark circle under his eyes, and his swollen abdomen were soon to follow. His stomach recovered on its own, as his paranoid worries disappeared. He felt twenty years younger; his refreshed blood pumped strong in his veins, ready to fuel his rekindled ambitions of infinite wealth and power, and a tireless lust for vengeance.

That bitch, she almost killed him. She was going to pay, and then some.

"Um... anything else, boss?"

The rest of the staffers had left, after packing diligently resource lists, deployed agents networks, asset banks, maps, organizational charts, and every single useful document Myatlev could think of. The last of them had vanished quietly, closing the door behind him.

"No, you can go, Ivan. We're set. Thanks."

Ivan approached Myatlev, extending his clipboard for him to view.

"What about her? Should I take care of her?"

A picture of Alex Hoffmann was attached onto Ivan's clipboard, held in place by a large metallic clamp. A little grainy and blurred, that was the image captured via satellite when the bitch had delivered her latest blow. Smiling defiantly, sure of herself, the Hoffmann bitch had laughed in his face. Her time to die was now.

"Yes, Ivan, take care of her, and of everyone she's ever loved, ever met, ever set eyes upon. You hear me?"

"Yes, boss. I'll get it done myself."

Myatlev stared into the grainy eyes of the woman in the photo. Not watching those defiant eyes blur as life left her body, not hearing her whimper and weep, not having her lying at his feet, begging for her life, that just didn't seem right. Why should Ivan have that privilege?

"Never mind, I'll take care of this one myself."

"You sure, boss?"

"Yeah. I want to hear her scream."

~~~End Preview~~~

Like *Operation Sunset*?

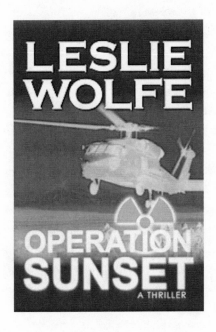

Buy it now!

ABOUT THE AUTHOR

Leslie Wolfe is a bestselling author whose novels break the mold of traditional thrillers. She creates unforgettable, brilliant, strong women heroes who deliver fast-paced, satisfying suspense, backed up by extensive background research in technology and psychology.

Leslie released the first novel, *Executive,* in October 2011. Since then, she has written many more, continuing to break down barriers of traditional thrillers. Her style of fast-paced suspense, backed up by extensive background research in technology and psychology, has made Leslie one of the most read authors in the genre and she has created an array of unforgettable, brilliant and strong women heroes along the way.

Reminiscent of the television drama *Criminal Minds*, her series of books featuring the fierce and relentless FBI Agent **Tess Winnett** would be of great interest to readers of James Patterson, Melinda Leigh, and David Baldacci crime thrillers. Fans of Kendra Elliot and Robert Dugoni suspenseful mysteries would love the **Las Vegas Crime** series, featuring the tension-filled relationship between Baxter and Holt. Finally, her **Alex Hoffmann** series of political and espionage action adventure will enthrall readers of Tom Clancy, Brad Thor, and Lee Child.

Leslie has received much acclaim for her work, including inquiries from Hollywood, and her books offer something that is different and tangible, with readers becoming invested in not only the main characters and plot but also with the ruthless minds of the killers she creates.

A complete list of Leslie's titles is available at LeslieWolfe.com/books.

Leslie enjoys engaging with readers every day and would love to hear from you. Become an insider: gain early access to previews of Leslie's new novels.

- Email: LW@WolfeNovels.com
- Facebook: https://www.facebook.com/wolfenovels
- Follow Leslie on Amazon: http://bit.ly/WolfeAuthor
- Follow Leslie on BookBub: http://bit.ly/wolfebb
- Website: www.LeslieWolfe.com
- Visit Leslie's Amazon store: http://bit.ly/WolfeAll

Made in United States
North Haven, CT
18 October 2023

42899738R00148